BOOK
PURSUED

Book One of the
Pursued by Evil, Called by God series

BOOK
PURSUED

Woody Dahlberg

BEAVER'S POND
PRESS

Edited by Robert Schmidt and Alicia Ester

ISBN: 978-1-59298-770-2
Library of Congress Catalog Number: 2017954771
Printed in the United States of America
First Printing: 2017
21 20 19 18 17   5 4 3 2 1

Cover and interior design by Woody Dahlberg
Illustration and cover photo by Woody Dahlberg

For more information about the author, visit: woody.valleyhill.net.

Beaver's Pond Press, Inc.
7108 Ohms Lane
Edina, MN 55439–2129

(952) 829-8818
www.BeaversPondPress.com

To order, visit www.ItascaBooks.com or call
1-800-901-3480 ext. 118. Reseller discounts available.

Acknowledgments

I thank Eva, my wife, for the time she gave up for me to produce this work, and for encouraging me, reading the manuscript, and giving feedback. Ave Shalom, my daughter, helped by typing several chapters of the book and giving valuable feedback. Thad, my son, provided invaluable technical assistance.

I thank the following people for their help at various stages of writing and editing *Book Pursued*: Dr. Thomas Becknell from Bethel University, Patty Thomson, Lynn Hansen, Tricia Theurer, and Nancy Paulson.

I benefited greatly from the seminars and contacts I made at the Write to Publish Conference held on the Wheaton College campus. The Minnesota Christian Writers Guild meetings encouraged me to keep writing and editing.

Beaver's Pond Press has provided great support and editing. Robert Schmidt's content editing was extremely helpful, and Alicia Ester's management and quality text editing was essential to make this work possible. Athena Currier supplied me with many design essentials for book publishing.

In the beginning God created . . .
Genesis 1:1

————————

And the Lord God said,
"The man has now become
like one of us, knowing good and evil."
Genesis 3:22

1

Jane was reading the Sunday newspaper at breakfast. With a shocked expression on her face, she held the paper up in front of me. "Have you seen this?"

"No. What?"

"Page two. See, one of the librarians has disappeared from the Harrison Library. The picture they're showing of the missing librarian, Miss Mildred Bates, looks just like the woman who checked our books out. The police are asking for leads."

"Could she have been kidnapped by the man who was yelling and beating on the library door?"

Jane and I had stopped at the Harrison Library in Edenville, Illinois, just three days earlier looking for books filled with mystery and suspense to read on our upcoming vacation. We have both spent *a lot* of time in libraries and around books throughout our lives. As students at Great Lakes University, we loved to search out the back corners to study—and get to know each other more intimately. In our adult lives, our passion for books didn't let up. I was an editor for EAD Publishing, a small company publishing special-interest magazines and books.

Jane was an art history professor at Great Lakes University. She loved studying art and objects of antiquity. I fell in love with Jane, in part, because of her insatiable curiosity and creativity, and her appreciation of artistic beauty akin to mine. During our five years of marriage, our mutual interests had led us to seek common life goals.

We planned to have children once our careers were more firmly established, but were happy exploring our passions together for the time being.

———————

On that fateful day when we visited at the Harrison Library, we had gone straight to the mystery shelves. As I scanned the titles, I noticed a book bound in worn leather that looked out of place among the other books. A shiver of excitement shot through me as I pulled it off the shelf. I smelled its mustiness. The corners of the small leather volume were soft and rounded from wear. I could tell that I would need to handle it with great care.

I wasn't expecting to find an ancient book there. Books like those are usually housed in museums or in the archives of esteemed universities, where they are collected for research into subjects that don't matter to most of us.

I was, instead, in a modern library in a suburb of Chicago. Expansive windows provided ample light. Books were cataloged on computers and filed on long shelves, carefully categorized by author, subject, and number. More people were seated at computers than were reading books. Yet, it was there where I discovered the ancient book that would begin my journey of terror and hope.

My fingers slid over the worn leather cover, and I had an overwhelming sensation. *This book will change my life forever.* I cast the thought aside as pure emotion, but I couldn't dismiss the feeling.

I hardly dared touch its pages. They felt as soft as cloth, as if the fibers were returning to sawdust. The stitching that held the book together was yellowed with age, but the pages were still bound in its unrelenting grasp. A hint of gold leaf clung to their edges.

The inside-cover pages were hand-made marbled paper, exhibiting the richness of old art. Running my fingers across the marbling revealed a slight texture where the oil paints adhered to the paper. The purple, red, and blue colors looked like the delicate feathers of a tropical bird. I could tell this was no ordinary book!

I didn't see a library number, bar code, or any signs of ownership. Had someone carelessly left a book like this on the shelf? I couldn't imagine anyone forgetting such a prize. *Had I been destined to find this book, to claim it, to possess it?*

I didn't believe in divine destiny. I suppose I believed that you might have good genes or happen upon something that could change your life, but I didn't believe in supernatural premonitions or predestination.

Nevertheless, I couldn't ignore the attachment I felt for the book. As I touched its pages, I had an overwhelming feeling I had found it for a reason—that I was supposed to possess it.

An announcement blared over the intercom: "The library will close in fifteen minutes."

I didn't return the book to the shelf. I couldn't leave it behind. Instead, I carefully placed it on top of the other books I was going to check out.

Jane would be interested in my discovery. She was sitting at a table, skimming the pages of several novels. I smiled as I placed the small volume in front of her. She lifted the cover. Her eyes hardly blinked as she delicately turned the pages.

"I'm almost afraid to touch it," she whispered.

I nodded. "Can you feel the subtle impressions of the type? I'm guessing the pages were printed on an old letterpress."

With her index finger, Jane lifted a silk ribbon bound into the spine. "Did you notice the purple ribbon? See the diamond pattern of fine gold threads woven into it? I remember having a bookmark like this when I was a girl, except the threads of this ribbon look like real gold."

After she carefully closed the cover, I noticed a subtle embossing on the leather. I pointed at it. "What's that?"

Jane looked closely. "It's a tree. The left half has leaves. The right half has bare branches, and there's a small round shape on the leafy side. The color is faded, but it looks like the leaves might have had a green pigment and the circle was dyed a deep red." Looking at the spine, she added, "Odd. I don't see a title."

Jane opened the book again. Sliding her finger over a line of text without touching the page, she said, "The words and sentences look like a jumble of letters and fragmented thoughts. They don't make any sense. In some places, the words look like some ancient form of English. In other spots, they look more like Latin, Spanish, French— or childish gibberish."

"They have eyes to see," I said, "but do not see."

"What?" Jane asked.

"Just a quote I remember from when my parents took me to church."

For the most part, I thought the Bible was out of touch with the twenty-first century, but occasionally I recalled a relevant phrase from my Sunday school days.

We didn't have time to examine the book in detail. A second announcement warned us the library would close in five minutes.

As unwilling as I was to give the book up, Jane placed it on top of our novels as we rushed to the checkout counter. When the librarian opened the ancient-looking book and found no identification or bar code, she looked as confused as we had. "Is this your book?"

Jane and I looked at each other, and inspired by some selfish deviousness, I said, "Oh, of course, excuse us!"

In that moment, we claimed that beautiful text as our own.

The librarian, who we later learned was Miss Mildred Bates, stared over the top of her glasses at us, hesitated for a moment, and handed it to us before checking out the rest of the books.

Maybe we should have told the truth, but in a moment of weakness, we chose to assume the book belonged to us. I told myself it must have been left by some unknown person months—or even years—before we discovered it. We were only claiming what we had rightfully found. *Finders, keepers. Right?*

After checking out, we walked casually out the door. *Perhaps it really was our destiny to possess this book*, I thought.

Little did I foresee the day would come when I would believe *it* possessed *us*.

Jane and I were the last to leave the library. We walked to our car with the special little volume still on top of our library books.

I glanced back as I opened the car door. A black limousine had pulled up in front of the library entrance. *How odd*, I mused.

I asked Jane, "Have you ever seen a limo stop at a library?"

She looked back as a man walked to the door. "And you don't see many men come to the library in tuxes."

The man tried the door, but it was already locked. He swore and pounded on the glass. No one responded. He became more agitated, stamping his feet, and even from a distance we could hear him shouting obscenities.

"This doesn't look good. Let's get out of here," Jane said.

As we drove away, I could see the man peering through the glass door, waving his arms.

We somehow knew that we needed to protect our ancient find as much as possible. On the way home we stopped at a photo store and purchased an archival box designed to store photographs. As soon as we got into the house, we put the book into the new container and carefully placed it on the top shelf of our closet.

Jane and I got up late on Saturday morning. She had tests to grade over the weekend, and I had several projects to finish before our vacation began the next week. That didn't stop us from going to the hall closet after breakfast and pulling down the box that contained our prize book.

We had mixed feelings about examining it too closely. Its ancient pages were delicate, and we would have to handle them cautiously to keep them from deteriorating.

We draped a red satin scarf across our dining room table. Jane lifted the box's lid, and I carefully removed the book and placed it on the cloth.

"I have a box of cotton gloves that we used for a class project when we did a series on studying old photos stored in the university library," Jane said. "I think we should use those gloves when we handle the book." Jane went to her desk and took out a small box containing gloves of several sizes. I found a pair that fit and put them on before gently opening the book.

I turned one page at a time. Its beauty amazed us. Speculating about our find, we wondered if the book was valuable.

I had a growing awareness that we were beginning to treat its ancient pages like a cherished historical artifact.

"It's still amazing how you found it," Jane said.

I agreed. "I've a hunch I discovered it for a reason, like there's something lurking just beyond my understanding; maybe even sinister, but definitely mysterious."

"That's so unlike you," Jane said as she laughed.

"I know; I can reject the logic, but I can't ignore my attraction to it."

"Well, I hope you're wrong about the sinister part," Jane said.

2

"Where should we start?"

"Why not begin by looking at the cover and work in from there?" Jane suggested, pulling on a pair of the cotton gloves.

"Sounds good."

I found my magnifying glass and examined the etching of the tree. The workmanship was excellent. Every leaf had definition; every branch was etched into the leather with precision. The shape Jane had seen on the leafy side of the tree was perfectly round, and she was right, it looked like it had once been dyed deep red.

"There's a curved line at the base of the tree. It looks like a snake."

Jane looked at it through my glass. "You're right."

"It kind of reminds me of the Bible story of the tree in the Garden of Eden."

"Maybe it's a religious book," Jane said.

"Could be. Judging by how old this book looks, a lot of people were heavily into religion when it was printed."

"A lot still are."

Even with a magnifying glass, I couldn't see any other identification on the cover. We agreed to move on. I opened the book and slowly turned the pages. Again the appearance, texture, and smell suggested its antiquity.

"Maybe this was only a proof copy for a book," I said. "That could explain why the text is random and there's no title."

"But why would anyone keep the proof and not the book?" Jane said.

"You're right, it doesn't make sense. It's too well designed to be filled with gibberish. There's got to be something we're not seeing."

We decided to examine every page to see if we could make any sense out of it.

"Could the book be in some kind of code?" Jane said. "Maybe choosing every third word or letter will help us discover the meaning?"

"Finding the code's got to be harder than that."

"Or not," Jane sighed, frustrated that I always opted for the difficult answer. "But you're probably right."

We studied the book for the rest of the morning, turning every page with gloved hands.

After taking a break for lunch, we examined it for a few more hours, making pages of notes about the combinations and patterns we found. But nothing made sense. Jane said, "If there are codes here, I doubt we're going to find them today. And I've got to get to my grading."

I had to agree. My work was waiting, too.

Despite our care, dust from the pages was coming off on our gloves; I feared for the book and its hidden mysteries. We decided to put it back into its box for the time being.

"I can scan it at work on Monday," I said. "We can do our research from the copies. That way our book won't deteriorate."

On Sunday, when Jane saw the story of the missing librarian from the Harrison Library, we recognized her photo almost immediately. Miss Mildred Bates was wearing the same glasses in the photo as she had been wearing when we'd told her the book was ours. The article said the police were asking for any leads about what happened.

"Maybe we'd better call the police and let them know what we saw as we were leaving. It's too bizarre," Jane said.

I dialed the number. When a police officer answered, I said, "You asked for leads about the disappearance of Miss Bates. She was at the library when we checked out Thursday night."

I explained the angry scene Jane and I had observed at the library entrance.

"Sorry. No, I can't describe the man very well," I said. "He was wearing a tuxedo, and got out of a limousine. That's what first caught our attention . . . Yes, he was beating on the door of the library. He was yelling, pounding on the glass, and swearing. He looked really mad."

The officer asked several more questions to clarify my story, and then took my name and phone number in case they needed to get in touch with us. "You're not the first person to describe the door pounding incident," he said. "We're already following up on this lead."

As I prepared to leave for work on Monday, I put the box containing our book in a bag, leaving the notes we had made in a file folder on the coffee table in the sunroom. I gave Jane a long kiss before I headed for the garage. She would be home for another hour before leaving to teach her only art class of the day.

Jane looked lovely as the morning light danced on the reddish highlights in her brown hair. She hadn't put on her makeup yet. Her fresh-out-of-the-shower beauty almost convinced me to pull her back into the bedroom to make love, but I had appointments. I also needed time to copy the pages of the book.

Looking back, that was one of those magical moments I wish I hadn't passed up. Minutes later, I was pulling into traffic on my way to the office with a longing for what could have been a beautiful hour with Jane.

I knew I had to be careful as I scanned our fragile book into a single document file. I wore my gloves and cautiously held each page against the glass to minimize the damage. The binding struggled to survive, and I found that I had to dust off the glass several times. I hated the harm I was doing, but hoped it would cause less damage than if we were constantly turning the pages to compare its contents.

Scanning our book took all morning and put a crunch on my time in the office. The rest of my day was so busy that I didn't have a chance to talk to Jane until I got home.

I brought the file with me on a flash drive and printed out all the pages that night. When I showed Jane the printouts, she studied them for several minutes.

"This is really crisp. It's actually easier to read than the book. It would be even better to have the book in a text format on the computer, instead of as images. That way, we could electronically search for patterns and clues to its meaning."

"You're right. I should have converted it when I scanned the pages."

"I'll take the files in to the university tomorrow," Jane said. "I have a program on my computer to convert the scanned photo pages into text. It's usually fairly accurate and doesn't take long. I won't be able to get to it for a day or two because of my grading, but I'm sure I can have it ready before we leave on vacation. Of course, we'll need to proof all the copy against the pages to correct any scanned letters that didn't convert correctly."

"Let's do it. I'll store the book in our safety deposit box at the bank. That should keep it dry and safe."

On Tuesday, just before lunch, I called Jane to tell her the book was safely locked up. I felt relieved our mysterious book was secure.

Wednesday was Jane's last day of work for spring term at the university. She went to her office to turn in her grades and close up for the summer, hoping to be home by midafternoon.

At about 4:00 p.m., Jane called. I could hear the stress in her voice. "Come home as fast as you can."

"What? Why?" I asked.

"I'm at Ellen's. Someone broke into our house."

"When? How? Are you okay?"

"I'm fine. When I got home, I saw the back door was smashed in. The police are on the way."

While I was telling her I would be there as soon as I could, I heard distant sirens blaring from my phone. I told my editorial assistant I needed to leave immediately and rushed to my car.

When I got home, Jane was with a police officer, inspecting the house.

"So far, I haven't found anything missing," Jane explained when I walked into the room.

I looked around. I couldn't see anything out of place. One of the policemen said, "The thieves were probably scared off when your wife unlocked the front door."

Before he left, the policeman in charge promised they would patrol our neighborhood regularly for a few weeks.

On his recommendation, we decided that when we replaced the back door, it would be made out of hardwood, and would have a more secure lock. We called around and found a carpenter who promised we could have the new door installed by Friday.

Jane and I had planned to leave Saturday morning for our vacation to the North Shore of Lake Superior in Minnesota, but, after the break-in, we decided to put off leaving until Sunday.

We had reservations at Lake Superior Cabins in Grand Marais for the second week of June. We had planned to drive to St. Paul and stay there the first night, and get to the North Shore on Sunday night.

After the police left, I called the motel in the Twin Cities and told them we needed to change our reservation. Then I called about our cabin in Grand Marais to tell them we would be arriving on Monday night instead of Sunday.

On Thursday morning, as I was preparing to leave, Jane came up to me in the living room with a confused look on her face. "Do you know where we put the notes on our book?"

I looked at the coffee table, where I remembered leaving them and said, "They were there, but . . . the break-in—could they have been stolen?"

11

"That doesn't make sense. What would anyone want with our notes?"

I replied, "Unless that's the reason they broke in."

"Okay," Jane said. She paused, looked around the room and said, "I think I'm getting frightened now."

We decided to call the police. We explained that we had found something was missing after our house had been broken into. When we told them we couldn't find our notes on a book we were researching, the officer on the other end downplayed the connection. "Even if they did take the notes," the officer assured us, "it's not likely that's what they were after."

I recalled the scene we had witnessed as we were leaving the library. I didn't want to tell him more, but felt I had to at least allude to something we had considered.

"Unless that was also the reason the Bates woman is missing," I suggested. "We found the book we were researching at the library, and she was the one who checked us out."

"I still think it was probably a coincidence, but we'll take that into account," the police officer answered. "Thanks for the tip."

―――――――――

Jane brought home the text file she had made of our book, along with the printouts, on Thursday afternoon. I copied the files to the cloud, as well as to a couple of flash drives so we would have backups. We packed one of the drives in my laptop bag, and the other in Jane's purse.

On Friday, as Jane was home overseeing the installation of our new door, I talked with Carlos Frank, a friend of ours from Great Lakes University. As a professor in computer programming in the College of Technology, I hoped he might be able to help us find some ways to analyze the digital copy of our book.

After I explained what we were doing, Carlos smiled and said, "In fact, a couple of months ago I assigned a project to one of my advanced graduate classes to write software for uncovering patterns in files. Some of their programs were quite well written."

Carlos said he would copy a few of the best programs onto a flash drive so I could take them with me. In return, I promised to report back to him about how well they worked.

Jane and I were becoming increasingly obsessed with our book as we planned our summer vacation around discovering its hidden secrets. We realized that most people would have thought we were crazy. Even I thought we were a little bit nuts to spend our free time searching for a hidden code in an old manuscript.

On the other hand, we decided we didn't need to bring the mystery novels from the library on our vacation. We had our own mystery to solve, and we were the main characters. We, of course, planned to balance our work on the book with walks along the shore, trips up the Gunflint Trail, and drives along the lake.

Sunday morning, after the car was packed, we ate a quick breakfast. Jane was reading the newspaper when she looked at me in shock and said, "They've found the missing librarian's body. The police believe Miss Bates was tortured before she was killed."

"What? Why?" I asked.

"It says they don't have any clues."

3

After breakfast, we started our drive to Minnesota. We looked forward to eating freshwater fish and the home-baked pies we had been told were famous along the North Shore of Lake Superior.

The traffic coming out of Chicago was intense until we reached the Wisconsin Dells, a popular tourist stop known as "The Waterpark Capital of the World." After that, the congestion eased considerably and I began to relax.

It was a beautiful June day. As we drove, the sky transitioned from a bright to a deep blue, with a few fluffy clouds floating overhead. All the trees and grasses in the midwestern landscape that rushed passed us still had the bright-green look of early summer. Wildflowers exploded in color along the roadside and meadows. The day was perfect for a long drive.

When we pulled into the parking lot of our motel on the north side of the Twin Cities, the late-afternoon sun was still shining bright. After settling into our room at the Island Lake Motel, we began to get ready for a late dinner.

We watched the evening news while we washed up and changed out of our driving clothes. The long-range weather forecast indicated there would be instability in the air in northern Minnesota, but it was a vaguely worded prediction with a lot of *maybe* words.

There was no news in Minnesota about the librarian.

I was probably being paranoid, but I decided I didn't want to leave my computer bag in the room when we left for dinner. I grabbed it on the way out and stored it in the trunk. Jane, of course, also took her purse that contained the extra flash drive. We drove around until we found a restaurant, then, after dinner, we shopped to pick up a few last-minute items on our vacation list.

The last vestiges of deep mauve and purple glowed on the horizon as we pulled back into the motel parking lot. Feeling protective of our book project, I took my computer, along with the flash drives and the printout of the book, out of the trunk and back to our room.

———————

As soon as I opened the door, I had an uneasy feeling. Nothing seemed to be missing, but our belongings looked like they had been . . . rearranged.

When I expressed my concern to Jane, she said, "The maids probably did a little cleaning while we were out."

"Maids don't usually do that right *after* you've checked in," I said.

"Don't try to scare me," Jane said.

"Okay. Maybe I'm imagining things. The maid might have done a little last-minute cleaning."

———————

When I opened the car trunk the next morning as we got ready to leave, I noticed that the duffel bag I had left there was partially unzipped.

"Jane, did you open my duffel bag?"

"No, why?"

"It's unzipped. I distinctly remember zipping it up last night."

We pulled the bag out, went through all of the contents, and found everything was accounted for. I had to concede I might not have done a good job of securing it. After all, there was no evidence that the car had been broken into, and—again—nothing was missing.

Still, it seemed odd. I looked at Jane and said, "Could someone have gotten into our car and looked through our luggage?"

She glanced nervously around the parking lot.

"It's probably nothing," I said. "I was sure I'd closed it up tight, but the zipper must have stuck on some fabric."

Jane scrutinized the parking lot again, more slowly this time. I could tell that she wasn't convinced by my explanation and was as upset as I was. Somewhat apprehensively, we went back into the motel to take advantage of their free breakfast before our drive.

After we ate, we called the resort office in Grand Marais to confirm our reservation and let them know that we planned to check in around dinnertime. Soon we were cruising up Interstate 35 on our way to our relaxing week on the North Shore, leaving the last night's mysteries behind us.

As we neared Duluth, the terrain turned from rolling plains to trees and hills. At the top of the final rise, we looked down a long incline at the vast expanse of the city, its harbor, and Lake Superior.

We stopped at a scenic overlook and walked out onto a veranda to admire the panorama. A cobalt-blue sky spanned the horizon, but a brisk north wind slashed at our faces. We could see the rhythmic white-capped waves surging across the lake.

"I didn't expect such a fantastic view. It's even more dramatic than Frank and Sarah described," Jane said.

Leaving the overlook behind us, we drove down the freeway, got off on Lake Drive, and were at the waterfront in minutes. We ate lunch at the Lift Bridge Grill, a quaint restaurant with outdoor seating that overlooked the harbor. We left the car in the parking lot and walked along a few paths and the beach. Seagulls squawked overhead, sending their shrill cries across the water and diving toward anyone who looked like they might have food for them.

A buzzer sounded, and as we turned to see what was going on, the traffic to and from Duluth's historic lift bridge stopped. The steel midsection of the bridge rose. A freighter navigated under the bridge and through the short channel to Lake Superior. As the freighter cleared the channel, we watched the midsection of the bridge lower again, and car traffic continued across to the narrow island that separated the harbor from the lake.

A brisk wind tried to blow us backward as we walked along the quarter-mile shipping canal that extended into the lake. The bigger waves slapped a fine spray across our path as we approached the lighthouse. We climbed the steps leading up to its base and watched the whitecaps crashing into the shore.

Jane and I huddled together as we half-walked and half-ran back to the parking lot. The wind filled our jackets like the canvas on a sailboat, pushing us to our car. When we finally got the car doors shut and were out of the wind, we were exhausted and cold—even in mid-June. We sat for several minutes recovering from the chill.

Once we started on our journey again it didn't take us long to leave Duluth. Aiming the car northeast along Highway 61 toward Grand Marais, we stopped at Gooseberry Falls and Split Rock Lighthouse just long enough to appreciate the views and take a few more photos.

About a half hour out of Grand Marais, we pulled the car off at the Superior View Restaurant for a relaxing dinner next to a picture window, where we enjoyed a view of the lake. By now Lake Superior was so wide we couldn't see the other shore and the misty horizon blended into the sky.

I wanted to stay longer, but Jane reached over and squeezed my hand saying, "Let's get going. I really want to get to Grand Marais so we can settle into our cabin and enjoy the evening."

By the time we arrived at the resort, checked into our studio-sized cabin, and unpacked, the sun was sinking low in the sky. The air began to cool, but unlike in Duluth, only a light breeze was blowing.

Jane suggested a short walk before dark.

"Sounds good. Let's go." I knew I would enjoy walking along the waterfront, watching the boats' shimmering lights reflect on the waves against the backdrop of the darkening sky.

The breakwater that separates Grand Marais's southern bay from Lake Superior cast purple shadows across the rippling water. We planned to take a walk onto the narrow, rocky barrier the next day to look over the vast lake. As we strolled, I remembered the song about the wreck of the *Edmund Fitzgerald*, the huge freighter that sank with its crew in one of Lake Superior's storms. It still lay some-where on the bottom of the lake.

After sitting quietly on a ledge beside the bay for a half hour, we held hands as we walked back to our cabin.

Possibly it was the enormity of the lake that made us feel like small creatures thrown together in a huge world. Perhaps it was the sense of the two of us facing an enormous universe that prompted us to talk about our love for each other as we strolled to our cabin. Perhaps it was the common purpose we felt in trying to understand our little leather-bound book that brought us especially close that evening.

Or it may have been the beauty of the night. We had nothing to interfere with us concentrating on each other for the first time in weeks, and the break-in at our home had made us realize how quickly everything in our lives could change.

As soon as we reached the cabin we got ready for bed and snug-gled close. We made love and I fell asleep with Jane lying snuggling into my shoulder.

———————

Rising early, we walked, barely awake, down the street to Inspiration Harbor Coffee and Bakery for breakfast. We seated ourselves on their deck and ordered hot coffee and scones. Though mist hung over the lake, and wispy clouds floated lightly across the sky, the sun warmed our faces as we waited. A small sailboat was rounding the corner into the fog. "This is the kind of vacation we've needed," I said.

I didn't want the feeling to end, so when Jane suggested we take a walk along the lake, I didn't object. Our book could wait.

Few people were on the beach, and no one was swimming. I reached down to test the frigid water and understood why.

At the end of the beach, we walked down a paved road running the length of a narrow peninsula. As we passed the house at the end of the lot, an old man with white hair and a plaid shirt approached.

He fit the image of a local eccentric who had spent years weathering his face on these shores.

The stranger pointed at the lakeshore and said, "That rocky shoreline over there's called Artist's Point."

Jane and I looked in the direction he pointed.

"It's called that," he said, "because so many artists have drawn, painted, and photographed the rocky outcroppings from there. In fact, it's almost become a cliché for North Shore art."

Smiling, he opened his case and showed us a recent painting from Artist's Point.

"It's beautiful," Jane said.

"If you want to see more, they're in the Water's Edge Gallery," he said.

Jane smiled and said, "We might just do that."

We hiked onto the outcroppings that jutted out into Lake Superior and formed the northeast harbor at Grand Marais. The huge rocks were angular, but the incessant beating of the waves had smoothed many of their rough surfaces. We jumped from rock to rock until we found a craggy ledge where we could sit and watch the waves beat against the rough shoreline, sending sprays of water into the air. The sun was warm, so Jane and I lay down for several minutes to watch the sky and the sea gulls. Rising, we continued on around the breakwater to the northeast point and came back on the bay side.

We walked back to town, where we ended up shopping in a small general store crowded with so much merchandise that we could hardly walk through the aisles. The contents could have filled a store twice its size. We bought a few things we needed, but planned to buy more later in some of the trendy tourist shops.

After unloading our purchases, we drove back to a quaint restaurant we had seen on our walk through town. Torgie's FishN'Spaghetti House was almost too unique. Jane laughed when she first saw the sign. After eating our fish and spaghetti lunch, I took a selfie of the two of us in front of the restaurant. Friends back in Chicago would enjoy the humor.

We drove back to our cabin determined to begin our research. I set up my laptop on the small desk in the corner. Jane turned on the radio for some background music while I opened the text file of our book.

We began comparing the text file with the image scans of our mysterious book's pages. We were looking for errors that might have happened when the images were converted by the computer. "One error and a vital link could be lost," my nerdy friend Carlos had said.

The text conversion was pretty accurate, but we found some obvious problems. We were constantly looking for instances of *cl* that had converted to text as a *d*, or cases of *rn* that became *m*. Once we checked the file for accuracy, we could begin working with the code-breaking programs Carlos had given me.

Jane and I spent the entire afternoon proofing, and made it through forty-nine pages. It was mind-numbing work.

"Are we nuts spending our vacation proofing nonsense in the hope of finding some hidden messages?" I asked.

Jane laughed, but we continued to feel compelled to solve the book's mystery.

In the evening, we ate at the Grand Bayside Cafe. Sitting outside, we watched the rippling water splash against the posts of the dock, only yards from where we were being served. Boats bobbed up and down, keeping pace with the sound of splashing. Sea gulls squawked overhead.

We finished our glasses of wine and consumed the freshwater fish the waiter claimed had been caught that very morning in Lake Superior. Everything seemed so different from the pace of our normal life.

Jane reminded me, "Before you get too comfortable, remember we're going to walk out to the lighthouse at the end of the breakwater this evening."

I didn't need reminding.

After our walk, we were too tired to do more proofing. We lit a fire in the wood stove, which took up one corner of the room. Even in

June, it was nice to take the chill out of the air on a cool North Shore evening. A television mounted on the wall lured us into watching a movie and then the news. The weather forecast looked unsettling, promising fog, rain, and high winds for the next day.

"Tomorrow looks like a perfect day to stay in our cabin to proof the book—and spend a little quality time together," Jane said.

"I'd love that," I said.

That night I had my first dream challenging my comprehension of reality—and leaving me terrified of what I had seen.

4

I don't usually remember dreams, but this one was so intense I will never forget its terror.

I was walking on the rocks of the northern bay, stepping carefully over their slippery surface by the light of a full moon. As I sat on an angular boulder facing Lake Superior, I saw a corked bottle floating in a backwash behind an outcropping of rocks. In my dream, I imagined some lost person whose last act was placing a note into the bottle with the hope it would be found and a life-saving search would begin. But this bottle looked empty. I watched it for a long time, not noticing the massive clouds building up over the ridge behind me and billowing southeast in the direction of the great lake.

A flash of lightning, followed by an ear-deafening clap of thunder, shocked me back to an awareness of my surroundings.

The wind hit with such fury I was almost thrown into the churning waves, waves that only moments before had been rippling playfully against the rocks. An ominous thundercloud edged out the light of the moon, overwhelming the night with impenetrable darkness. I thought about trying to get back to town, but feared falling on the slippery boulders. My flashlight was useless against the foreboding storm.

Lightning was striking all around. I clawed, slipped, and climbed my way to a higher rock. The waves crashed across the boulder where I had been sitting moments before. I hoped the force of the wind would pass quickly like it often does once a storm front has passed.

I knew there was no point in yelling for help, as my screams would never be heard above the noise of the wind and the powerful waves that lashed at my feet. I fought against the force of the wind. The waves threatened to drag me into the roiling waters. My fingers felt like they were going to break as I clung onto cracks in the cold rocks, grasping them for my very life. The fury of the storm dashed me against their brutal surface.

A flash of lightning shot across the sky. It reflected off a shiny object bouncing in the frothy water within a cleft in the rocks beside me. I recognized it as the bottle I had seen earlier.

Then, in another flash of lightning, I saw the storm from inside the bottle. Everything I was grasping onto was *in* the bottle. The entire rock outcropping I was clinging to—and a portion of the lake—had materialized inside the bottle.

I yelled above the thunder of the storm, *"No! This isn't possible. I can't be inside. The bottle is there, in the waves. I'm on the rocks."*

My objection didn't change my dreaming perception.

Horrified, I realized I was experiencing the impossible. The rock I was clinging to was now inside the bottle with the storm raging all around me. Its violence attacked without mercy. I struggled for my life as the waves lifted, tossed, and slammed the bottle against the giant boulders outside of my glass enclosure. At the same time, the storm raged on inside the bottle, forcing me to cling to crevices in the boulder until my hands bled.

As I struggled against impossible odds, I looked up at the surrounding glass of the bottle. I saw, etched in it, the symbol from the cover of our book—the same tree, but this time I was seeing it from the inside out, so the leaves were on the right and bare branches on the left. The small circle was etched into the glass on the leafy side. The snake curled in the opposite direction. How was it possible that the same image was etched onto the surface of the bottle? What was the connection? The meaning eluded me.

My fear turned to panic when I saw a crack opening along the edge of the cork in the neck of the bottle. Water was seeping in every time it dipped below the surface.

The bottle was huge; its neck looked like it was a hundred feet above me. Every time more water came rushing into the bottle it cascaded down like a waterfall, and the waves inside grew angrier and higher.

The storm continued to strengthen, both inside and outside of my glass enclosure. My stomach churned. I retched, and then threw up. A moment later, the Lake Superior in my bottle claimed my vomit.

The waves grabbed at me until finally I lost my grip and grasped for fresh handholds. I fought against the waves with all my strength, but I was sliding down toward the lake, still inside the bottle. At the same time, the bottle itself was beginning to sink.

In a final effort to save myself, I somehow jolted myself awake and the endless storm disappeared instantly. I looked around and realized I was lying, not on the rocks, but on the torn pages of our mysterious book that I must have, in my agitated state, ripped to shreds.

I cried out as I felt Jane shaking me to free me from my dream. It was only then that I realized my first sense of awakening was still part of the nightmare. As I opened my eyes I realized that I wasn't standing on a torn-up copy of our book. The book was still stored in the safety deposit box at our bank, and our copy was stacked carefully on the table. I realized I had, instead, ripped all the pages out of the Gideon Bible that had been on the bedside stand next to me.

I had obviously been grasping and flailing for some time in my nightmare, fighting for my life on the rocks.

I questioned, *What is my reality? Have I always been inside a bottle while the real storm rages outside?*

Jane looked frightened. "George!" she screamed.

I dropped into her arms. I had never experienced such intense emotions.

Jane held me for a long time before I had the strength to tell her about the horrors of my dream. I relived the nightmare as I described it to her.

"I am a rational man," I said. "Visions are for mystics—and nightmares with that kind of vividness are for children scared of monsters under the bed."

"Count on me to check under the bed whenever you feel the urge," Jane said.

We laughed. My tension eased.

"Besides," she said, "your dream sounds a lot like our walks along the lake, except for the storm, of course."

"You're right. The images of the rocks, the lake, and our mysterious book must have combined in my subconscious to cause my nightmare."

Nevertheless, my dream had taken on the qualities of a vision to me, as would those that followed. Jane said she could never forget how scared and alone she felt when she found me yelling and half delirious, with torn pages of the bedside Bible spread out across the covers.

The sun was beginning to rise in the east. Since we were both awake, we decided to get up.

A steady rain beat against the window. Jane put her arm around me and said, "Even the weather report may have played into your dream."

"Maybe, but they didn't predict a storm."

"They did predict high winds," Jane said.

After I finally stopped shaking, we relit the fire, showered, and dressed, then began our proofreading. We read every letter, page after page. We were about a quarter of the way through when we became so hungry and exhausted that we couldn't proof another line until we had something to eat.

We had Wi-Fi in our cabin, so I backed up our corrected book file onto my cloud drive. By then it was almost noon, and the sun was shining through breaks in the rain clouds. We decided to walk to a downtown restaurant where we stayed longer than we had planned, enjoying the quiet atmosphere. After our second cup of coffee, the day looked like it was going to turn unpredictably nice, and we decided we were far too energetic to go back to work just yet.

"Let's go out to Artist's Point to confront the fear of your nightmare—and maybe enjoy the walk, too," Jane said.

"Sounds good to me. The walk won't take long, and we'll feel a lot better."

We were about halfway along the rocky formations on the Lake Superior side of the peninsula when I looked down into the water and saw a bottle bouncing along the rocks. It twisted and turned in the frothy water. I immediately stopped. My body language must have betrayed my shock.

Jane grabbed my arm. "What's wrong?"

I pointed at the bottle. "That bottle, it's floating in the rocks *exactly* as I remember seeing it in my nightmare. Exactly."

Jane's first reaction was, "You're kidding!" Then she looked directly into my eyes, and said, "You're not kidding."

"I swear I'm not. It's like I'm reliving the dream. That's the bottle."

Jane studied it as it bobbed along the rocks. She said, "Maybe you saw the bottle on our walk yesterday. You probably didn't think about it then, but for some reason you remembered it in your dream. Look at it. Does it have the tree on it?"

The bottle was about ten feet below us. I couldn't tell for sure, but I didn't think I saw the image from our book on it as it splashed and bobbed in the crevice. It looked like a plain, old wine bottle with the label missing.

"No," I said. "You're probably right."

I couldn't face any other possibility.

We found a dry spot on one of the large boulders, where we sat down and watched the waves race across the lake, splashing across the lower rocks.

"I know we wanted to research our book on vacation, but sometimes don't you wish we'd left the research at home?" Jane said.

"I've got to admit, proofing any book can be darn boring," I said. "But I'm so intrigued. I want to find out what our book is all about. I know it's kind of mind numbing, but the book's captured my imagination, in the same way that looking for buried treasure would tempt an explorer."

In many ways, I really did think about the research as looking for buried treasure. I still had the same uneasy feeling I'd had the first time I touched the book, a feeling that somehow it would change the whole focus of our lives.

Jane and I both shivered. The air definitely felt colder. I looked back to see billowing black clouds forming over the top of the ridge that overshadowed Grand Marais. I cringed, thinking that this was too much like my nightmare. If it had the same strength as the storm I had dreamed about, I wanted to get off the rocks as soon as possible.

"Let's get out of here before that storm hits," I urged.

Jane looked back, gasped, and said, "I'm with you."

We scurried along the outcroppings, jumping from rock to rock, racing against the wild fury advancing toward us. We worked our way through the brush in the middle of the peninsula as fast as we could and sprinted into town just as the first bolt of lightning cracked overhead.

In moments, the street was as dark as night. Giant raindrops poured down as we reached the first shop. The wind nearly knocked us off our feet as I reached for the door handle. I flung the door open, and the stormy blast tried to rip it off its hinges as I held on with all of my strength, forcing it shut behind me. I turned to look out the window. I could hardly see across the sidewalk through the falling sheets of water. The rain slammed down the street at such an angle it looked like a flood driving at us sideways.

I was terrified. "That was close."

Jane looked equally scared. "For sure. Your dream may have saved us."

As we walked deeper into the store, I saw a brighter-than-usual flash of lightning. The store's power went out, and it looked like the darkest of nights, like in my dream.

The rain was blasting against the store so hard that the clerks yelled, "Everyone, stay away from the windows, and please move to the back of the store."

Jane and I didn't need to be convinced. We moved behind some shelves, sitting on the floor. Flashes of lightning punctuated the darkness with piercing light, creating shadowy black outlines of the merchandise against the back wall.

As we huddled in our small refuge, I thought back over the dream and rationalized aloud, "I couldn't have seen the storm yesterday. It was almost exactly like my dream, except I couldn't get off the rocks when it struck. And I saw the bottle. Heck, I was *in* the bottle."

Jane squeezed my arm and said, "You keep trying to scare me. Stop it."

All I could say was, "Well, I survived the nightmare, didn't I? I think we'll be fine."

"It's the 'I think' part that bothers me," Jane said.

The storm continued for almost an hour before its intensity abated enough for us to feel comfortable walking to the front of the still-dark store. We looked out the window toward the waterfront. The waves beat against the breakwater between the lake and the harbor, splashing foam over its top like it was trying to beat the land into submission. I could only imagine what it must have been like fifteen minutes earlier.

Jane and I would never have survived on the rocks.

5

We were pretty shaken by our close call with tragedy.

We eventually walked back to our cabin through a light drizzle. The atmosphere was beginning to recover, though tree branches were down everywhere and rivers of water flowed down the streets.

"I'm glad that's over. All my muscles hurt—and I'm starved," Jane said.

"Not much hope of stopping at a restaurant," I said, looking around. "The power's out everywhere. Everything's closed."

"I'll make some sandwiches as soon as we get back to the cabin."

Safe in our cabin, we ate standing by the window as the sun began to peek around the edges of the purple clouds. Beams of sunlight shot across the sky and a rainbow colored an arch of hope.

We watched until the effect began to fade and I said, "Let's get back to work."

Fortunately, I had unplugged the computer before we left so the lightning hadn't damaged it. While the power was still off, my laptop was fully charged. I figured we could do several hours of proofing before the batteries died.

We had proofed for about an hour when the lights flickered and came back on for good. Jane and I worked, snacked, and worked some more. We continued proofing late into the night, and we had more than half of the book done when we went to bed.

I woke the next morning and peeked around the curtains. The day was cloudy; a light mist was drizzling against the window. A few minutes later, I ran out to the car to get a bag of coffee I had left in the trunk. The damp wind hit me with a cold blast. It would be another great day to hunker down and keep working. Jane and I desperately wanted to finish so we could begin using our computer programs to analyze the file.

By late evening, we had finished the entire document, correcting hundreds of errors. We probably should have also read it again backwards, but we wanted to get started on the analysis with the decoding software.

———————

Since lightning had already knocked out the power once, I felt even more insecure about losing the work we had done on the book over the past few days. I immediately backed up my file to my cloud drive. I also backed up the file of the corrected book onto my flash drive and two separate CDs.

I put one of the CDs into a padded envelope and addressed it to my office, and I hid the second one in our car. I put the flash drive into my computer bag.

"I know the precautions are a bit extreme, but I want to know the files are safe," I explained to Jane.

"I think it's a good plan," Jane said. "Our notes have already been stolen once. I don't want to have to start over."

How many more things can go wrong? I thought as I sensed the lure of the book and my desire to understand its meaning. The intensity of my yearning was becoming obsessive. I had to keep searching.

I felt a lot more secure once I had dropped the backup copy into the mailbox. I could relax when Jane and I went for a late dinner just as the sun was beginning to set. We decided once again to eat at the Grand Bayside Cafe.

As soon as we entered, they put up their *Closed* sign. We would be the evening's last customers.

Jane whispered, "I hate when they do that. It makes me feel like I need to hurry to finish."

The restaurant staff, however, seemed genuinely pleased that we had come to dine with them, and we felt comfortable as they joked with us.

We sat outside on the deck, looking across the misty bay and enjoying the cool night air. Lake water lapped against the stones under the wooden boards of the dock we were eating on.

By mutual consent, Jane and I had avoided talking about the book during our meal. As we were eating our desserts, however, Jane gave me one of her "a-ha" looks. "Have you noticed how many numbers are in the book? Do you think they might be a clue to cracking the code?"

As I thought about her revelation, I realized she was right. There were more numbers than you would expect to find in most books, math books being excluded.

As soon as we finished our desserts, Jane and I rushed back to our cabin and began to search. Why hadn't we discovered the numbers earlier? Now they seemed to stand out on nearly every page.

"Most of the numbers are single digits, except I'm seeing the number 28 several times," Jane said. "This number must have some special significance."

We had found our first clue since discovering our book in the mystery section of the library, but that only added to the mystery.

It was nearly midnight by the time we finished searching the book for numerals, so we decided to make a fresh start in the morning.

We had established a morning vacation ritual by now. After we got up and dressed, we would go straight to the bakery, where the waitress remembered our names and how we took our coffee. Jane and I would eat our breakfast while watching the sun progressing higher over Lake Superior.

This morning we discussed the storm from a couple of days earlier. As we were leaving, Jane said, "This really is a dangerous lake."

I nodded in agreement. "No question about that. The storm was terrible. I can only imagine what it must be like on a ship in the middle of the lake when a gale like that hits. There are a lot of vessels on the bottom, including the *Edmund Fitzgerald*, to testify to the power of the storms here." I took her hand as I thought back to my dream. "I'm just glad I wasn't inside a bottle when it hit."

After coffee, we went back to the cabin and started searching for more patterns in the text. As we looked at all of the times we found the number 28, Jane said, "It looks like the numbers that follow the number 28 often repeat themselves, even if they're pages apart. See, every sixth number is repeating itself until the next number 28 appears."

"How did you ever figure that out?" I said.

Jane showed me her notes. She was writing every number in a column, adding a new row every time the number 28 appeared. "See, other sequences have different numbers, except that every sixth number is always the same. Several numbers that seem to always stay in a consistent order are 1, 2, 4, and 7."

"I think we've found our second clue—or perhaps it's an expansion on our first clue," I said. "There probably are a lot more number patterns, but we've at least found one of them."

"But we still don't have any idea what the numbers *mean*," Jane said.

"True, but if I remember my college math right, the number 28 is a perfect number—just don't ask me why."

Jane and I were artists, writers, and editors; not mathematicians. What did Jane or I know about math? At the time, however, we felt that all the numbers had to point to some way of deciphering the content, and the number 28 had to be important.

I did a computer search for "perfect numbers," and found I was right—it meant that the number was also the sum of all of the whole numbers you could use to divide it.

Of course we were just beginning. The numbers—even the perfect ones—could still mean nothing. We had to face the possibility that, as beautiful and mysterious as our book was, it really might have been meaningless, but that now seemed less likely. We were becoming increasingly compelled to unravel the puzzles we believed the book contained.

"These aren't just game puzzles," Jane said. "If they're the kind of puzzles I think they are, they'll likely change our lives dramatically."

We ate lunch in the cabin and, after relaxing for an hour, charged ahead at trying to solve the mystery. But the results of our afternoon's search for keys to unlock the book's hidden meaning were less rewarding.

That evening, we finally ran one of Carlos's computer programs. The software was designed to look for sequences that repeated themselves. I would have run it sooner, but we had to figure out how to use it from some rather sketchy notes. Plus, even though I knew how the program was *supposed* to work, I had no idea how effective it would be.

On the plus side, I wasn't worried about corrupting our book file because I had multiple backups. We started the program by pointing it to the file and selecting the Start Analysis button. Though our laptop was supposed to be one of the fastest on the market, the program took a while to process all the combinations in the book. When it finished, it had found several instances when the numbers four, nine, and six had occurred together with a comma between the four and nine, and an ampersand between the nine and six.

Now we weren't certain whether that key number was "4, 9 & 6"; or "496"; or all of the above. In addition to that combination, the number sequence eight, one, two, and eight occurred at least five times. Were those individual numbers, or did they indicate the number 8,128?

I couldn't exactly remember, but I was pretty certain 496 and 8,128 were other perfect numbers. Again, I searched online, and confirmed that they were, indeed, perfect numbers.

Along with the repeated numerals, there were also hundreds of text sequences that duplicated themselves.

"The text combinations might mean something as a group, or they may simply be repeated phrases," I said.

"They may be clues that help us figure out the meaning of the language—or languages—used in the book," Jane suggested. "If we can even figure out one or two of the words, we can match them up to other places they occur. I think we should back up these findings, too, before we move on."

I agreed. I again backed up the results of our research to my cloud drive and both of our flash drives, and put everything on two new CDs. I put the flash drive back into the computer bag, put one CD in the car, and put the third one in a padded envelope to mail to my office.

We felt we had made real progress, but we were burned out from the intense effort. Our vacation was almost over, and it felt like we'd been working all week. "As soon as we mail the CD in the morning, let's take the rest of the day to have some fun," I suggested.

"I'd like to drive up the Gunflint Trail to see the forest and lakes we've heard so much about from the Fosters," Jane agreed.

We woke up a little later than we had planned. When we slid from under the sheets it was nearly eight.

"I must have forgotten to set the alarm," Jane said.

I peeked through the curtains. The day was bright, but the ground was wet from more rain during the night.

We dressed quickly. When we stepped out, the cool breeze made us shiver, so we put on the sweatshirts we had purchased downtown. They had matching loons on them with lettering that said, "A Loon in Minnesota, Sure Nuff!" Touristy, yes; corny, very; but they were somehow fitting for the day.

Even though we were starting off a little later than planned, we walked down the street for our coffee. Along with our usual breakfast order, we bought a couple of multigrain sandwiches and some chips to take with us for lunch.

We went back to the cabin where I picked up the envelope containing the CD to send back to my office. I didn't want to leave without mailing it, so I drove to the post office and dropped it into the mailbox while Jane finished preparing for the drive.

Am I being overly cautious? I again questioned. *It's always better to be a little too careful, isn't it? Mistakes happen. Things go wrong.*

6

We drove up the steep incline leading out of Grand Marais and onto the Gunflint Trail. When we reached the top of the ridge that over-looked Grand Marais and Lake Superior, I pulled off the road and Jane and I took a moment to gaze across the expanse of the silver-blue water glistening as far as we could see. The clear sky brightened in the distance until it seemed to merge with the lake. In the bay, far below us, a single sailboat with white sails whisked silently past the lighthouse and out onto the lake.

I took a panoramic photo, but it was flat and could never begin to capture the vast expanse below. While the view was captivating, our journey had barely begun, so we continued our drive over the hill.

We had been told the Gunflint Trail was one of those rare roads that ends at the edge of the wilderness and that we would find a parking lot and a place to turn around about sixty miles from Grand Marais.

On the inland side of the ridge, the landscape became rolling hills and thick forest. As we drove, lush green trees swept past. Wild grasses brushed the edge of the road. Purple, yellow, and white flow-ers dotted the ditches, filling the air with their rich fragrances.

We stopped abruptly about ten miles down the trail as a bull moose casually crossed the road. Without even glancing our way, it ambled across just fifty feet in front of our bumper and continued down into a small swamp; after all, we were the intruders—he lived here.

We pulled to the side of the road.

Jane smiled. "Don't you feel close to nature?"

"I think nature just walked in front of us. Hand me my camera," I said.

Jane passed it to me and then grabbed the binoculars. Once the moose had moved a respectable distance away, we got out of the car. He took his time, and I was able to take several photos as he grazed his way into the forest.

I felt, for a moment, like I had a special relationship with the huge creature, almost as if he had allowed me to be a part of his world.

Yet, as suddenly as the moose had appeared, he left. Jane and I watched the branches close in behind him.

After traveling over the hills and through the forest for many more awe-inspiring miles, we parked near a pristine lake. The lush trees and gray rocks were reflected on the water's surface with just enough of a ripple to let us know which scene was real. A lone bird with black and white feathers, a loon, created the only disturbance to the reflection; its lonesome cry echoed across the water.

Jane sat quietly, absorbing the scene. I took several photos, attempting to capture the elusive beauty.

The tranquil mood was shattered when a blue SUV with a canoe on top sped down the road. It pulled off, dust flying, and parked next to us. A young couple got out; the woman grabbed a camera off the seat and called to the young man. "James, go stand by the lake so I can get a couple pictures of you."

He walked down to the water's edge and waited while she took several photos, the beauty of the lake glistening behind him. Then she gave him the camera and he took her picture.

Although they had interrupted the serene atmosphere, we couldn't be upset with them.

"Beautiful, isn't it?" I said.

They nodded. The woman said, "Gorgeous."

"Would you like me to take a photo of the two of you by the lake?"

They seemed pleased by my suggestion and handed me their camera. When we'd finished, they offered to return the favor, so I gave them my camera. Jane and I hugged on the shore while the young woman carefully framed us in the viewfinder.

We talked with them for a few minutes about camping and canoeing. Then, almost as quickly as our moose had come into our lives and disappeared into the forest, our new acquaintances got into their car and drove off. The sounds of the forest again reigned supreme. A few minutes later, we continued our own journey up the Gunflint Trail.

We stopped at a scenic overlook on a ridge that must have been hundreds of feet above a wide valley. A hawk flew circles over a long thin lake in the distance.

Jane looked at our map, pointed at the lake, and said, "According to this, Canada's on the other side of that lake."

We were so far north we could see Canada. Short of canoeing or a long hike, however, there didn't appear to be any way to get there.

We wanted the road to continue forever, carrying us to new wildlife discoveries, but we soon came to its end. We could either go around the loop and begin our trip back, or pull into the trail's end parking lot. Choosing the latter, we were amazed at how many vehicles had traveled up the narrow road. We took one of the last parking places in a lot filled with cars, SUVs, and trucks, many with trailers attached.

Jane and I found a tree to throw a blanket under, and sat enjoying the warmth of the midday sun. Mostly, we cherished being with each other with nothing to distract us.

After a light lunch, we walked to the lake to watch a group of young people launch canoes for a wilderness adventure, staying until the canoes disappeared around a bend.

As we left the parking lot to begin our drive back to Grand Marais, Jane said, "Let's come back here when we have more time."

"And let's get a canoe and be the ones paddling into the wilderness," I said.

About halfway back, we turned off the Gunflint Trail and drove down a gravel road past some more lakes. After driving to the far end of a lake, we pulled into another parking lot. A few people were canoeing along the shore near a primitive lodge, creating the only ripples on the lake.

The scene was almost *too* peaceful. Most of our lives had been spent in such noise and tension we hardly knew what to do with the quiet. The haunting calls of loons echoing across the lake, the rustling of the forest behind us, and the splashing of the water along the shore whispered to us, "Relax."

We drove down the gravel road to see if we could find the way to the lodge we had seen. Discovering its location almost immediately, we continued bouncing along a rougher road than anything we had yet driven on. The picturesque lodge was constructed of dark brown logs, and a number of smaller log cabins flanked it on each side.

We went in and I asked the desk clerk if we could make reservations to stay there sometime. He introduced himself as Wally and nodded his head in agreement. He handed me a business card with a website and an 800 number to call.

I joked with Wally that these woods would be a great place to hide. Wally said, "Yah, it might be a good place for two or three months, but the winters are dangerous this far north. In January, wind chill can feel like its 100 degrees below zero. Even summers can be dangerous for those not prepared."

"That's *cold*," I said.

Wally looked at me. "Last August, not far from here, someone died in the woods from exposure."

I shivered at the thought.

We stopped a few more times at various lakes and scenic overlooks on our drive back. The sun was beginning to set as we pulled off the road atop the ridge overlooking Grand Marais. The lights of the town flickered on, defining the shoreline against the dark lake and sky. We took our flashlights, walked about thirty yards along the ridge, and sat down to watch the evening landscape.

I put my arm around Jane, feeling her warmth in the cool air. I gently brushed my hands through her soft hair and down her cheek. "I wish this day could last forever."

"Wouldn't it be great if we could leave everything behind in Chicago and move up here?" Jane said.

"Nice dream," I said.

Jane put her head on my shoulder. "Yeah, nice dream until it feels like 100 degrees below zero."

I brushed her hair back and gazed into her eyes. I whispered, "I have my dream."

Though the thoughts were warm, we shivered in the night air creeping up the hill from the lake. It was time to move on. Hand in hand, we walked back to the car. This was a day Jane and I would remember. Looking back, maybe the closeness we felt gave us the strength to survive the trials we would soon face. Granted, there had been countless moments that bound us together. Who can say which ones were most important? But this had been a rare day to strengthen our bond and marvel at the world around us.

It was dark by the time we got back to our cabin. One street lamp projected its light across our walk and a small light over our door dimly lit the entrance.

————————

At first we didn't notice anything unusual, but when I tried to put the key into the lock, the door pushed open with no resistance. I reached around the corner and flipped the light switch on, but the room remained dark.

I jumped back and collided with Jane, who yelled, "What's with you?"

I yanked her back toward the car. As calmly as I could, I whispered, "The door was open, the lights didn't come on, and I think there might be someone in our cabin."

I opened the car and pushed Jane in as I said, "Get away as fast as you can and call the police."

Jane tugged on my arm as she slid over to the passenger side. "Don't be stupid. I'm not leaving you here."

"Okay, you're probably right." I slid into the driver's seat and started the car.

We drove downtown to a place near the lake where our cell phones had coverage and called the police. Then we drove back to the cabin.

"The burglar must have left by now," I said. "We weren't quiet about what we were going to do. Besides, I want to find out what happened before the police arrive."

Jane grabbed my arm and whispered harshly, "Don't."

I pulled free and whispered back, "I'll be careful."

I grabbed the flashlight and crept to the cabin. Jane watched from the car. I pushed the door open and shined the beam of light into the darkness. Stepping into the room, I looked around.

Surprisingly, the laptop was where I had left it, but our research notes were gone. I looked into the bathroom. No one was there.

I waved for Jane to come in. She looked scared when she entered. I probably looked just as frightened. What was happening? The fears we had suppressed after the break-in of our house haunted us again. Were we in danger? What was so important about the notes that someone kept taking them?

After studying the room, I said, "The software and flash drive I left by the computer are also missing."

Jane looked down at the table where I had left them. "Do you think there might be something about the research itself they're after?"

I decided to risk starting the computer to see if our files were intact. Since I didn't want to disturb any possible evidence, I pulled out a napkin and pressed the Start button. Nothing happened.

Not only were the files gone, but the whole hard drive had been wiped clean. Whoever had broken in appeared to have only one purpose: destroy our work.

I stared at Jane with a shocked look on my face. "How did they even know we were working on the book up here?"

What was the book all about? Who had put it in the library to begin with? How did they—whoever *they* were—know we had their book? Did they follow us from Chicago? Had someone been secretly watching us? Was it the same people who we thought had broken into our car in the Twin Cities? Could they be the same ones who broke into our house?

And, most frightening of all, was the librarian killed because she had given us this very book?

We were asking so many questions that we were working ourselves into a state of shock and bewilderment.

"What do we tell the police?" Jane said. "Should we tell them everything, including about taking the book from the library? That has to be a minor infraction, one they probably won't prosecute us for."

"Maybe," I said, "but that would complicate things, and I doubt they'd believe us. We only need to tell them the door was kicked in, and our notes on a book we were researching have been stolen."

"So, we won't say anything about the mystery surrounding our book," Jane said.

"No, but what if they ask why the computer wasn't stolen?" I said as I heard sirens growing louder.

"I don't know," Jane said.

I didn't have much time to think. I packed the computer and slid it under the couch. "If the police find it there, they won't question why it wasn't taken."

7

We were exhausted from our day of traveling the Gunflint Trail. Our privacy had again been invaded. We were afraid. Now we had to re-evaluate everything we were doing and undergo questioning by the police.

A squad car pulled into the drive, siren blaring, lights flashing. The police officers looked over the entire scene and took our statements. An officer interviewed John and Madge Johansen, the owners of the cabin, who had rushed down from the office as soon as they heard the police pulling into their drive.

The police went around the complex taking statements from guests staying in the neighboring cabins. Apparently no one had seen or heard anything.

We went up to the resort office to sign off that our statements to the police were accurate. One of the officers gave an official-looking report to John. They suggested we call our insurance company, but nothing of value to anyone but us had been taken. While the resort owner called a locksmith and scheduled a time for the door to be fixed, the desk clerk told us that she had another cabin open for the night and gave us a new key.

Before the police left, they explained that, in cases like this, the burglar is rarely caught. Jane and I had assumed that. After all, without witnesses or fingerprints—or *any* obvious physical evidence—what chance would there be of catching the culprits, or convicting them if they were caught?

Later, after settling into the new cabin, Jane and I spent a long time discussing our situation. "I was really nervous about holding back on some of the details," Jane said. "I know we'd discussed not telling them, but I also thought the police might think we were nuts if we told them about researching a book filled with gibberish. What's weird though . . . I felt like something *inside me* also demanded I shouldn't tell them."

"I had the same feeling. What kind of hold does this book have over us?"

It didn't make sense, and that bothered us.

By the time we got to bed, my travel clock had clicked past 2:00 a.m. Even then, I didn't go right to sleep. I stayed awake worrying.

I worried about Jane. How was she coping with the stress? What if next time they threatened us personally—or worse? It would probably be best to turn our book and all of our research over to the police, but I just couldn't. I wasn't ready to give it up yet. We still needed to crack the mystery of our book.

I remembered the backup CD I had made of the files and stored in the car before we left on our journey. Would it work? I couldn't check it on my computer because they had erased its hard drive, but it would be comforting to have the CD with me.

Sleep must have finally overtaken me because, when I woke up, sunlight was shining in the window. When I rolled over, I saw Jane was already dressed and making coffee.

I sat up and said, "When you're done, will you run out to the car and get the CD of our research? I left it in the bin between the seats."

I had just finished brushing my teeth when she charged into the cabin. "It's gone!"

I pulled on some pants and ran out to check for myself. I was positive I had left the CD there, but it was indeed missing. We looked everywhere in and around the vehicle, not so much because we thought we would find it, but to convince ourselves it really had been stolen.

We figured that, whoever the thieves were, they must have waited until all was quiet, slipped back, and then searched our car. We were pretty shaken up.

"Should we call the police again?" I said.

"No. Let's just get out of here. This place is giving me the creeps."

"You're right. Let's get packed. At least we have our original CD of the book."

Jane immediately checked her purse.

"No!" Jane cried. "I forgot. I pulled it out yesterday morning and put it on the sink when I was looking for my makeup bag. They must have taken it when they stole everything else."

"Well," I said, "we still have the original on my cloud drive, and on the two CDs I sent back to my office. And the book's in our safety deposit box."

"I also wrote some notes from our research onto a sheet of paper as I was recording them into the computer," Jane said as she pulled out a folded note from her purse.

I let out a cheer and threw my arms around her. "Very clever!"

Now the notes took on greater urgency, as did any other coded messages in the book. We both decided to memorize the numbers. I felt better that we at least had a few key elements to use in our research.

"What have we gotten ourselves into?" Jane said.

"Perhaps we've stumbled onto secret directions to a hidden treasure or a message for an underworld scheme—but not likely," I said. "Based on the movies, mobsters would have killed us, and we're still alive."

"Maybe they're following us because they don't know where we've hidden the book. They could be waiting for us to lead them to it and, after they have the book, they'll kill us," Jane suggested.

"That's a depressing thought. Wouldn't it be more positive to assume our predator was choosing to destroy our resources rather than attack us? Of course, if they killed the librarian, then you're right. We're probably in serious danger.

"On the other hand," I said, "maybe it's the good guys who want the book. Could the FBI or CIA be trying to retrieve it, and they followed us because the book contains the code for CIA agents worldwide? The FBI or CIA could track us because we've used our credit cards."

Our ideas were beginning to sound more and more like radical conspiracy theories.

Jane added one more to the mix. "Or is the book some kind of guide to secret cult rituals? Could cult worshipers be looking for their book? If they don't find it, they'll keep attacking us. And if they *do* find it, we become human sacrifices on one of their altars."

These are the nightmarish plots of horror movies—and we are living in one of them.

The more questions we asked, the more we realized how little we knew.

Jane peeked out the window to see if anyone was lurking in the bushes. Were we exaggerating our fears, or were we understating our danger? Was someone—or some clan, gang, occult society, or government organization—out to get our book at any cost?

We wanted to believe that all of the strange occurrences that had happened since we had taken the book were just coincidences. But that was unlikely.

Jane and I discussed what danger we might be in, but we had no idea what we would do if our worst fears became reality.

"If these guys are as good as we think they are, I doubt the police will be able to protect us," I said.

"Of course, we haven't been totally honest with them," Jane said.

"We could tell them everything we know and plead for protection. But, if we do that, they'll most likely consider us crackpots and protect us only long enough for us to get out of town."

Jane laughed. "Yeah, our story's so bizarre I'll bet they'd think we faked the whole break-in just to get attention."

I still didn't want to believe we had been followed from Chicago, but considering all of the evidence, this was the most likely conclusion.

Whoever had broken into our cabin appeared to be professional. They had destroyed exactly what they wanted and had left no evidence behind, but they weren't perfect. We still had backups, and we had the number sequences we had found, thanks to Jane. We also still had the original book locked safely away—or at least I hoped we did.

The question was: How likely was it that whoever was behind the break-ins might still try to kill us?

While we didn't know what to do, we were certain we didn't want to spend another night in Grand Marais, especially in this cabin.

We loaded our car and stopped at the office to check out. When we had reserved the cabin, we were told a twenty-four-hour notice would be required if we weren't going to stay for the duration of our reservation. We expected to have to pay for the night's lodging, but given the circumstances, Madge said she wouldn't charge us. John even offered to give us the previous night free since, as he said, "You couldn't have slept much after what happened."

"We want our guests to feel safe here," Madge affirmed, though I wasn't sure whether she meant us, or the other guests who might feel safer after we were gone.

We thanked them profusely and drove into downtown Grand Marais to get gas. From there we drove along the coast toward Duluth. The waves of Lake Superior glistened in the distance on the left side of the road now as we headed towards home. When we drove over a small rise in the road and saw the Superior View Restaurant, Jane said, "The restaurant has a great view of the lake. I need a break after getting out of Grand Marais. Let's stop for an early lunch."

I agreed. We needed to stop somewhere to reflect and relax after everything that had happened. After coffee, we decided to walk over to the Superior View Lodge to ask if they had any vacancies for the night.

"We've just received a cancellation for a couple of rooms," the desk clerk said. One room was on the ground floor, which we declined. We chose the room on the second floor, feeling safer there.

The room wouldn't be ready until early afternoon, so we left our bags in the car, walking across the road and down to the shore of Lake Superior. We hiked along the water's edge until we reached some rock outcroppings.

We sat on a large boulder and once again talked about our search for clues in our book. The probability that we had stumbled onto something dangerous still worried us.

"Maybe, when we get back, we should stop researching our book," Jane said.

I tossed a pebble into the water. "After everything that's happened, I doubt it would do any good."

Jane stared across the lake. "If only we could put the book back where we found it, and our lives could return to normal." She looked into my eyes. "Of course, I know that can't happen. We had to find that book, didn't we?"

We both still held an irrational feeling that we were, somehow, supposed to possess the book. If our book led us to a great discovery or changed our lives through solving its secret, it would be worth the risk. The longer we talked, the more we realized that whatever the consequences, we believed the book was *our* treasure, and we would continue to investigate its hidden meanings. We were too intrigued by its mystery to quit.

Jane said, "Let's make a solemn pact between us."

"What?" I said. "What kind of pact?"

"Okay," she said, "here it is: Do you covenant with me that, short of death, we will continue our research into our book with the mysterious tree embossed on the leather cover and its unreadable copy until we discover the hidden mysteries it contains?"

She was so serious that I wasn't sure, at first, how to react. She took my hand, and I knew what I had to do. "Okay, I do declare this with you," I pledged.

"I do, as well," Jane said. "That sounded a lot like our wedding vows, didn't it?"

I hugged her saying, "Maybe it was a refreshing of our vows."

We held hands as we leisurely walked back to the lodge for lunch. Then we walked up the road to Cascade State Park and spent the rest of the afternoon hiking the trails, a welcome break from the tension of the previous few days.

We watched the Cascade River plunge over several misty waterfalls, and then flow down to Lake Superior. Craggy rocks bound the water to its course. Wildflowers were in bloom everywhere along the trails. We stopped once to watch fish swimming along the bottom of one of the shallow pools that swirled away from the river.

We stood on an outcropping high on the side of a ridge where we looked out for miles over dense forest and the lake. We stepped further out on the ledge to see a hawk flying in large swooping circles over the tree-covered hills before disappearing into the trees.

We took dozens of photos and left only when our tired muscles reminded us that we still needed to make the trek back to the lodge. We stopped at the front desk to see if we could get into our room, happy that the desk clerk said it was ready and handed us our keys.

The first thing we did was to check the room for anything suspicious. To our relief everything looked normal—and we reminded ourselves that there was nothing left that could be taken. After changing our clothes and showering, we went back to the restaurant for a relaxing dinner, but we were exhausted from the stresses of the last few days, not to mention our hike, and ate quickly before returning to our room.

———————

The next morning, when I woke up, I noticed the Gideon Bible on the bedside table. I remembered how, a couple of nights earlier, I had ripped one to shreds in my dream. I decided to flip through its pages while Jane was in the bathroom.

The book was cheaply made and most of the language was archaic. I was fascinated, however, when I noticed the book called "Numbers." I remembered the book from my childhood classes in church. Genesis, Exodus, L-something, and then Numbers, wasn't it? I had almost forgotten. The book itself was meaningless to me, but the idea that even ancient people valued numbers made me think about the meaning of those we had found in our book.

I realized that my reflections on our book went to extremes. Sometimes I remembered its ancient beauty. The random writings piqued my imagination. The number patterns made me wonder about its origin and purpose. Why code mysterious information in a book? Most important of all, why did this book have such a hold on me?

At other times, I wanted to burn the book, but I knew that if I tried, I would never have the courage to actually go through with it. Its beauty and mystery held me hostage.

Everything from the rich leather cover to the strange type on its dusty pages called to me. The tree design etched into the leather seemed to be telling me something about myself that I couldn't quite define. Why did the image look like the description of the tree in the Garden of Eden? Why had the symbol imprinted itself in my memory so powerfully that it appeared on the bottle in my dream? If I were superstitious, I might have worried about the relationship of the book to my frightening dream—and the real storm that followed.

After packing, Jane and I had a quick breakfast and took another walk to the lake. We stood with our arms around each other's waists for a few quiet moments. The only sounds were the chirping of birds and the ripple of water against the stones. Our quiet was broken when a semi-truck slowed down with foreboding gear crunching and diesel popping to the reduced speed limit on the road behind us.

We walked back to the lodge and checked out. Minutes later, we were driving south.

As Jane drove toward Minneapolis and St. Paul, I dozed and wondered, what disasters might yet occur in our search for answers to our mysterious book's dark secrets?

8

We pulled into the driveway of our home shortly after midnight on Tuesday. Luckily, we hadn't encountered any problems on our way back to Chicago. Jane and I unloaded our car, but the suitcases stayed in the living room for the night.

Our own bed felt good. This had been an unforgettable vacation. In a strange way, our time had been exhilarating because we had survived, without injury, the kinds of disasters and intrigues usually found only in movies.

My dream of the storm and the bottle still lingered as a dreadful premonition, but I had rationalized the similarity to the real storm that followed as a coincidence, a *dramatic* coincidence, but a coincidence nonetheless.

Having been the victims of a bizarre burglary connected somehow to our research on the book, we remained apprehensive. Neither of us had been personally threatened, but our privacy had been invaded. That made us nervous—and we still worried that the murder of the librarian might be somehow connected to it all.

Despite the dangers, Jane and I figured we had unlocked some of our book's code. If it did contain hidden messages, we might well be on our way to figuring them out.

I was glad I had taken Tuesday morning off as part of our vacation. I figured that would give me time to relax in bed with Jane, and still have a late morning cup of coffee before plunging into my work. Jane had the morning free because she was teaching a summer course that met only on Tuesday and Thursday afternoons. We turned off our alarms so we could sleep in.

When I woke up at about nine, I felt Jane hugging me tightly from behind. She had thrown off all the covers except for the sheet.

We clung together for what seemed like only a few minutes in our dreamy state, but when I reopened my eyes the clock showed it had been more like an hour. We needed this time with each other, knowing how busy we would be in the next several weeks.

Finally we admitted we had to get up. I kissed Jane one last time before sliding out of bed and, soon, I was driving down the freeway, leaving Jane behind to prepare for her class.

———

When I got to my office, I immediately went through the mail, but I couldn't find the envelopes I had sent from Grand Marais. I felt like I couldn't breathe. Had the thieves tracked the mail to my office and stolen the backup CDs? If so, how did they know I had sent them, unless they were watching when I dropped them into the mailbox? This was getting creepy.

I asked my staff, Carla and Linda, if they had seen any padded envelopes with a return address from Grand Marais. Both of them agreed that the envelopes had been delivered and put into my inbox, but Linda, my secretary, said, "I saw someone I didn't recognize leaving your office with at least one envelope like the one you described."

"Didn't you stop him?" I said.

"Well, I asked him what he was doing," Linda said, defensively. "He said you had called and asked him to pick up the envelope for your insurance company."

"He *what*?"

"He told me Carla let him into the office to find the letter. At the time, I assumed it was fine, even though it seemed odd."

"Carla wouldn't let him in my office," I said, glancing at Carla who was shaking her head.

"I thought that, too, but he knew her name. I assumed she must have said it was okay and then she was called away," Linda said. Her defensive tone had become mixed with confusion and apology.

"When Carla got back, did you ask her about what he was doing here?"

"No," she said, "I completely forgot."

When I asked Linda if she could describe the man, all she said was, "He was tall. He was quite tan, and had dark brown or black hair, and was maybe in his mid-forties. He wore a gray sport coat, but no tie. Oh, he also wore glasses with a black frame. I can't remember anything else."

Both Carla and Linda looked upset. Linda said, "I can't believe it. He simply walked right in during the day and walked out with your mail. I'm sorry. I should have been more careful."

I knew I was coming across as perturbed, but I let them know that I wasn't angry with them. "These crooks are smart," I said. "I suspect they were the same ones who broke into our home—and our cabin on vacation. If you ever see that man or anyone suspicious around here again, call security immediately.

"In fact, Linda, you'd better call building security now and tell them what's happened. See if they have any information."

I went into my office. The first thing I did was start my computer and go to my cloud drive to retrieve the file. I tried logging in, but I was so nervous it took three tries to get my password right. When the drive opened, it was empty. Every file had been deleted. Not only were the book files missing, but so were ten gigabytes of work files I had backed up onto the drive. Since most of them were on the office network server, I wasn't too worried, but how could this have happened? How could someone get into my drive? I was the only one using it—though I did have a couple of directories I used for sharing files with the art director.

I called Jane. I tried to remain calm as I told her that my cloud drive had been compromised and all the files had been deleted. Then I explained how the CDs we had mailed had been stolen.

"You mean they got into your drive and destroyed it, like your laptop? And then they walked right in and . . . "

"Yes, they carried it out flawlessly. They must have excellent computer skills. And a lot of preparation must have gone into finding and stealing the discs. They seemed to know the envelopes were there—and where to look for them."

Jane sounded shocked. "Do you think they're watching us?"

"I don't know. Probably. I had Linda call our security office."

"Shouldn't you call the police, too?"

"If I did, what would I tell them? Everything?"

"What would they do if we told them about the book?" Jane said. "Would they believe us? Would they demand we give it up?"

"If that happens, we'll lose all of our research—and the book, too."

We spent some time considering how we had acquired the book; basically, we had taken it. Since it wasn't cataloged, however, we could argue that it was simply a lost item we had claimed.

Maybe we should have handed it over to the library's lost and found. And perhaps we should have given it to the police, but we both were obsessed with it. After all, we had made a pact to keep researching the book until we found its secret. I wasn't ready to give up on our plan—at least not yet.

"The crooks are the ones invading our privacy because we found a lost book that they want. If they have a legitimate claim to the book, why haven't they come forward and said it was missing?" I asked, trying to rationalize what I was feeling. "We would be disappointed, but under those circumstances, we would give it to them, wouldn't we? At least I think we would."

As it was, we didn't know anything about the crooks—or how we could return the book, even if we wanted to.

"If our lives are in real danger, they've had plenty of chances to kill us," I pointed out.

"What if we just left the book out and they stole it back from us; then everything might return to normal. Right?" Jane suggested.

"On the other hand, they might wait until they get the book back before they kill us, or arrange for a convenient 'accident' to kill us. Remember what happened to Miss Bates."

We decided not to call the police, yet. Instead, Jane and I would stay alert for anything unusual and keep each other informed of any troubling events. If we felt personally threatened, we could contact the police then.

In the end, the police showed up at my work anyway because our security officer had reported the theft. I hadn't counted on him doing that, but realized it would be standard procedure.

I explained to the officer that I had been researching some archival material, that all my backup files had been deleted, and that the CDs on which I had saved my notes had been stolen. I also told him that copies of the notes had been stolen in Minnesota.

The officer was as mystified as I was. He said he would look into the case but would need more information about the material I was researching. After I told him it was an old book I had found but hadn't figured out how to read, he asked to see it. I made the split-second decision to lie. I said, "Don't you understand? Everything was stolen."

He left shaking his head, probably thinking I was crazy. Since security had made the call, he couldn't accuse me of overreacting. Still, I am certain he must have thought I was on the strange side of sane. Chicago police have better things to do than search for missing files and CDs for some half-crazed editor.

After the police left and I had calmed down Linda and Carla, I informed my boss and the other offices in EAD Publishing about what had happened. Then I tried to get back to some semblance of a normal day as I continued to sort my mail, listen to my phone messages, and respond to those needing immediate attention.

Sometime midafternoon I logged back on to my computer to check my e-mail and found more than two hundred unread messages in my inbox. I rapidly deleted about three-fourths of them as junk.

I was about to open my first e-mail message when I noticed a mailer like the ones I had sent from Minnesota. It had slipped off the top of my "IN" basket and fallen down behind my printer. I grabbed it and saw it was the second package I had mailed. The thief had only stolen the first envelope. I quickly opened the brown bubble-wrap envelope and slipped the CD into my computer. I clicked on each of the files, then ran my cursor to the end of each document to make sure it was okay. When I was completely satisfied that all of my files of our book were intact, I closed them, copied them to our network server, and put the disc into my briefcase to take home.

I contemplated making another backup copy and putting it in my safety deposit box at the bank where I had stored our book, but I was afraid that I might be followed. I didn't want to give away where the original book was being kept.

Of course, I had no way of knowing if the book was still there, and a part of me was scared it wasn't. Whoever was stalking us was good at finding out where we were keeping our research. The thought of going to my bank box and discovering the book had been taken was unpleasant, both because of how much I valued our mystery book, and because it would confirm that still one more intrusion had been made into our personal lives.

I remembered that Jane had a second safety deposit box at a credit union near the university, and considered that it might be a good option for hiding a second disc. I made a duplicate copy of the CD and put it into my briefcase with the first. Maybe we could still outsmart these guys—whoever they were.

I was going to call Jane again, but then the realization struck me: *my phone could be tapped.* I also considered the possibility that the thief could have even hidden a microphone in my office. I would have to search the whole office.

While thinking about those possibilities, I leaned back in my chair and, by chance, looked up at the ceiling. I spotted something odd in the ceiling vent. I stood on the chair and looked into the louvers. I discovered not only a microphone but a device with a tiny lens protruding from it. I was not only being listened to, I was being watched!

I left my office and called security again from the phone at Linda's desk. This time, Bill Mackey, the director of security, came up. He determined the camera had probably been placed quickly because the vent louvers kept it from being very effective. From its placement, all that could be recorded was the doorway. Everything I had discussed with Jane, however, had probably been transmitted to the thieves.

Bill then checked my phone, and my anxiety increased when he discovered another listening device implanted in it. At that point, I didn't know what the thieves might have heard. I couldn't remember what I had said aloud, or what I had only thought to myself. I realized they might know I had found the missing CD.

I was becoming increasingly paranoid. Whoever was after our book and research was apparently part of a sophisticated spy organization. I wished I knew what was motivating them to be so aggressive. What I did know was that Jane and I would need to take extreme care in our work and personal lives from now on. After all, if they had bugged my office, they probably had bugged our house and cars, too.

We were in over our heads, but we were being driven by an unexplainable desire to discover the hidden mysteries of the book—*our* book.

It belonged to *us*.

———————

I needed to talk to Jane without the threat of surveillance. It was crucial that we discuss what was happening.

I whispered to Linda, "May I borrow your cell phone to call Jane?" She handed me her phone. I walked outside of the office to make my call.

As soon as Jane answered the phone in her office, I blurted out: "We've got another problem. My office and phone have been bugged. They even had a video camera in my ceiling vents. We've got to be careful what we say."

"Okay . . . now what?"

She sounded upset. I understood. I was upset, too.

I explained how we had found the bugs, but tried not to give any details away, since I had to assume that her phone was bugged, too. Then I suggested, "Let's go out to eat this evening. You don't have anything going on, do you?"

I waited for a moment before she answered, "I'm free. What time?"

"About a quarter to six?"

"Where should we go?"

I didn't want to provide any clues ahead of time. "Let's decide on the way."

"I'll meet you outside of Calley Arts Hall."

When I left the office, I carried the envelope containing the CD I had mailed from Grand Marais in my hand to make it obvious I had the files with me. When I got into the car, I put the envelope where it could barely be seen sticking out from under the seat. My intention was to use it as a decoy to see if they were still tailing me.

I hoped that, if they were following me, they would recognize the mailing envelope containing the CD and steal it, thinking it was the one they had missed—and the last remaining copy of our research.

I wasn't sure how much the crooks really knew. Maybe they still had other surveillance devices in and around the office. I speculated they might even have uploaded a malicious program to my computer to track my keystrokes. I doubted they would have had time to do that without being seen by security, but I couldn't be certain. Perhaps they had done it remotely through the network. They had, after all, accessed my cloud drive and deleted all its files. And one or more of them may have even been in my office before, unobserved by my staff.

When I got into my car, I looked around for bugs, but cars have so many gadgets under the dash I would have been challenged to find one even if it were there. I speculated they might be using GPS to track us. I turned off my cell phone to minimize the possibility of using that to locate me.

By now, I was tired and just wanted to find Jane. Driving to campus would take forty-five minutes in rush-hour traffic. I pulled away from the curb and began the stress-filled commute.

When I met Jane I said, "Let's take a short walk before we go so I can fill you in on what's happened."

I explained as much as I could. She appeared to grow more and more nervous. We both attempted to look casual, though we were actively observing more of the activity around us than usual.

I didn't want to needlessly worry her, so I didn't tell her about the decoy CD I had left half hidden under the seat, which I could just make out as I opened my door.

We got into the car and drove in the direction of one of the campus restaurants, a pizza-burger kind of place where the sound system is always blaring youth culture at high decibels. Once inside, I ordered a Hawaiian pizza. While we waited, Jane spoke over the noise, asking, "So, now what?"

"I'm not sure, but I think we should stop our research for a while. Maybe, given a little time, things will settle down."

"I doubt we'll ever get back to normal, but I think you're right," Jane said. "I've got lots of planning to do for my classes. We should put this project aside for a while."

I nodded. "I'm behind on my editing, too, and I have several articles to write."

"So what do we do with our research?"

I pulled the second CD I had burned from my pocket and slid it across the table. "We need to store this in a safe place for now. I don't want to risk putting it in the same bank box where our book is. You still have your credit union safety deposit box, right? Could you put this copy in there?"

"Good idea, but what can we do to get them to stop chasing us?"

I considered the question. "Maybe we could begin dropping hints around our house and offices that we're giving up on our research. If they're still eavesdropping—and if it's our research they're after instead of the book—they might stop, but I doubt it."

"Would they stop if we gave the book back?" Jane said.

"I'm still not sure about that. If we did, they might not need us anymore. Once they've got the book, we both know the best way to stop us would be to kill us."

"We just can't bring ourselves to give our little book back, can we?" Jane said.

"You're reading my mind," I said. "But we'll have to be careful what we say from now on, unless we're in a noisy place like this."

It suddenly dawned on me that they might even have listening devices on us that could hear over the noise.

"Jane," I said as I leaned over and whispered in her ear, "don't say anything more. We should check everything we have on us for microphones. They might have put one in your purse or in my coat pocket."

We stopped and checked everywhere we could think of. We even went to the restrooms and checked our clothing. I was relieved when I didn't find anything. I was doubly relieved when Jane returned and said, "I think I'm clean."

We were getting jumpy, but we weren't ready to give in. *We must have high tolerances for danger*, I thought.

9

My car looked fine when we returned from the restaurant. All the doors and windows were intact. A glance showed me that the envelope containing the CD was still where I had placed it.

During our silent drive back to Jane's car at the university, we stopped at a drugstore to buy prepaid burner phones so we could call each other on phones we knew weren't being traced.

After returning Jane to her car, the solitude of my drive home was disquieting. As I thought about what needed to be accomplished in the next few weeks, I grew increasingly anxious. I guess Jane must have been feeling the same because we grumbled at each other all evening.

I was so tired, I hurt; but after I went to bed, I couldn't turn my brain off.

In that delusional state between consciousness and sleep, I rehashed our situation. The events of the last two weeks, combined with the day's crisis, had caused emotional overload. Knowing that someone had been watching us, keeping track of our movements, and invading our lives was disconcerting.

At the same time, the feeling of *we are supposed to have the book, and it will change our lives forever* gnawed at me. How the book would change our lives, I didn't know—and that was frightening, too.

I could tell Jane was having trouble sleeping as well, but I didn't want to disturb her. I kept checking the digital readout of our clock radio and measuring the slow passage of the night.

In my semiconscious state, I dreamed about being trapped once more in the bottle in Lake Superior. It wasn't as vivid as the first time, but even though the second dream was vaguely distant, it compounded my fears.

In my first dream, the waters of Lake Superior were beating against the rocks, and I was hanging on with all my strength to keep from being washed out into the turbulent lake. This time, I was outside of the bottle, and there was a message inside—but the storm was still raging on. I wasn't panicking as water poured into it, but I somehow knew I had to save it from sinking. That would be risky in the storm, and I would need to time my rescue to happen between the crashing waves. In my semiconscious state, I realized that this might explain my anxiety: I was trapped in a plot I didn't want any part of, but had to finish it in order to get the message hidden in the bottle.

We had found some hopeful keys to unlocking our book's hidden code, but we were still missing the formula to discover its secrets. Though we had been stalked and robbed, Jane and I still felt compelled to continue searching for its hidden meaning. There were still so many questions we could only answer by plumbing the depths of the book's content.

Jane and I understood we had to be careful. We hoped we weren't personally in danger, but we couldn't ignore the possibility our fate would be the same as the librarian's. We felt like we had no choice. We had vowed to each other to search until we solved the mystery.

We had an agreement.

No wonder I was anxious. Even my dreams and my half-sleeping thoughts were filled with paranoia. *Are the people following us attracted to the book as much as we are? If they are . . .*

I struggled through the unforgiving night. In the morning, Jane and I had coffee and bagels on the patio because we couldn't be sure the house was free of eavesdropping devices.

One of our great strengths as a couple has always been our willingness to talk to each other about nearly everything. No matter how upset we were, we always talked. Because of that long pattern, we dared to face each other in our current state, exhausted and short-tempered.

On this particular morning, however, we drove each other emotionally down. The more we grouched at each other, the more upset we became. The more upset we became, the more we grouched at each other. Then, in a sudden flash of enthusiasm, Jane said, "Why don't you call in sick today? Let's get away from all of this!"

I was ready to snap back, *This has to be one of the stupidest ideas you've ever had,* but it wasn't. After a brief hesitation, I answered, "I'm with you. Great idea."

I called Fred Erickson, my boss, as he was driving to work. All I said was, "I know I'm just back from my vacation, but I desperately need to take a mental health day."

Our company's policy actually did allow for that, provided it was approved.

He asked why, and I explained, "First, our cabin and car were broken into while we were on vacation. Then, my office was robbed. And yesterday, bugs and a camera were found in my office."

He kept saying, "I understand," but I could sense the tension building in his voice.

Finally, he said, "Okay, go ahead and take the day off. You certainly need it. But when you come in on Thursday, I'll want to see you in my office with a full report. I have to understand what's going on."

After hanging up, we practically ran to Jane's car and drove to Lincoln Park Zoo, having lunch and staying there until about three in the afternoon. After that, we took a leisurely drive along Lake Michigan and stopped for a short walk along the waterfront. We avoided discussing our present situation and the dangers we faced. Instead, we hugged, laughed, and talked about the fun things we had done that day. When we drove home that night, we felt more hopeful.

The next morning, I woke refreshed. I got to work a half hour early and jumped into editing my highest-priority project. By 9:00 a.m., I had finished the article and needed a break. I rushed down three floors to the cafeteria to grab some coffee and a muffin.

When I got back, my voicemail light was blinking. It turned out to be the call from Fred I had both expected and dreaded, telling me to call him back immediately to set up a meeting.

My newly felt optimism began to slip. How could I explain the theft of my mail and the electronic bugs in my office? Would I need to mention our book? If I did, what would I say?

The answers were dependent on Fred's questions. I wasn't able to come up with a *safe* response. I sighed, and called Ann, his assistant, to set up the meeting for 1:30 that afternoon.

Ann checked the schedule. "I know Fred's anxious for your meeting, but he's busy until two. Will that work?"

"Okay, that'll do," I said. That would buy me more time to think about how to deal with his request, but would still be early enough that I'd be fresh when he confronted me with difficult questions.

I considered calling Jane, but there was nothing new to discuss. And I didn't want to add to her worries.

I got to Fred's office five minutes early. Ann called him on the intercom while I tried to look calm. I was afraid my voice was going to crack when I talked to her or my hands would shake, giving away how nervous I was.

I waited for several minutes. My anxiety grew. Finally, Fred came to the door. A tall, handsome man in his fifties, he acted cordial enough, but I felt like he was trying to suppress his emotions. Was this a friendly meeting, or a formality—or was he going to take drastic measures? He sat down behind his desk, facing me across its massive mahogany surface. This would be a tense meeting. Usually he sat in one of the side chairs when we had our sessions.

From where I sat, I could see the diplomas on his wall pointing out that he was a graduate of New Cove University, with a doctorate in journalism. He was also an editorial genius as well as a good administrator. Although Fred was a master at building up confidence, he could also be cold and calculating when he decided to take action.

Fred leaned over his desk and stated the facts he had from two days earlier. This was his way of making certain I understood that he was well informed. He paused after every comment so I could add or correct him. His account was too accurate for my comfort.

"Now, here are some new developments you are not aware of," Fred said.

He paused between words for emphasis.

I didn't want to hear about any *new* developments. I stared past him, looking out the window, trying to project a calm composure. Fred didn't begin again until he had made eye contact with me.

"Security found someone hiding in a restroom Tuesday night," he said. "As you probably know, the building's security guards don't carry loaded guns and, frankly, are usually just athletic college students."

I nodded that I understood, but this didn't sound good.

"The guard that night was a muscular twenty-one-year-old male weightlifter named Jake," Fred said. "As he made his rounds, he heard a muted cough coming from the women's restroom on this floor. No one was supposed to be up here at that time of night, but he was so certain he'd heard someone he knocked on the door and asked who was in there. When no one answered, Jake started pushing the door open. Without warning, a man slammed the door back against him with such force it knocked him down."

I knew the shock showed on my face, though I tried to contain it. How far would this go? I hoped it had nothing to do with the book, but I was pretty certain it did. I didn't want to confirm my fear with Fred, however.

"That's terrible," I said. "Is he okay?"

"Jake should have reported the incident to the security company before he investigated the bathroom, but he wasn't expecting anything to happen. When the door hit him, he was thrown so hard that one of his ribs was cracked. The attacker apparently wasn't interested in doing him any additional harm and escaped down the hall. Jake was able to report to his office what had happened. Ten minutes later, the police arrived and found him doubled over in pain. They immediately called for an ambulance."

Fred paused. I thought back to the librarian who had been murdered. Could this have been the second violent act by this group?

I was too stunned to say anything except, "Then what?"

"When the police checked the bathroom, they found a penny-sized microphone and transmitter lying on the floor behind the door, which sparked a full investigation. The police brought in a technical specialist to check the entire floor of offices for more devices. Several were found. One was discovered near the coffee pot, another by the copier, and still another was found in this office. In *my* office!"

Fred stood up, leaned over his desk, and looked directly at me. Without blinking, he said, "I can't tell you how upset I am. The investigators have found *thirteen* eavesdropping devices—and two relay transmitters in storage rooms."

This was serious. I sat facing Fred in stunned silence. Perhaps this whole affair was bigger than just the book. Fred must have figured that out, too.

He said, "Tell me more about the research you say was stolen in Minnesota. I need to know if it's linked in any way to broader corporate espionage, or if you are into something that's going to cause legal problems for EAD Publishing. If there's anything that will get us into trouble, I want to know about it—now. And I want your 100 percent cooperation with the police investigation."

I wasn't about to turn my work over to the authorities. However, I didn't want to lie to my boss, either. I just didn't want to tell Fred the whole truth. I ended up putting a spin on what had happened.

"I never did figure out what the book I was researching was about because it was in coded languages I couldn't understand. And since my research was stolen in Minnesota, how can I turn it over to anyone?"

Fred seemed to accept this, but he made a nasty threat. "I don't want EAD Publishing tied to anything illegal. If you're involved in anything that even *resembles* a crime, I'll terminate you immediately."

The threat was direct. I wasn't sure how to react. I hoped things would calm down, but I doubted my life would ever return to normal. For a brief moment, I considered turning over all of my research, but then I would have had to admit that I had lied to Fred. And he would fire me. I also didn't want to give up my discoveries.

The book is ours, Jane's and mine. We have a pact. We found the book. It belongs to us. Even now the book seemed to be calling me, asking me to find out what deep secrets it contained.

As I sat in stunned silence, I had a sudden realization. *I've got to delete the files from my drive on the company server so they can't cause EAD any problems—or get me fired.*

I excused myself from Fred's office and promised to update him with any information I thought of, then rushed back to my office and hurried to my computer. I was about to hit the delete key for my book directory when I realized what kind of chain reaction that might set off. By now Ralph, our computer guru, must have backed up my data and he could easily cross-reference my files. If I deleted my research files now, wouldn't that call attention to them as the files I was trying to hide? Maybe I was overanalyzing the situation. They had no clue about the documents on the book I was researching. But I couldn't take any unnecessary risks.

I wanted to believe that the hidden microphones found around the office had nothing to do with our research on our book. They could have been a part of some conspiracy to discover what we were doing as a publishing company.

The reality of the thefts in my home, in Grand Marais, and most recently, from my office, told me otherwise. I had clearly been the target of the robberies—not my company. Besides, what deep secrets did the company have to hide?

Whoever was stalking us must have been watching us for some time to know that Jane and I were trying to unlock the mysteries of the book we had taken from the library. Even before our vacation, someone must have been listening in on our conversations to find out what we knew and to discover where our research was hidden. Did they hear us discussing our plans to work on it in Grand Marais? Maybe they even knew where the original book was hidden.

"No," I cried out loud, startling Carla at her desk. I didn't want to admit that possibility.

It had been weeks since we had discovered *our* book. We found it intriguing, but I was mystified by what might make it so important. Why was someone going through the effort to track us to Minnesota in order to sabotage our research? It didn't make sense.

I resolved to have my house checked for hidden surveillance devices. Whoever was tracking us gave me the creeps. That they might be listening to our dinner conversations, or worse, our bedroom conversations, was disconcerting.

I went outside and down the block. Then I called the building's security office using my burner phone and asked to talk to Mackey, the head of security. I was hoping his phone wasn't tapped.

"Because of all the bugs we've found around here, could you put me in touch with the specialists who checked our offices? I'd like them to look for hidden microphones in my house, too."

"I've got just about as much equipment as the police," Mackey said. "Doing sweeps was one of my jobs when I was in military security. I'd be happy to search your place for a little extra cash. How about a hundred 'n' fifty bucks?"

"How about a hundred dollars and dinner?" I countered.

He agreed.

I called Jane, and asked her to call me back. Jane understood that meant she should go outside and use her burner phone. When she called back, we discussed Mackey coming to do the security check of our home. Jane decided to ask the university to do one in her office, too.

After we hung up, I called Mackey back. "What night will work best for you to do our project?"

"Tonight's the only time I can do it for at least a week."

"Okay, then tonight it is."

I called Jane again and asked her to prepare a meal for "a friend" who was coming over.

After work, Mackey followed me home in his car. When we arrived at the house, he took several electronic gadgets out of his back seat and began to check for stray transmissions. He methodically roamed the house, listening and watching his equipment. He meticulously checked every room, scanning the television, stereo, DVD player, telephones, computer, Wi-Fi router, and even our coffee pot. He looked in and under desks and drawers, and behind furniture and mirrors. Mackey even investigated the wiring, inspecting behind the switches and power plates on the walls for electronics that might send signals to an outside receiver. He climbed into our attic and looked in every place he could envision a transmitter might be hidden. He even walked around the neighborhood to see if anything appeared to be *aimed at* our house.

Finally, Mackey scanned the house one more time with some other kind of an electronic device that could pick up local transmissions. Other than our secured Wi-Fi, he found nothing. Our house appeared to be clean.

Jane and I were relieved. We gladly served him dinner and paid him a hundred dollars.

After he left, I discussed with Jane how we would proceed. Now we were doubly puzzled. How did the crooks know we would be taking the book files with us to Minnesota if they weren't listening to our conversations? Jane raised her eyebrows and said, "Maybe they found out Mackey was coming over tonight. When I went shopping this afternoon, they could have cleared out all the evidence."

We both decided that we should go with our first plan to lay low for a while. After all, there was nothing we needed to do immediately. While we were still convinced we were on a mission to understand our book, Jane and I agreed we would back off for a bit.

Of course, that would have been easier to do if I didn't still face an investigation at my office. We talked late into the night, discussing how we would respond to that. The possibilities for what might happen at work were staggering. I decided we would need to cooperate in every way possible—short of telling them we had CD copies of the manuscript and the original book was in our safety deposit box.

10

As calm as Friday and the weekend were, I wasn't prepared for what I encountered the following Monday. Two FBI agents met me at my office door with a search warrant. Fred, my boss, had already cleared them, and the computer center had given them an administrative password, both for my office computer and for the network. So much for personal privacy at work.

The agents used their own computer to copy all of my files from the network to their hard drive. They also hooked up an external drive to my computer and duplicated my entire hard drive. By lunchtime, they were gone.

Were they onto something? I nervously speculated that they had hidden their own bugs in my office, tapped my phone, and put software in my computer to trace what I was doing. More of the same— only this time, the *good guys* were listening in on me.

I didn't know how to react. I desperately needed some normalcy in my life, for at least a few hours. I settled down to do my job, getting into some serious editing. I closed my door, something I almost never did. I opened a document on the computer and immersed myself in editing an article that, a few days earlier, I would have considered monotonous. I reveled in the tedium of giving a boring document some life, making it readable to architects who saw beauty in structural functionality.

Around midafternoon, I had a quick coffee break, and then jumped back into the same work pattern for the rest of the day. At quitting time, I picked up Jane and we went grocery shopping.

Tuesday was uneventful. All of the tragedies, robberies, and spying seemed like part of a bad dream. I hoped our lives could return to normal.

As I approached the office building on Wednesday morning, however, I looked in my rearview mirror. *Haven't I seen that car several times before? Wasn't it on the freeway—and didn't it get off at the same exit I did?*

If I weren't so sensitive these days, I wouldn't have noticed it.

I reminded myself, *I might be imagining all of this. After all, I haven't been watching that closely. I could be seeing several cars that look alike, or someone could have a similar destination to mine.*

I decided not to let my tenuous observation bother me. I was probably being paranoid, but remembered the old saying, "Just because you're paranoid doesn't mean someone isn't out to get you."

I began my day as usual. Late in the afternoon, Alice asked, "Would you have time to take a look at my computer? I saved an important file a couple of weeks ago and can't find it."

Alice wasn't one of our more computer-savvy editors, so occasionally she would ask me to come down the hall to help her. As soon as I stepped into her office, I asked, "What's the name of your file, and when did you save it?" She remembered the day, and that it was saved late in the afternoon, but could only remember part of the name. I wrote the information down on a sticky note and posted it on the side of her monitor, then began to search.

While I was typing keywords into Alice's search window, she got a call from the design department and had to leave. I figured she would be out of her office for at least fifteen minutes, and decided this would be a good time to make a copy of my files. While I assumed my computer was probably compromised with software designed to track what I was doing, hers likely was not.

I walked back to my office as fast as I could without calling attention to myself, and grabbed a CD from my stash. I hurried back to her office and pushed the disc into the computer. If the FBI was monitoring my network history, they would know exactly what had been copied, but I figured that was unlikely, so I would take a chance.

I logged out of Alice's account and logged in under mine. Then I went to my directory, and copied the book files in less than three minutes. Moments later, I logged back in under Alice's name. (It wasn't hard to do because I knew she kept her password conveniently written on a card in her desk drawer.)

I had just pocketed the disc and resumed searching for Alice's missing files when she returned. I now had another copy of the book and, a minute later, I found her missing file in her photo directory, exactly where you would never expect it. I moved the file to one of her directories that was appropriately labeled, and told her where to look for it.

If my computer activity had been monitored, I guessed that my new disc might be confiscated; but if I copied the new disc to yet another CD on someone else's computer, no one should be able to detect that. I glanced around and saw Jim Morgan moving in the direction of the break room. Since his office was empty, I used his computer to copy my first CD to a second one.

I didn't want to risk returning to my office with both of the incriminating discs on me, so I stopped by the office supply room and grabbed a couple envelopes. I stuck each CD into its own envelope, and then I went to the restroom. After making sure it was empty, I stood on a toilet seat, lifted a ceiling tile, and stuck one of the discs above the tiles. In less than a minute, I was walking back to my office with the original disc in my pocket. If government agents discovered I had copied the files, there would be no documentation that I had duplicated them onto another disc—and I couldn't imagine anyone looking above the bathroom ceiling. I wasn't sure whether I was being stealthy, or grossly overreacting. I didn't care.

The rest of the day was completely normal. Normal, that is, until I drove home.

I kept checking in my rearview mirror for the car I thought had been following me on my drive in. It didn't appear, but I was almost certain that two other cars had moved in and out of my field of vision several times as I drove toward home. Again, I wasn't sure whether or not I was being followed. The cars never got close enough for me to read their license plates, and they were ordinary enough tan and gray vehicles.

I had planned on going to the library after dinner, but decided to take a short diversion in that direction before going home. *Would one or both follow me?* The route to the Harrison Library was about two miles out of my direct route home. I kept watching. Then, about a block from the library, I looked in my rearview mirror and thought I saw one of the cars again. I began to panic.

I knew I needed to get into a public place for safety—and to calm myself. I also decided I had better get rid of the CD in my brief-case. If I were stopped, I didn't want them to find it.

The car I had observed came around the final corner as I turned into the library parking lot. I found an open spot near the front door and pulled into it.

I jumped out of the car and forced myself to calmly walk to the entrance. I didn't look back because I didn't want to let the driver know I was aware I was being followed, but I saw a reflection in the glass door of the car pulling into the lot. This was the same door where, only weeks ago, Jane and I had witnessed the man beating against the glass and cursing because it was locked.

I walked into the library and went straight to the magazine section. In case someone followed me in, I wanted to be able to look like I had stopped to read a magazine. I pulled a random magazine from the rack and attempted to look like I was searching its contents. From where I stood, I could see the doorway, and I looked up often to see who was coming through the front entrance. Several people did, but none looked suspicious. Still, I was nervous and worried about what might happen if they caught me with the CD.

I stayed in the library for about a half hour. Before I left, I stopped by the historical books section. I searched for a boring book that appeared not to have been checked out in years. When no one was looking, I noted the name and file number of the book, slipped the CD into the middle of its pages, and put it back on the shelf. Now the CD of our book was in the same library where I had found the original book. I would come back and get it later.

As I stepped out of the library, I casually scanned the street. None of the cars matched the one I was looking for, so I walked to my car. I kept checking my rearview mirror on my way home, but didn't notice anyone following me.

By the time I got home, Jane had dinner on the table. "You're late," she said, annoyance tinged with fear in her voice.

"I'm sorry, I should've called. I was afraid someone might be tailing me. I stopped at the library to see if the car would follow me there."

"Well, did it?"

"It appeared to." I told her about all the strange things that had happened in the course of the day, making us both edgy. For a brief moment, we once again considered quitting and turning everything over to the police. And, once again, we couldn't. The book was ours.

Instead, we discussed getting a handgun. We had never owned one, but now having a handgun seemed like a wise idea.

"But wouldn't it be dangerous for us to even have a gun? Guns scare me," Jane said.

"If we're going to keep our book, I think I'd better buy one anyway. Don't worry, I'll take classes on how to shoot it."

"You're probably right," Jane said. "In the meantime, we'd better take some other precautions."

Jane checked to make sure her pepper spray was in her purse. I put my heavy four-battery flashlight under my car seat. We double-checked our new alarm system to make certain it was set. Only then did we go to bed. Still, we didn't sleep well. Even if we only suspected I had been followed, enough had happened to make us nervous. And if I *had* been followed, was it by the police, the FBI, or the criminals? At the thought of the police or the FBI following me, I felt a mixture of relief and uncertainty. At the thought of criminals doing the same, I was downright scared.

About 3:30 in the morning, I got up to go to the bathroom, and then, without turning on any lights, stumbled into the living room. I decided it wouldn't hurt to check out on the street, so I peeked around the edge of the curtains.

A car was parked a house or two down the block. *That's strange. The city has an ordinance about not parking overnight on city streets.*

I couldn't see what kind of car it was or if anyone was in it because a tree shaded most of the car from the streetlight. I tried to convince myself it was nothing to worry about and by morning there would be a ticket on its front window for illegal parking.

The light, however, was reflecting off the license plate, and I could just make out the number. I reached into the coffee table drawer and pulled out a notepad and pencil. After jotting down the number, I went back to the bedroom. Jane was sitting upright in bed with fear disfiguring her face. She whispered, "Did you see a bright light flash across the shade?"

Now I was just as frightened. "No. But there's a car parked out front. Do you think we should call the police?"

"Yes, hurry." Jane said.

I reached for the phone. When I put the receiver to my ear, there was no dial tone. I pushed the Talk button several times, but got nothing.

"Quick," Jane whispered, "get your cell phone—now!"

I raced for our home office to get it off the charger on my desk. As I opened the bedroom door, I heard a loud crash, which I guessed was the back door being kicked in. *Why didn't the blasted alarm go off?* I wanted to scream. I could only assume they were professionals who knew how to bypass it or shut it down.

I ran to the office, desperately searching for my phone in the dark. I had just found it when I heard running in the hall. I pushed the On button. I waited in vain for it to make a connection to the outside world, but it was too late.

A command of "Stop, or you're dead" brought me to a halt.

The intruder dragged me back to the bedroom. Jane must have shut the door. We were met by a second intruder who kicked it open.

Jane, who had been standing behind the door with my baseball bat, tried to slam the bat into his face, but the force of the door had broken her swing. The bat went flying across the room, bounced wildly back, and almost hit her as she fell sideways to the floor. Before she could move, the man aimed a gun at her head. With his other hand, he picked up the bat and struck our vanity mirror, shattering the glass and scattering sharp shards around the room.

Jane jumped. Terror contorted her face.

I was pushed beside her and got my first look at the men. Both were in ski masks, and the taller one, who seemed to be in command, was about six-foot-six. They told us to strip off our nightclothes, while they leered at Jane. I feared they would kill me and rape her. Instead, the gunman said, "Do what we say, and we won't touch you. Give us an excuse and we can do what we want." After we had stripped to nothing, he said, "Now put on your clothes. We need to get out of here fast."

Not cooperating was not an option.

The tall man's voice sounded raspy, but his accomplice, who was shorter and stockier and looked like the kind of guy who could carry a keg of beer over each shoulder without flinching was silent. Although I had no frame of reference, they appeared to be professionals, responding quickly to situations and seeming to understand each other with little talking.

We dressed in minutes, avoiding the broken glass from the mirror as much as possible. As soon as we were clothed, the men taped our mouths shut and bound our wrists behind us with duct tape. They forced us to the door that opened into the garage. I heard someone, likely a third kidnapper, move the car from the street into our driveway. They pushed Jane and I through the garage, out through the side doorway, and over to a full-sized car. Jane was blindfolded and thrust into the back seat. Then they shoved me in and one of the thugs slid in beside me. The other climbed into the front seat. I was blindfolded as the car pulled out of the drive. They seemed to have thought of everything. It was dark and the car windows were heavily tinted. No one would see that we were blindfolded, bound, and gagged.

Claustrophobia closed its grip tightly around me as we drove through the night streets of Chicago. To maintain my sanity and to give myself some clues as to where we were going, I tried to count the streets by the dips in the road at intersections. Eventually, I lost track, and gave up. After multiple turns and twists, I had no idea where we were. I tried to listen for any sounds that might give me a clue, but they kept the radio blaring so loud I couldn't clearly hear any of the outside noises. Eventually, I felt the bumps of railroad tracks and shortly after that we pulled onto a freeway.

Jane struggled. Her breathing was heavy. I shifted, trying to give her a little more room. Sensing her pain intensified my own hysteria.

After what I guessed was an hour, we left the freeway. A short time later, we drove over some rough roads that jostled us around, then down a curvy hill, and stopped. I went stiff and my heart raced. I could feel Jane's body tense up, too.

I worried that they had taken us to a remote place to kill us—somewhere hunters or hikers wouldn't find our bodies for years. I could imagine pathologists examining our teeth to identify our decomposed corpses. When the car shifted, I could tell the two in the front seat had gotten out and opened the trunk. The trunk lid slammed and our doors flung open. I was yanked from one door. Jane was pulled out of the other.

I stumbled out and someone jerked me along sideways by my bound hands. We were still alive and moving, but I feared they were taking us deeper into the woods to shoot us. Gradually, I heard less road noise. To my horror, I also realized I could barely hear Jane stumbling through the brush in the distance. Were they moving her in a different direction?

I fell once or twice, and lost track of how far we'd gone. With no way to catch myself, my knees and torso were taking the brunt of their aggression.

Some minutes later, I heard what sounded like a muffled shot. My imagination tore angrily at the possibilities. *Did they murder Jane? Will I be killed in a few seconds or minutes?* My wrists were chafed. My knees were scraped and sore from falling; my heart despaired. I had the horrible feeling that, even if I lived through my ordeal, I would never see Jane again. I stumbled on, no longer caring what happened to me.

Finally, I was jerked to a stop. I heard talking, but I couldn't understand what was being said. I felt a tug on my arm. We moved ahead slowly. I felt the rough terrain become what I speculated must be mowed grass; soon that changed to a hard surface. A gruff voice commanded, "Stop! Step up." I raised my foot higher and brought it down onto a small ledge.

I was pushed through a door and shoved through one room and into the next. When we finally stopped, I felt the excruciating pain of duct tape being ripped from my face. Stifling a scream, I remained silent, gritting my teeth to fight the throbbing of my face. My blindfold came off, and I got the first glimpse of my situation. The crooks, "the enemy," all had black ski masks on. Maybe that was a good sign.

If they planned to kill me, they wouldn't care if I could identify them, right?

I looked around at the dimly lit room. It was not much bigger than a large walk-in closet. There were no windows. The walls were finished with what looked like oak paneling. The door appeared to be constructed of metal and painted dark brown. A small, foldout army-style cot sat along one side of the room, and there was one chair in the adjacent corner. Some early morning light shone through a small skylight in the ceiling. I couldn't see any electric lights in the room. A door to what seemed to be a tiny bathroom stood open on one side, but with no additional light I couldn't make out what was inside.

Choking back tears, I tried, somewhat incoherently, to ask about Jane. They didn't answer. Instead, they shoved me onto the cot with my hands still taped together and left the room, locking the door behind them.

———————

I was so emotionally drained all I could do was lie on the cot and weep. Was Jane alive or dead?

I was certain our abduction had something to do with the book. This was no longer paranoia. This was gut-wrenching reality.

BOOK PURSUED

What felt like an hour later, the door opened. Two masked men entered. One held a gun to my head while the other ripped the tape off my wrists. He pulled my hands in front of me and bound them with a coarse rope. They left a couple of cold buns and a paper cup of lukewarm water on the floor before locking the door behind them.

I felt faint when I tried to sit up. I wasn't ready to eat anything. Nevertheless, I chewed and swallowed the bread, not knowing when or if I would eat again. I sipped the tepid water, drinking just enough of it to keep the bread from sticking in my throat. I sat on the side of my cot with my head buried in my bound hands.

My whole body throbbed in pain, making it hard to think, much less rest. My face felt like it was on fire, and my wrists had been rubbed raw. The light coming through the skylight was getting brighter. Night was turning into day. My head hurt and my muscles were knotting up. I was becoming more claustrophobic the longer I was stuck in the room, a feeling that made my muscles tense up even more.

I kept mumbling Jane's name, as if saying it would bring her back to me. I didn't know whether she was dead or alive. One moment, I was sure she would turn up alive, and my heart would beat with joy. Minutes later, I would be convinced they had shot her, and I would weep.

My world had stopped and would not start again until I heard Jane's voice. If she was dead, my whole life lay as a wasteland before me.

I struggled to find sleep and escape, but thoughts of the last weeks kept revolving in my head unmercifully. During that time, Jane and I had felt closer than we had since our wedding more than seven years earlier. But more disasters had happened since discovering our little leather book than we had experienced in our entire lives.

I feared this might be the last great disaster for Jane, and I would soon meet my own demise.

11

I don't remember falling asleep. One moment, I was tossing around on the uncomfortable cot; the next, I was the main character in a nightmare. This nightmare was remarkably similar to the one I'd had in Grand Marais.

I was again lying prostrate on the rocks that jutted out into the waters of Lake Superior; the storm was raging. Cold waves of water crashed over me. I would have been swept into the depths of the lake if the heavy ring I was grasping onto hadn't been anchored to a giant boulder.

Lightning flashed from foreboding clouds, reflecting off the froth of the breaking waves. Thunder rumbled warnings as rain pounded me. The dark waters called for my death: *Let go! Give up! Release your grip!* They cried out for my damnation as they dashed me against the rocks, as they thrashed against my body. Still I hung onto life, refusing to let go of the metal ring, refusing to give up.

The same bottle I had seen in my Grand Marais dream was bobbing in the violent waves near the very rock that I was so precariously hanging onto.

In the next terrifying moment, the bottle expanded to twice its size. I blinked once and it grew to ten times its size. As it twisted in the foam, I saw an embossed symbol on its side, the same one as on the book—the tree, leaves on one side and dead branches on the other, and a snake at its base.

I blinked again and the bottle became a thousand times bigger, enough to hold entire boulders and a gigantic portion of the lake. As I struggled to understand, a new horror struck me. Instead of fighting for my life inside the bottle, this time I saw Jane. She was holding onto the same ring inside the bottle that I was clinging to outside. The noise of the storm was so loud that it overwhelmed all other sounds, but Jane's face betrayed her desperate cries for help.

I yelled at the storm. "Stop! Stop!" I screamed into the deafening wind.

Jane was fighting for her life. I had to save her.

I blinked water out of my eyes, and in the next moment, the bottle appeared to be its normal size, but I could see into it like it was still huge. I fought to understand how I could comprehend this reality in three dimensions, but I didn't have time to work out the logic. That would have to wait.

Lowering myself as far as I could on my rock ledge, while gripping the ring with my left hand, I reached for the bottle. The waves slapped at my face. I felt like my body was going to break, like I was stretching so far that it would be torn apart.

My distress was further compounded as, to my horror, in the enlarged bottle, I saw Jane's grip slipping from the ring as she slid farther down the rock.

"Jane!" I yelled against the howling wind. "Jane!" I cried out as loud as I could, but it was hopeless. The bottle had floated to within an inch of my fingers to torment me before an angry wave carried it in the direction of the lake of death. Then it slipped under a breaking wave, and I could no longer see it.

I couldn't save Jane, and in that instant my life lost all meaning. The tormenting waves tempted me, *Let go. Enter into the lake of death. Release yourself from your horrors.*

But I couldn't give up. Something inside me cried, *Hang on!* So I grasped firmly onto the ring that anchored me so solidly to the unmovable boulder. I wanted to let go and be done with the pain, but the ring kept challenging me to hold on. I gripped it with all my strength because the life I wanted to give up also held out just enough hope to demand I challenge the odds. I would endure the pain for that hope.

I was startled from my horrifying dream by several loud thumps on the door. For a few moments, I hung between reality and my dream as the thumps echoed those of my own heart.

When I finally woke, my hand was bleeding. I had been grasping the metal hinges at the sides of the cot so tightly that a deep gash cut into my palm. My wrists were still tied, and they were so raw from rubbing against the rope that I groaned in agony as I became more alert. The cut on my hand added to the excruciating pain of my wrists. My arms hurt like they had been pulled out of joint by my efforts to hang onto the cot.

But the hurt in my heart surpassed all of my physical pain. The dream had confirmed my loss.

The door opened a few inches and someone slid in a couple more plain bread buns and a hot drink that smelled like coffee.

I forced myself into a sitting position. I sat for about a minute and then leaned forward until my weight shifted enough to allow me to stand. I quickly collapsed and shuffled along on my knees toward the food. I hoped the coffee, by some miracle, might be both hot and good this morning. It was hot, but it looked more like tea. Still, it was appreciated.

The flimsy plastic cup was challenging to pick up with my wrists still tied and chafing from the fibrous rope. The cut on my hand added to the difficulty, which was further complicated because I could hardly make my arms respond after stretching them so intensely in my nightmare.

I ate everything, and drank every drop of the coffee, though it tasted like piss. I even chewed the grounds on the bottom of the cup.

A few minutes later, the door flew open and another muscular man in a black ski mask stepped into the room. He must have been at least six feet tall and three hundred pounds—the kind of person who could body-slam me effortlessly. *Are all the guards musclemen?*

All he said was "Get up, asshole!"

I had no choice. I would have to negotiate a successful launch to my feet in spite of my bound wrists and my joints refusing to support my weight.

I grabbed onto the side of the chair and leveraged myself to a standing position, though I wasn't sure I could stay that way for long. Gravity was calling me back down with great force. My hands and wrists throbbed. My head felt like it had been hit with a hammer. Yet, somehow, I remained vertical while he both blindfolded me and dropped a black hood over my head.

Finally, the muscle-bound thug grabbed the rope around my wrist and began pulling me out the door. Disoriented and claustrophobic, I cursed in agony as I stumbled into another room. I sensed the presence of others as I was forced down onto a hard, straight-back chair.

I was relieved to be sitting. I gasped from the pain as my wrists were untied, but my hands were free for the first time in hours. They were raw, but I no longer felt fresh blood oozing from my palm, and the tingling in my fingers gradually began to diminish.

Someone came into the room, and in an unexpected act of kindness, I felt him putting salve on my open sores and taping gauze over my bloodied flesh.

After that, he pulled some kind of tape, probably packing tape, around my torso, upper arms, and the chair so that only my lower arms and hands were free. He then proceeded to tape my lower legs and ankles to the chair, as well.

He left me to contemplate my predicament. The tape around my chest allowed me to breathe, but was constraining enough that I couldn't take a deep breath without feeling a dull pain. I had no idea what their plans might be. They had certainly put great effort into preparing for my torment.

Alone and in the dark, my thoughts returned to Jane. I recalled the times we had made love, her soft skin against mine. I remembered early morning walks along the beaches north of Chicago, watching the sunrise over Lake Michigan. The wind would blow her hair. We would laugh as the waves receded, only to crash back in and splash at our feet, trying to trick us into walking too close to the water's edge.

I missed her with an intensity I had never felt before.

The isolation overwhelmed me, and fearing the worst, I lost hope. As in my dream, there was nothing I could do to save Jane, if indeed, she might still be alive. I could do nothing to save myself, either. I sat for a long time in the pitch-blackness of my despair.

My tormentors seemed to know how to attack me where I was most vulnerable. They probably were so well trained in torture they had planned exactly what would break me. They were manipulating my mind, and even though I knew what they were doing, I couldn't stop myself from experiencing terrifying emotions.

———————

I heard the door open. At least three people came in. This time they seemed bent on serious confrontation.

At first, they were cordial, asking me easy questions about myself, things I figured they already knew. I played along, which is what I assumed they wanted. I was in no hurry to experience what I was certain would come soon enough.

"How old are you?"

"Where were you born?"

"What is your job?"

"Where did you go to school?"

The initial questions were general in nature and exclusively about me.

Then they shifted to questions about Jane and me.

"Where were you married?"

"When is your anniversary?"

"Where did you go on your honeymoon?"

I answered these questions with a carefully controlled tone before I screwed up my courage and asked, "Where's Jane? What've you done with her?"

No one answered, and it took a few minutes before I realized I was alone. I couldn't figure out why they had left so quietly and suddenly. I thought they should have anticipated the question. I could only assume this was part of their strategy.

About an hour later, they walked back in. This time they started by immediately asking if I had a book of theirs.

I lied. "I don't know what you're talking about," I said. "What book?"

"Look, we're trying to be reasonable," one of them said. "If you tell us where our book is, we'll let you go. If you don't, well, let me put it this way: newspapers will be printing your obituary."

I had known since we were captured that this was likely, but actually hearing their words made me flinch. I could almost feel a cold coffin boxing me in its silky enclosure.

I wanted to blurt out, "Okay, I have your book! Now let me go so I can get on with my life." Instead, I said, "I won't say anything unless I know Jane is alive."

"Forget about Jane," they replied. "Tell us where our book is, or you'll end up just as dead."

My heart beat with anger when I realized what they were saying. I tried to stand, jerking and thrashing futilely in my chair. I flung my body against my restraints with all the energy I could and suddenly found myself falling forward.

For a fraction of a second, I felt suspended in midfall; then my knees hit the floor. Flying forward, my face encountered the hard surface. I felt a pain shoot through my lower jaw and a trickle of blood run down my chin. Tears burned my eyes as my chair was yanked upright with me in it. I twisted several more times in disgust and excruciating pain before I settled back in defeat. All I could do was groan.

One of them demanded in a surly voice, "We know you've got our book, so tell us where it is and all of this shit'll end!"

Spitting blood, I shot back, "And what is this freaking book that I'm supposed to have?"

"The book you stole. We know you've got it. It should've been a flawless transfer, but you got in the way."

"What makes you think I've got it?"

"We hacked the library records to see who might have taken it. We found everyone who'd checked out books between our drop-off and when it was to be picked up. We narrowed the search to you. The librarian confirmed your identity before we killed her.

"We know you have our book because we found the discs and notes in your room in Grand Marais. You have our book or know where it is. Now tell us where you put it or—"

I felt the sharp edge of a knife blade on my neck for several seconds, just long enough to get his point across.

I sat stunned. The knife at my throat left no doubt about the consequences of not cooperating. I reflected on the fate of the librarian. *Our* act had doomed her to death.

The pieces were beginning to fit into the puzzle; we had stumbled onto a valuable book that had been put in the library before we arrived, and the pickup must have been scheduled to take place before the library closed.

I asked myself, *Was the man in the limo we saw as we left the library the pickup person?*

The nature of the book, however, remained unclear. Did it contain some ancient knowledge, or were there hidden codes or directions in the text leading to some buried treasure?

I was baffled. *Maybe, the book was secondary to their purpose. Could they have embedded the information into the spine or under the leather cover?* I wasn't about to ask.

Whatever their reason for finding it, our book must have contained something valuable. Otherwise, why would they have carried out such an elaborate, and deadly, search for us? Were they crooks, spies, terrorists, or some ancient cult or secret society? Or were they attracted to the book even more than Jane and I were?

The nature of our crime had seemed trivial. We didn't think we had done anything to deserve this. We had simply lied to get an unclaimed book, and now they had as much as admitted that Jane was dead. And that I would also be dead soon if I didn't confess.

Yet, the fact they hadn't killed me meant that they probably wouldn't until they either got the book or were certain I would never tell them where it was.

They taped my wrists and added more tape to my ankles, pulling it tighter. They pulled more tape across my chest, making it even harder to breathe.

I sensed a new level of intensity. I got the feeling their questioning was going to become more demanding. I steeled myself for the worst.

"Tell us where our book is, or we'll kill you like the librarian."

Their threat was clear. I didn't answer. Their response was a slap across the face and another threat: "You'll die just like your precious Jane!"

First, I was too angry to respond.

Second, it now became a matter of loyalty to Jane. I couldn't let her death be in vain. I had committed myself to keeping our secret. I wouldn't tell them anything. I would die first.

The sting of another hard slap across the face almost knocked me off the chair, letting me know my death would be extremely painful.

Every time I said "No!" they slapped or punched me. I kept refusing. After each episode, it took me longer to recover. I was facing death by torture if I didn't tell them where I had hidden our book.

I began to hallucinate. I was feeling the ancient book again with its soft pages and smelling its musty odor. I didn't want to tell them where it was, but in my painful stupor, I began to reconsider my options. *This is still just a book and I'm alive. Jane is dead. Why not tell them?*

I kept changing my mind. One moment, under no circumstances would I give in. The next moment, I was ready to tell them its exact location as a last desperate act to end this madness. But I couldn't.

They yelled at me again, "Where is our book?"

My face stung from another slap that rattled my teeth. The impact was compounded by the fact that I couldn't see when they were going to hit me and couldn't brace myself.

As the pain edged its way down my spine, I wanted to cry out, *The book's in our safety deposit box.* But deep inside, as dazed as I was, I couldn't tell them.

Then I felt a needle prick my arm. I felt my awareness slip. Reality became like a thick fog.

They asked the question again. I heard it, but like one might hear someone from across a cavern.

As I was going under, I relived another episode of my nightmare from Grand Marais. I was again trapped in the bottle as the storm ravaged the rocks. I could do nothing to save myself. I heard their words repeated over and over in my mind, and I sensed the truth in the last moment of my consciousness: they were playing with me. They would never let me go. As I slipped into oblivion, this realization stood out like a beacon, directing all of my future responses.

I repeated to myself, *They'll never let me go!* As I passed out, or maybe it was as I was coming back out of my stupor, I whispered the words, "Book. No!"

I woke up flat on my back on the army cot. This time I was strapped down. A dim light was coming through the skylight. I assumed it was either almost night or early Saturday morning; or was this Sunday?

Only my head and my arms below the elbows could move freely. My back felt like it might snap in half if I moved. My arms and legs felt like they had been hit with sledgehammers. I feared I was going to suffocate from the mucus in the back of my throat. I gagged and was able to turn my head sideways just enough to spit on the floor. Phlegm drooled out of my mouth. My stomach cried for food and drink.

———————

It was so quiet I began to think they had left me there to die.

For the first time in years, I seriously reflected on the Sunday school classes I had attended as a child. While I rejected their teachings as naive, I found myself wishing they might be true. I couldn't quite bring myself to believe the ancient stories of a god who rushed in to save his followers when they cried for help. I wished I could believe. If only a god existed who could help me out of this, I could yell out in my distress, *God, get me out of this mess!*

As the room began to get brighter, I heard footsteps.

Two men wearing ski masks entered. They lashed two long poles to my cot, providing handles. They blindfolded me and covered my head with the hood like they had before. I struggled to breathe. I guess they saw my difficulty because they cut a hole in the hood just under my nose. Then they carried me into the next room.

Before they left, they lifted the bottom of my hood, stuck a straw into my mouth, and told me to drink. I was able to get several swallows of sugary water into me before they pulled the straw away and left. My stomach ached for more.

I was alone again. In spite of everything, I was grateful to be alive; but Jane, Jane was gone forever.

I felt so weak I didn't think that I could make it through another day. The day felt like it was going to be hot, and I lay strapped to the cot with the hood over my face. I began to sweat profusely, sure I was being slowly cooked. Perhaps this was how they intended to kill me.

Stay calm! I kept telling myself. *Stay calm!* I imagined how a fly caught in a spider's web must feel. I could fight against my bonds with all of my might and they wouldn't come loose. I had no options other than to stay calm or to fight uselessly, like the fly.

When I began to worry that I could no longer survive, the door opened and a cool breeze filled the room. I realized the rest of the building must have been air-conditioned. They simply wanted me to feel the heat.

Someone untied me and two people lifted me into a chair. After taping my upper arms to the chair, they held a straw to my mouth again and said, "Drink this. You'll feel better."

I wanted to gulp the sweet juice down, but they only let me drink through one thin straw.

They finished taping me to the chair, and the interrogation began. "You don't want today to be like yesterday, do you? Where's our book?"

They slapped me when I didn't answer the way they wanted. By now my face was bloated and painful from being repeatedly slapped the day before. One eye was swollen shut, though they couldn't have seen that through the hood.

After a couple more rounds of questions, they left once again.

———————

When they returned, they changed their tactics.

First, the same two thugs with the ski masks took off my hood and blindfold. They wiped my face thoroughly with a wet cloth, and put fresh ointment on my scrapes and sores. They then blindfolded me again, but this time they left the hood off.

These little comforts were refreshing. How could they terrorize me one minute, and in the next, do something to make me feel better? I assumed I must have looked pretty bad, and they didn't want to kill me just yet. They wanted to keep me alive, to wear me down until I told them what they wanted to hear.

This belief was quickly confirmed. Within a few minutes they were interrogating me again.

This time, when the voice demanded that I tell him where the book was, he added, "If you want to save Jane's life, you'll tell us where the book is!"

What? Is Jane still alive? They had led me to believe she was dead.

A spark of hope surged through me. "Are you telling me Jane is alive?"

"Yes, but if you ever want to see her, you'll tell us where our book is."

Brazenly, I said, "How do I know she's alive? You told me she was dead."

"Wait," was all he said in response, and they left me alone to think about the revelation.

12

I was overwhelmed with hope. Maybe Jane wasn't dead.

I had assumed she was lost forever, and I'd doubted I would survive. Eventually, I'd guessed, we would both be listed as missing. Or if somehow I made it through this tragic ordeal, I would end up attending Jane's funeral with an empty coffin.

My belief that Jane was alive had been crushed and those responsible for beating that belief to death were now attempting to resurrect it to new life. Still, my emotions were going back and forth. One moment, I was grateful Jane was alive, if indeed I could trust that they were telling me the truth. In the next, I was angry they had used such a hellish trick on me. They had lied about the most important person in my life when they led me to believe they had killed Jane.

Or are they lying now? Was she really dead? I was under their complete control. I had no way of knowing.

I was more unsettled than ever. I had been willing to die over something as stupid as a book. Now I didn't know what to do. Assuming Jane was alive, I would do anything to save her life.

For an instant I felt everything would turn out fine if I cooperated with them. In the next instant, I feared the worst possible outcome was the most likely one—they would kill both of us.

After about an hour, the lying scoundrels came back into the room. They loosened one of my arms and gave me a mug of soup to drink. I drank it thankfully while still building my resolve to stand firm.

Then, as if I had control of the situation, I asked, "Why didn't you bring Jane?"

One of them exploded with a string of vile swear words before saying, "You'll get to see her when we're good and ready. If you tell us where our book is, you'll be with her in a couple of hours—and free by evening. Otherwise, forget it."

I wanted to believe them. I hoped they would be as relieved as me if they got their book back and we could go free, but I didn't trust them. They had seemed totally honest when they led me to believe that they had killed Jane. How could I trust them now?

"Prove she's alive. I'm not talking until I see her."

They didn't respond, but instead played a recording of Jane's voice. She identified herself and, with no inflections, recited the date she was making the recording. I calculated in my mind that it was either made the same day or the day before. I was pretty sure it was earlier the same day I was hearing it. She sounded terribly weak.

I was encouraged, but still wary. These crooks had no integrity. She could have made the recording before she was killed.

The recording continued, "Please tell them where the book is."

She knew full well where the book was, and I was certain she was just as resolved not to tell them as I was. Her plea was a clue for me to keep silent. She was letting me know she hadn't revealed anything—and that I shouldn't either.

Yet, if I could save her—save us—simply by telling them, I was ready to disclose everything.

Or was I? The book seemed to be reaching out to me, encouraging me to remain silent. I wasn't sure I could ever give it up, even to save Jane. *No, I have to save Jane.*

The thugs demanded once more that I tell them where they could find the book, exchanging our lives for the information.

I wanted to tell. I wanted all of this to end. Instead, I heard myself say, "I'll never tell you bastards anything until I see Jane."

They swore again and one of them said, "Forget it. We're not bringing her here until we know where our book is. We need to protect our assets."

"Assets?" I spat back. "Is that what we are? Assets?"

"Shut up," the voice said. "We don't need any of your drivel. Where's our book?"

Their book? No, it's ours.

"I refuse to tell you anything until I see Jane. I want my wife!"

I suddenly realized just how much I wanted to see her again. If we didn't survive, I at least wanted to be with her one last time.

One of them demanded, "Talk first, and then we'll bring her. If you don't tell us where to find our book, we will kill her!" He paused, then added, "And I can assure you her last hours won't be pleasant. She's quite sexy, you know."

I lunged against my restraints. This time they grabbed me before I knocked myself to the floor. I was now more tormented than ever. She might still be alive, but my response could free her—or bring her to a horrible death. I agonized over what to say, but I decided my only option was to remain firm in my demands. Trembling with fear at what might happen, I restated, "I won't talk until you bring Jane here."

"You're an idiot!" one of them yelled, and then he slapped me so hard I completely lost my equilibrium. My chair flew backwards, but someone caught me again before I crashed onto the floor.

I was pulled upright, the door opened, and I heard people leaving.

I had no doubt that they would have killed Jane if it weren't for our knowledge of the book we had claimed as our own; the book we treated as if its leather covers contained our destiny.

I still couldn't shake the attraction I'd felt when I first found the book; the feeling that it would change our lives forever. It certainly had done that, though not in the way we'd hoped.

I was alone. My face stung for a long time, but eventually fatigue set in. In spite of my uncomfortable position, I fell into a delirious sleep. I dreamed of making love to Jane in our own bed, a dream that vanished too quickly, turning abruptly into still another version of my Grand Marais nightmare.

In this episode, Jane and I were both inside the bottle with the Lake Superior storm raging around us. The bottle rose and fell in the tempest outside, and the waves thrashed against us inside. Lake water was seeping in around the cork, and with each lightning flash I could see the agony on Jane's face.

I was sick and dizzy. With one hand, I frantically held onto the metallic ring bolted into the same gray boulder as before. With my other hand, I clung to Jane's wrist.

The ferocious waves of the lake beat against us, trying to rip us from the rocks and bury us in the unforgiving waves. A huge wave washed over us and Jane lost her grip. She screamed for help, and I hollered back at the deafening storm.

I was sure I had lost her, but I was relieved to see she had grasped hold of a crevice in one of the lower rocks. By some force of her will, and a lot of luck, she was hanging on. As the wave subsided she leaped up and grabbed the ring with her hand. This time I knew there was nothing I could do to save either of us. Eventually, the bottle would fill with water, and we would drown in the depths of Lake Superior.

The force of one wave threw me onto my back, and I looked up at the glass above me. Embossed on the surface was the shape of the tree—half with the healthy leaves, half with the naked branches. The round shape on the leafy side refracted a reddish light. As I stared in amazement, I felt an overwhelming satisfaction that I possessed this book. It was mine to keep.

Another great wave washed over us. I tightened my grip on the ring and held my breath until I thought I could no longer resist inhaling the deadly waters.

When the wave dropped back, my eyes were filled with water, and for several seconds everything was fuzzy. I fought to see Jane, to make sure she was still there. I couldn't reach out because I was using all of my energy to hang on, and my hand was so numb I couldn't feel the ring anymore.

Finally, through bleary eyes, I saw she still had a grip on her ring, too. She had been pulled sideways, perpendicular to me. I blinked, and using all the energy I could muster, I smiled at her, figuring this might be the last time I saw her. One more powerful wave washed over us, but we held on through that one, too.

Then something marvelous happened. I saw a rainbow inside the bottle, and a matching rainbow arched across the sky outside. The storm stopped as quickly as it had started. The neck of the bottle looked like it rose several feet above the water from my perspective, but was probably only fractions of an inch if you were observing it from outside. No more water was seeping into our small biosphere. As Jane pulled herself up beside me, I passed out from exhaustion.

When I woke up, the translucent rainbow lingered in my memory. I hoped against all odds this was some kind of premonition.

I silently mouthed the words, "If by chance there is some power out there, please save us!" I considered this as a response to the dream, a hope to get out of this mess. I refused to call it a prayer.

I really doubted we would walk away alive, but at least I hoped the dream was true enough that I could see Jane and smile at her one last time.

I dozed in and out of reality. My neck and back felt like they were about to break.

Finally, I heard footsteps. At least two people entered who, with some difficulty, loosened my arms. After removing my hood and blindfold, the two thugs in ski masks handed me some slimy soup, toast, and a cup of water.

"Eat this," was all they said the entire time they were in the room. When I was done, they removed the tape that bound me to the chair, lifted me off, and pushed me back onto the cot. They then carried the cot back to my prison room, where they left me with an unsatisfied hunger.

This time I wasn't tied down, but my body ached. I stumbled into the bathroom as fast as I could before I staggered back to my cot and lay down. I was exhausted, but the best I could do was to doze in and out of sleep. Still, when light began to filter into the room the next morning, I found myself amazingly optimistic. Was it possible I would see Jane that day?

In the past few days I had lost a lot of weight. My face felt raw. One eye was still swollen shut. I could only imagine how awful I must have looked. Touching my face hurt. My hair and beard were tangled with dried blood. I felt battered and bruised. I wondered how Jane would react to seeing me like this.

I realized I needed to prepare myself to see Jane, too, because she must have been treated as brutally as I had. *If I see her alive, I'll need to restrain myself from expressing any shock at her appearance.* I loved her, and I wanted our meeting to be as positive as possible.

I was alone until midmorning when the door opened. A couple of pieces of buttered toast and a glass of lukewarm water were placed inside the door. I crawled to the food, and ate the meager breakfast. Then I waited until, finally, the door opened again.

They again blindfolded me, pulled a hood over my head, and led me back into the next room where I was firmly taped to the chair.

"Tell us where our book is."

I screwed up my courage and told them, "I'm not telling you anything until I see Jane."

To my surprise they said, "If that'll get you to talk, we'll arrange it. But then if you refuse to tell us, all hell will break loose. You'll watch your sweet Jane die—painfully. We'll rape her; then we'll cut her to pieces, beginning with her tongue. After that, it'll be your turn—piece by piece."

The prospect of seeing Jane under these circumstances terrified me. Their threats were too possible, too real. I began to think the only two options left were to tell them where the book was and die quickly, or to not tell them, and die a painful, barbaric death. If neither of us cooperated, first Jane would be brutalized in front of me; then I would face the same horrible death.

I heard one of them leave. A few minutes later he returned, shoving someone into the room.

Is it Jane? My heart raced. It had to be her. I blurted out, "Jane, I love you!"

13

I heard a heavily muffled response, and I envisioned Jane with a hood over her head and her mouth gagged. I heard struggling as they shoved her across the room. A chair scraped against the hardwood floor. They cursed each other and Jane as they strapped her to it.

The door creaked again. Shuffling feet left the room, and the door slammed. My blindfold was removed. I didn't open my eyes for a couple of seconds as I prepared myself mentally for what I might see.

When I opened my eyes, I saw that Jane and I were in a large room with high, narrow windows across the top edge of a slanted high-beamed ceiling.

I assumed the large mirror on the opposite wall was made of one-way glass to observe us. I was sitting in one corner of the room. Jane sat in the adjacent corner. If we were being observed, we could both be seen from the mirror.

No matter how hard I had tried to prepare for this moment, I was shocked by her appearance. One of her checks was black and blue. Her blouse hung loose because most of the buttons had been ripped off. Her hair was greasy and matted with dried blood. She looked thin, fragile, and all I could think of was holding her in my arms and caressing the pain away forever.

I had vowed not to show any shock if she looked my way. I thought this would be hard, but I was so thrilled to see her, I bubbled over with joy. "Jane!" I cried and laughed at the same time as I exclaimed, "I love you! I was afraid I'd never ever see you again!"

Jane didn't look at me. She hung her head and wept.

My head flooded with the awful things they could have done to her, and I wept, too. I cried inside for what had happened to her.

I forgot my own suffering. My beloved was in such terrible pain.

"Jane, I love you! Jane, I missed you! Jane! Jane!" I said.

She didn't look up for a long time. Tears continued to flow down her face.

Finally, after what seemed like a lifetime, she lifted her head and sobbed, "I feel so dirty."

I suffered with her. I wanted to hug her and tell her everything would be fine. If I could only caress her and run my fingers through her hair, we would both feel better. I wanted to ease my own hurt by holding her in my arms and letting our tears flow together.

"I feel so dirty," Jane said again. "I don't see how you can still love me."

I was angry and totally helpless. I didn't want to know what they had done to her, but I needed to accept the worst so I could comfort her.

"Why did you ask to see me?" she cried. "I wanted to die alone."

I mustered all of the love and hope I could. "Nothing could ever destroy my love for you."

She lowered her head again. Then she uttered the words so softly that I could barely hear her, "I love you, but I don't think I can go on living. Forgive me . . . please understand." Her voice whispered into silence.

One of our guards had stayed in the room. I noticed that even he looked down and away when she spoke. His posture had lost some of its aggressive edge. When he looked up, the eyes peering through his ski mask didn't seem to glare at us so harshly. He offered both of us a drink of water. I drank as much as I could.

Jane was crying too much to drink, but the guard surprised us both when he wiped her lips with the liquid.

This touching moment was just that—another few caring seconds in a ruthless assault on our lives.

When the others came back into the room, it didn't matter to them that Jane was weeping. Jane moaned as the blindfold was tied into place and a hood was pulled over her bruised face.

If they were trying to make a point about how serious their intentions were to terrorize Jane, it had certainly been effective. I was livid with anger, but I could do nothing except imagine ways to get even. I wanted to slam a sledgehammer into their faces. I wanted to cut their throats with a rusty knife.

When they blindfolded me and pulled the hood over my head, all I could do was sit and fume.

I heard more people enter the room. These, I discovered, would be our real tormentors. I heard a chair slide close to me. A man's voice demanded, "You'd better tell me where our book is now, or we'll begin torturing your wife in front of you." He waited a few seconds, and then said, "She'll die as horrible a death as you can possibly imagine unless you tell us where you've hidden our book."

I was so distraught and angry that I had trouble talking. I struggled to whimper, "I need a little time to think."

He replied with a sneer, "You've got one minute to make up your mind."

One minute to determine Jane's fate. We might both die, but I held the key to saving her from a horrible death.

I reminded myself that she also knew where the book was and had stood up to our tormentors, enduring terrible traumas to protect that knowledge. If I told them now, I would be betraying her trust in me. I thought that might be even more horrible than the torture they could still inflict on her.

Of course, if they tortured us as severely as they had promised, perhaps telling them would be better for both of us.

On the other hand, if I told them where the book was hidden, and we lived through this ordeal, would Jane ever be able to trust me again? Could our marriage survive either way I responded to them? Jane would be hurt if I gave in. We were both so messed up, I wasn't sure if hope was even an option.

If I told them where the book was, where *my* book was, where *our* book was, we would have to give it up. I could still feel its leather cover and smell its soft pages.

I didn't know what to do. In the end, would it matter? They would do whatever they wanted.

———————

I heard the dreaded words: "Time's up."

I'd rather have been slapped in the face. They could do anything to me, but they had already hurt Jane so much she wanted to die.

I was almost ready to give in when I recalled my dream. The storm was raging around us. We were trapped in the bottle, and it was slowly sinking. I was reaching out to save Jane, but she was slipping down the rocks into the abyss of the merciless waters.

I recalled two impressions I had at the height of my nightmare.

First, I realized there was nothing I could do to save Jane, absolutely nothing. I didn't really believe they would let us go, and they might rape and torture Jane to death even if I told them where our precious book was. They would do it to spite me. They would do it to destroy Jane.

Second, I remembered the image from the book embossed on the bottle's glass surface, along with the feeling that I was supposed to have the book. It was *mine*. I craved possessing it like an addict craves drugs.

I heard myself say, "I can't do it. I can't betray Jane's trust by talking!"

"Trust?" my tormentor yelled. "What trust? If you won't tell us where our book is, what kind of idiot is she trusting?"

I didn't say a word. I hoped Jane knew the answer to that question.

"Very well. That's it. Neither of you'll leave here alive. The only question will be how much you suffer before you crack."

From the other side of the room, I heard, "Go ahead and take their blindfolds off. It doesn't matter if they see us now. They're dead."

I had a sudden flash of foreboding. What if I had chosen the wrong response? Maybe they would have set us free, but now it was too late.

They ripped off our hoods and blindfolds.

I looked around and saw our tormentors for the first time. They wore expensive, tailored silk suits. Black shoes, designer ties, and flashy watches told me these were wealthy people of distinctive breeding.

We stared into their well-tanned faces, so now they would have to kill us. They would never allow us to reveal their identities.

"Why is this book so important to you?" I asked. "I'd at least like to know why you're killing us."

They laughed and the man who looked like their leader said, "You're kidding me, right? You don't know? You have this book and you don't know its power? Yet, you're going to die because you're not willing to give it up? Okay. It's too late to help you anyway. Here's the short version."

I interrupted him. "Go ahead. Give us the long version."

He looked at me, then at Jane. "No, the short version will do. It is, of course, the *Book of the Knowledge of Good and Evil*."

"The book of *what*?" I said.

"The content of the book goes back to the beginning of human existence," he said. "Surely you've heard the story of how Eve was tempted by the serpent to eat the fruit from the tree of the knowledge of good and evil, and then Adam was tempted to do the same. And he ate it, too. They were kicked out of Eden for eating that fruit. They were kicked out of paradise."

I didn't know how to respond. *These people are nuts.*

He looked at my blank stare and said, "You really don't get it, do you?

"Jews and Christians believe Adam and Eve made the wrong choice. We, however, believe they made the right choice. They chose knowledge in its entirety. They chose to know both the knowledge of good *and* the knowledge of evil. They chose to become their own gods, knowing everything. They chose to know all that God knows, and to rule the world as they chose to run it."

"You're nuts," I said. "I've never heard such insanity."

"Call us what you want. Our Guild for the Knowledge of Good and Evil has been around since the beginning of time."

"But what's so important about this book? Surely you've got others," I said.

"Of course our guild has other copies, but we're protective of our books. Not everyone can handle them—or the knowledge they contain. The copy you stole is from the fifteenth century. It was one of the first books ever printed."

"So why leave it in a public library?" I said.

"This plan has worked for five centuries with no interceptions—that is, until you stole our book. We've always passed it to other branches of our guild by transferring it through a library because libraries have historically been centers for the transfer of human knowledge.

"While we have computers and the Internet now, we still value the historic traditions. Of course we embrace the power of the new technologies to finally make us into gods. One day we will have the power to create life. One day we will rule the world, and even the universe. As we create computers with more power, we will become gods. We will control our own fates and the fate of the world. No one will ever need to trust God again. We will live forever in our own land, and it will be our paradise."

"Wait . . . you've got a guild for what—human knowledge to control? Good and evil? What the heck?" I said.

"We represent all knowledge," the leader said. "We support knowing evil, but also doing good when it's in our best interest. We support the side of good when it brings us closer to our goals, but we must always take the side of evil when it advances knowledge. And when we do good, it's for our own good. It has nothing to do with God. By that definition, even our good would be considered evil to those who believe in God."

"How can you want to be gods?" I said. "That's ridiculous. How can you want evil as much as good, and how can you even believe there's a God and a Satan? Hasn't science proven they're myths?"

"Believe what you want, but we still believe there's a real God. Sure, even a few in our guild think those beliefs are merely metaphors for the knowledge of good and evil. But all of us believe we must know all that's evil, as well as what's good. We must know *everything* to control our destinies."

"What?" I said in frustration.

"We believe in the eternal struggle to control our own lives," my captor explained. "Not achieving that is our hell. I, for one, believe God is real, but we cannot worship him. We honor the serpent for inspiring Eve to set us free from God, but we don't worship him any more than we worship God. We believe there's a Satan, but we don't worship him either. We worship ourselves."

I shook my head in disgust.

"Let me put it this way," he said. "We choose the freedom to do whatever we want, whenever we want. Someday we'll have eternal life, like the life stolen from us when mankind was sent out of Eden.

"Our guild always supports war because a lot of technological advances happen when the military develops weapons and defenses. We always have members on both sides of every war—even religious wars—but we concentrate on controlling our own destinies, our own lives. We simply use wars to advance our own cause.

"We encourage the rich to live for their wealth. We also encourage a few to give some of their wealth to the poor, but we limit our support because we need the poor. We support slavery and suppression of the poor so we can understand the nature of power. We support both racism and civil rights, especially if we can inspire a riot that helps our cause. We focus on making evil become our good, and good look like evil.

"We are the true humans. We are our own gods. One day the Guild for the Knowledge of Good and Evil will become the Guild of God. We will control the world and all destiny."

The image on the cover of the book was beginning to make sense. Here was the image of the tree I remembered studying in Sunday school when I was a kid. The round shape represented the fruit Eve was supposed to have eaten and given to Adam, who willingly consumed it. I imagined that the leafy side of the tree represented the good, and the side with bare branches represented the fallen world.

"We've learned how to control evil for our own good," the guild leader continued, "or evil would most certainly destroy us. Controlled evil has become our good."

"That's insane," I said.

"Not as insane as you think," he said. "What kinds of programs do you watch on television—news, murder mysteries, sports?"

"I don't know, probably all of them," I said.

"When you watch the news or a murder mystery, you want the good to win, but you would be bored to death if there was no evil to fight. Right? We want both the good guys and the bad to play their parts. We, of course, always want our team to win and the other team to lose. In the end, we choose ourselves over all else. We will fight and kill to win. We choose to be our own gods.

"Because we humans ate of the tree of the knowledge of good and evil, we're all in the same situation. We all want good for ourselves, but we also want evil to make our lives exciting."

The room seemed to spin as I thought about what this all meant. Had the book been calling me to choose to make evil into my good, or did I now need to choose between good and evil? I still didn't believe there was a God who created us, much less one who placed humans in a garden called Eden, but was I being called to be my own god? Or had I already chosen that?

"Jesus, you're crazy as—" I said.

"Don't ever say that name!" one of the guards yelled, and slapped me across the cheek.

When I recovered, I said, "I'm sorry. I didn't mean to swear."

"You didn't," the leader said. He leaned over and stared into my eyes. "But that is the name of the only human who ever lived who *always* chose good. We tried everything possible to tempt him. We offered him the world, but he never chose evil. We hate that name!"

"How can you believe evil is as important as good?" I asked, still trying to wrap my head around what they were telling me.

"Don't you ever want to do any wickedness that makes you feel good, even if it hurts someone else? Haven't you ever wanted to kill someone to get even, or rape someone for the fun of it?"

"No!" Jane screamed so loud my eardrums hurt.

"That's enough," the man stood up and yelled. "It's time to kill you. Remember, the sooner you tell us where the book is, the quicker you'll die."

He looked at the two men who stood guard over us. Pointing at the muscle-bound one, he said, "That's Cain." Nodding at the other thug, he said, "And he's Abel."

"Cain and Abel?" I recalled Abel was the good brother and Cain was the evil one.

"Amuse yourselves," he said as he nodded at them. "I'll come back to check on your progress after I've had a couple glasses of wine."

He left with his bodyguard, who carried a large pistol at his side.

To my surprise, a young woman I hadn't seen sitting behind me got up to leave. She was wearing an expensive floor-length dress. A diamond necklace adorned her dipping neckline. Without looking at either of us, she followed them to the door, but stopped momentarily. She looked straight at Jane and commented sulkily, "I won't be back. I hate the sight of tortured corpses."

Her comment terrified me.

As soon as the others left, Cain and Abel looked lustily at Jane, then at me. They began to add extra strapping to hold our arms and legs to the chair, laughing as they taped the chairs to the floor.

I was shaking from fear. Jane was trembling.

Abel took my shoes off, rubbed a gel under my feet, and then taped them to a metal plate. He also rubbed the gel onto my wrists and taped metal electrodes to them. Heavy gauge wires were attached to the electrodes.

Sweat dripped from my face. So we were going to be electrocuted! My insides began to churn from the anticipated shock.

I remembered reading about electrocutions once in a piece I had to edit. They were terrifying, even when there was an attempt to make them as humane as possible. I was sure, when used for torture, they could make death unbearably slow and painful.

The men followed the same procedure for hooking Jane to the wires. Her face had gone ghostly white. Her body strained against the bonds holding her. She looked like she wanted to scream, but was, by sheer force of will, not giving them that satisfaction.

Cain and Abel stepped outside the door and brought a device that looked like some kind of electrical charger into the room. They proceeded to hook the other ends of the heavy wire to large terminals on the surface of the machine. A large cable was plugged into what looked like a 220-volt outlet for an electric stove.

"The electrocution control has ten settings," Cain said in a monotone. "We'll start with one and move up one number every time you don't tell us what we want to know. Number eight will probably knock you out from the shock. Numbers nine or ten should kill you." He paused, then added, "If not, we'll add electrodes to your head. If that doesn't work—" He pointed at my head with a sly smile. "We'll just shoot you between the eyes.

"To test the equipment," Cain said, "I'll zap you with a number one jolt just to see what happens."

He smiled at me as he swung a large lever upward and, in a flash, it hit me. I was sure my hair turned gray. My feet and wrists felt like hot flames were burning them. I screamed. My body twisted as I fought against my restraints until my veins felt like they would burst. When I thought I couldn't stand any more, Cain pulled the lever back. My trial was over—for the moment. I had wet my pants.

"That one works pissing well," he spat with a leer.

An instant later, Jane was jolted with the electricity. The pain on her face was beyond horrible. She shrieked and flung herself back, fighting against her restraints. Her body shook violently. Her eyes bulged in their sockets. The air smelled like hot wires and burning flesh. Then the power was shut off for her, too.

Her head fell forward against her chest. I worried for a brief moment that she might have died, but finally she groaned. Jane slowly lifted her head and stared straight ahead.

"That works, too. Ain't this going to be fun?" Cain said, smiling at Abel, who sneered back and said, "Freak'n' fun!"

14

If this was only the test, what would the numbers eight, nine, or ten be like? Was tortured death the destiny this book had in store for us?

The power the book held over me was mysterious and frightening, but also, somehow, exciting. My pledge to Jane was firm. I thought about the pact we had made to keep everything we knew about our book a secret. Without that, I doubted I would be able to endure either my pain or seeing her agony. Telling them where our book was hidden would break my commitment to her, and when we made our oath the commitment to keep our book had become a commitment to each other, even *unto death*.

I could see Jane felt the same deep conviction. Perhaps it was a sadly misguided commitment—or at least a misguided expression of our commitment to each other—but I knew that if I broke down and told them where our book was, Jane would take that as a breach of trust. I couldn't do that. I *wouldn't* do that.

This was a frightening cult. I realized that if its members wanted our book this much, it must hold great power over them—and promise tremendous power *to* them. I didn't want them to have any more power. They had too much already.

This time when they demanded "Tell us where our book is!" I gathered all my strength, gasped for a breath of air, and blurted out, "I'm not telling! I'll never tell!"

They glared at me like I was worthless trash; then they walked over to Jane. She had tilted her head to the side when she heard my reply. She looked pleased with my response, but also frightened. One of the thugs grabbed her hair and pulled her head upright, repeating the demand.

"No," she yelled back, "I'll never tell!"

Jane was experiencing the same pain I was, but wasn't willing to tell them what they wanted to hear. We would die together with our secret.

A moment of calm came over me. It was almost funny. I had never imagined I would die because I was committed to any cause, especially something as strange and compelling as a rare book. Now, however, that book stood for much more. As much as it had attracted us, it had also become part of a greater bond between Jane and me. Our purpose—yes, even our very will to live and die for a cause— was being tested. It wasn't many weeks earlier that I would have been far more likely to die from a lack of commitment to anything. I was as surprised as our captors that I had such reserves of strength.

Cain walked back to the electrical switches. "Let's zap both of them at the same time."

All of my muscles went tense as the current charged through me.

My hands burned where they contacted the metal plates. I felt the tree of the knowledge of good and evil's etching being seared into my palms. I could feel its leaves and sharp branches. The tempting fruit scorched deeper into my flesh, calling me to the book. I tried to yell but my bindings held me too tight across the chest. I groaned, though I'm not sure any sound escaped. *Am I the new Adam? Is Jane the new Eve?*

From deep inside of me, a whisper contrary to all my desires to search for the meaning of our book said, *Flee. Flee from the book, for you are, indeed, Adam and Jane is Eve. You must choose.*

As quickly as the charge had entered my body, it stopped. My head bounced back, and then fell forward. I wanted to look to see whether my hands actually had a permanent etching of the tree burned into them or if that was all a pain-induced hallucination.

I wanted to take a deep breath, but my bindings were too tight. I could barely breathe, and when I did, a metallic smell of electricity and burnt flesh filled my nostrils.

When I looked at Jane, she stared back at me and grimaced.

Abel left the room. Cain added more gel under our hands to make sure the electric current would have maximum impact—or maybe he did it just to scare us. He seemed to be enjoying our torture.

I wondered if Jane and I would die in vain, or if keeping our book from this demented guild was really worth dying for. Their whole existence was built on being devious and controlling everything around them. How could they want all the knowledge of evil, and believe it was as important as the knowledge of good?

At the same time, I felt compelled by their logic. There had been times in my life when I wanted to rationalize that Adam and Eve had made the right choice. We had to know evil to make life challenging, didn't we? I wanted good to win, but I wanted it to win *against evil*. Or did I want it to win no matter what the cost? If there were no evil . . .

At any rate, we deserved this book. I had to keep it out of their hands. It was ours, Jane's and mine. I still wanted to find *our* book's hidden meaning, but I doubted we would ever have the chance. And what if we did discover the hidden code? Would the book's hidden meaning then destroy us?

And what about the whisper I had heard so clearly only moments before? *Flee*, it had said.

No! I screamed inside. *The book is ours.*

I wasn't sure how long we had been waiting. I heard some noise in the hall and looked up, expecting to see Abel enter. Instead, the door flew open with such force that the handle punched a hole in the wall. A man I'd never seen plunged into the room and immediately dropped to one knee. He lifted a large revolver with both hands.

To my horror, I saw Cain frantically twist the dial on the generator. *This is it*, I thought, but before he could throw the switch, my ears cracked with a deafening pain at the sound of a gun firing. Blood spattered around the room like spray paint, and Cain flipped backwards, his hand flying off the switch. He crashed violently to the floor.

I started shaking and crying uncontrollably. I felt clammy and dizzy. The room went out of focus, then disappeared completely.

———————

I felt myself slipping in and out of consciousness. When I became aware of my surroundings, I was lying on a bed. That realization was all I could handle for the moment. I slipped back into a dull fog.

I remember hearing footsteps, doors opening and closing, and the sound of people talking. A damp cloth wiped my forehead, and a blanket was thrown over me. I felt claustrophobic . . . trapped.

Stark impressions of terror kept flashing through my mind: a bottle floating in a storm, caught in the rocks; a woman's face, agony etched into every feature. In my nightmare, I twitched involuntarily, screaming as I heard a gun shot and saw blood splash against a wall. *Am I going crazy?*

A needle was injected into my arm and I passed out.

The next thing I remembered was waking up and feeling a soft bed under me. I felt warm. Slowly opening one eye, then the other, I saw someone standing beside the bed. As my eyes focused, I saw a nurse watching me. I guessed I was in a hospital.

Why was I there? As I tried to understand my situation, I realized I couldn't remember anything about my life prior to waking up. I didn't even know my name. I knew I must have had one, but as hard as I tried, I couldn't recall it.

The nurse finished adjusting the drip of an IV going into my arm. She looked down and, seeing I was awake, said, "It's good to have you back among the living."

I didn't know what she meant. I tried to ask, but my mouth felt like it was full of cotton. I couldn't get it to work.

She smiled, saying, "Rest now. We can talk later."

The advice sounded good. I closed my eyes. All I could do was lie still and try to remember—*anything*—but my mind was blank. I had only been awake for a few minutes, but I craved sleep, and gave in.

As I became aware of my surroundings again, I recalled the name *Jane*. I couldn't remember who Jane was—but I associated her name with warmth and goodness, and in some strange way, also terror. I couldn't quite understand why I should know her, but I had a driving need to find out who she was. Something must have happened to her, or to us.

To us? Why did I think *us*?

No one was in the room when I woke up the second time. The sun was shining through a large window on my right, and light streamed across the floor, over my bed covers, and up the opposite wall. I lay still for a few minutes; then tried to move my arms. They seemed to work. An IV drip poked into my lower left arm. I had strength enough to push myself up in bed, but my wrists ached from the effort. My hands were blistered. Something in the back of my mind told me the blisters came from burns. My arms, neck, and back throbbed with pain. *Could I have been in a fire?*

I glanced around the room. The walls were painted minty green. A vase of multicolored flowers sat on a dresser opposite the foot of the bed. The room smelled of antiseptic.

I twisted to my side and looked past my feet to see what I looked like in a mirror on the wall behind the flowers. My eyes had dark circles around them; my head was wrapped in bandages.

I tried in vain to remember what had happened—and who I was. *If only I could see my face more clearly, that might help.*

A nurse entered the room and smiled broadly. "Wow," she said. Her eyes met mine. "You're looking a lot better. How are you feeling?"

I ignored the question. As loudly as I could, I whispered, "Who am I?"

I wasn't sure she could understand me, but she responded by reading my name off the chart. "George Mercy. You're George Mercy. I'll need to get the doctor before I tell you any more."

Now, at least, I knew my name, and it seemed natural that it should be George Mercy.

She turned to leave, but stopped and said, "Just so you know, two FBI agents are guarding your door."

Even in my state, I knew who the FBI were. *What have I done?* I thought.

"I'll send the doctor in as soon as he's finished with his patient rounds," she said on her way out.

I wanted to ask her who Jane was, but I couldn't get the words out. There was nothing I could do but wait. I whispered my name several times, hoping it would connect with some clues.

I closed my eyes and, as I said the name "Jane," a face flashed to the surface of my mind. I guessed that it must be Jane's face. She was beautiful.

The pieces seemed to be slowly revealing themselves. It would take some time, however, to sort, organize, and put the puzzle together. At least I hoped it would be possible and that none of the pieces had been lost.

The door to my room opened, and three men in suits entered. "Good afternoon, George. I'm Dr. Gray and this is Dr. Frank. He's a psychologist." Nodding at the third person, Gray said, "That is FBI agent Joseph—you can call him Joe."

"You're a doctor, he's a psychologist, and he's FBI? What did I do?" I said in my raspy whisper.

"Sorry," FBI Joe said, "we can't tell you any more right now. We don't want to influence how you remember the events of the last few days."

"What events?" I asked.

"As I said, we can't tell you yet, but we need you to answer some questions."

The first question Joe asked was, "What's your name?"

"The nurse said I'm George Mercy, but you already knew that," I whispered.

They nodded their heads in unison, and Joe immediately asked, "Where do you live?"

"I . . . don't know," I answered truthfully.

"Do you remember anything about what's happened to you?" Dr. Frank asked.

I shook my head. "No. What's happened? Why?"

"I can tell you this much so you understand why we're here," Joe said. "You could be a witness in court and there are a few people who don't want you to testify."

"So you're protecting me?"

"Yes, but I can't tell you any more. You've got to remember on your own."

"Our greatest concern right now is for your recovery and protection," Dr. Gray said.

Dr. Gray examined me while the others waited quietly by the door. He checked my wrists, hands, and the bottoms of my feet. I could see that all were burned and blistered. He removed the bandages from my face and touched what felt like cuts and bruises. He entered some notes into a computer on a stand by the wall.

When he finished, Dr. Frank asked me again, "Do you remember anything?"

"Almost nothing." I paused, coughed, and added, "I did remember someone—Jane, but I don't know who she is."

"Jane is your wife. You're both recovering from traumas," Dr. Frank said. "It's not uncommon to experience a period of amnesia after a shock to the body and mind like you've had, but you should eventually regain most, if not all, of your memory. My goal is to help you in every way possible."

"How's Jane . . . my wife?" I asked.

Dr. Gray smiled and said, "She's recovering well, but we're keeping her in a coma for now to help her body heal. I think you'll be able to see her in a couple of days."

That both excited and scared me. What was my wife like? How could I forget my own wife? Oh, I knew her name, *Jane*, but what had attracted me to her? What had attracted her to me?

They had assured me that my memory should come back. I had to remember!

The last thing Dr. Gray said before they left me to my worried thoughts was, "I think you're ready to start eating a soft diet."

A few minutes later, Dr. Frank returned and handed me several biographical pages about my life. "I hope this brings back some mental images that'll help you recall your past."

After he left, I leaned back and rested for a few minutes before I picked up the half-a-dozen pages about my forgotten life. I read my history like it was a biography of someone I didn't know. There were names, dates, anniversaries, and places from a life I couldn't remember. I knew I could memorize them. I could take a test on them. In some sense, they were me because my present was fashioned by those facts. Still, I couldn't know or really understand how they fit together to form my reality until I recovered my own memory, remembered my personal links to the past, and understood my emotional connections to the otherwise dry statistics.

How could I know so much about myself and still not remember who I was? It didn't make sense.

As I began to feel better over the next days, I started to sit up in a chair, and move from soft foods to a normal diet. My feet were still tender and hurt when I put weight on them, but I was able, with the aid of crutches, to take several short walks down the hospital corridor and back to my room.

I began to grow suspicious about the FBI agents who always seemed to be following me. I didn't understand why they were still needed. What was I missing? I couldn't remember anything I had done that would make me a witness to any crime, much less to one so important that it required a cadre of FBI agents to protect me. Did Jane have personal guards, too? When I asked why all the agents were needed, I was only told that I would eventually be briefed.

When I asked about Jane, I was asking about a woman whom I hardly remembered, but who, I was certain, had been a huge part of my life.

They assured me that Jane's health was improving slowly, but she needed more time to heal. I began to wonder if they were putting off telling me bad news, but they truly seemed optimistic. Maybe she couldn't remember me, either.

Dr. Frank showed up for about an hour every day and we did the psychologist–patient routine. My memory was a mosaic with the pieces all jumbled. I would remember some little detail and fit that piece into place. Then I would remember another. I felt like a detective putting my life back together. I kept looking for the magic piece . . . the moment when whole sections and histories would begin to make sense.

Dr. Frank kept reminding me to be patient. "You should eventually recover most of your memory. However, you may always have holes in your history, especially from the period of time when you faced your most serious traumas."

I wasn't sure how to adjust to what he was saying. I wanted to remember everything and move on with my life. Or did I? Maybe a few memories were better forgotten, but Dr. Frank had warned me they would still be in my subconscious, conditioning my mental health in ways I may not know how to deal with.

Gradually, the days fell into a routine, and I began to track the passage of time. On a Monday a couple of weeks after I first found myself in the hospital, Dr. Gray came into my room and said, "I think Jane has recovered enough for you to see her. I've scheduled a meeting with her for tomorrow."

I was thrilled. I had begun to remember Jane and I was pretty certain that I had pieced together most of our life up until our recent ordeal—though there were still gaps I wanted to ask her about. I'd also rediscovered how much I loved her, not only intellectually, but also emotionally.

As much as I wanted to see her, I was terrified about the moment we would meet face to face. I wasn't sure how Jane would react to me.

I discussed my fears with Dr. Frank that afternoon. "Don't worry. You'll be fine," he said. "Jane is missing you as much as you're missing her, and being with her will likely help you fill in many of the lost pieces of your memory."

I knew he was right—for better or worse. I hardly slept that night.

As early morning light filtered into my room, I noticed a book lying on the nightstand next to me. Looking at it more closely, I recognized it as a Gideon Bible, and it reminded me of some other book I wanted to touch but couldn't. The recollection gave me goose bumps. Whatever book it resembled must have had a major impact on my life. I couldn't take my eyes off the Bible with its fake leather cover. I imaged it into my consciousness like a burning brand.

The effort to concentrate on discovering its importance—combined with a need for sleep—soon exhausted me, and I dozed off.

When I woke up later in the morning, the room was bright. In a flash, I remembered the Harrison Library where I had discovered a book. I had pulled the little leather book off the shelf and shown it to Jane. Suddenly, my memory was so clear that the events could have happened yesterday. This was the book the Gideon Bible had reminded me of. I also remembered tearing up a copy of the Gideon Bible in Grand Marais, thinking I had destroyed the book Jane and I had found—our book. I had a hunch that the contents of the two books were somehow in conflict.

I remembered how, immediately after finding our book in the library, I ran my fingers across the ancient paper, and I visualized the rich leather cover. I could almost feel the image of the tree as I imagined touching its subtle imprint. That tree also evoked a feeling in my gut, a power I both wanted and was repulsed by. The book's ancient beauty awed me as I mentally caressed its mysterious pages.

As I thought back, I recalled that the content of the book was unreadable, and I had been working with Jane to find the code to unlock its secret meaning. We had not succeeded. Yet, as I had sensed when I first found the book, I had the feeling that doing so would change our lives forever.

I began to understand the impact of the events leading up to my current situation. I remembered how Jane and I seemed to encounter danger whenever we tried to research the meaning of our mysterious little book. We were constantly trying to escape from whoever was attempting to find our book and destroy our research. The memories were coming back quickly—and with a power of their own.

I didn't know how to deal with all I was remembering.

The FBI was somehow connected to the recent incidents related to the book. If I could only remember the details of what had happened before I was hospitalized, I might understand how dangerous our situation had become.

15

Dr. Gray knocked on my door and pushed it open. FBI Joe followed him into the room carrying a small travel bag in one hand. He walked over to the bed and dropped the bag beside me. He pulled out some clothes, and said gruffly, though not without a touch of concern in his voice, "Get dressed in these, ASAP."

"Why? Am I going to see Jane?"

"Sorry. No. We fear there may be people in the hospital who want you dead," he said. "I'm trying to save your life. You need to get dressed. Quickly."

"What? What people? Who wants me dead?"

While I knew I was being protected, I was shocked by the revelation of how immediate the danger had suddenly become.

"Several more FBI agents have been assigned to guard the hospital because we believe they know where you are," Joe said, again pushing the bag of clothing toward me.

"What about Jane?" I asked. "Do they know about her, too? Is she okay?"

Dr. Frank entered the room and whispered something to Joe. Then Joe said, "The FBI has received information from a confidential source. Those who want you dead have confirmed you're a patient in this hospital. It's time to leave—immediately and discreetly." My questions must have been obvious from my face, as Joe continued almost immediately.

"Two days ago an agent was admitted into the hospital; he's in the next room," Joe said. "He was picked because he has your build and your general facial features. You'll be checked out of the hospital under his name instead of George Mercy. He will become you."

As I tried to process all of this new information while dressing, Dr. Frank pressed me once more about what I remembered.

"I think I remember pretty much everything—up until the last week," I said.

I wasn't about to tell them about our book. I wanted to discuss the details with Jane, first. I remembered enough to know we had already gone through a lot to keep it a secret, and just because this was the FBI, I wasn't going to say anything without Jane's input. We were in this together.

I remembered that Jane and I had made a pact of silence about our book. Our secret understanding was important to me, and I sensed it was critical to our relationship. I didn't know where all of this was taking us, but I believed the book held the key to some deeper mystery—a key that was just waiting to be discovered. I also knew there was still something about the book I couldn't remember, something that both captivated and frightened me.

As soon as I was dressed in my new clothes, I was handed a pair of glasses. A dark wig was adjusted over my natural hair. An extraordinarily real-looking paste-on mustache was attached to my upper lip. It all reminded me of dressing up as a kid, pretending I was a spy. A small scar was then very carefully added over my left eye. I guessed that every detail had been crafted to make me look like the person I was replacing. As they worked, Joe checked and double-checked my appearance against eight photos taken from various angles of the man I was impersonating.

I was encouraged not to worry. I was told that the person I was replacing was an agent himself, and tomorrow he would vanish, too. My temporary name was to be Michael Ward—"Mike" for short—the name the agent had used when he checked into the hospital. His name would temporarily become George Mercy.

Vanish, I thought. *That's what they want me to do. They want me to vanish. They want me to become someone else, and make George Mercy disappear.*

Just as I was beginning to figure myself out, I was going to become someone else.

FBI Joe outlined the plan. "We're going to move you next door, and move the agent into your bed. Then, a few minutes later, you'll be wheeled out of the room by a nursing assistant and brought to the front desk to be checked out. You'll meet a woman at the desk who will walk with you to a car at the hospital entrance. You are to act like she's your wife. When you're still several yards away, say to her, 'It's wonderful to see you, my dear.' She will answer, 'You're looking good, Mike. I've missed you.'"

The whole plan made me nervous. This was obviously a far more dangerous escape than I had anticipated. Who were these people who were so determined to kill me? I still had no clue.

I was also beginning to worry about Jane. What were they trying to keep from me? Was she also in danger? Why couldn't we escape together?

Unable to constrain myself, I asked, "When will I see Jane? It seems like you're trying to keep us apart."

Dr. Frank said, "Hopefully, later today. Getting both of you away from here is our first priority, and it will be easier to get you out separately."

This sounded like a lame excuse to me. I felt like they were playing games with us, but I also got the impression that if we didn't play along, we might never walk out of the hospital alive. I couldn't take any chances. I didn't have any idea where Jane's room was, and I had little choice but to go along with their plan.

"Good luck," Dr. Frank said as he and Dr. Gray left.

FBI Joe waited quietly, looking at his watch. After about a minute he said, "Stay here while I check the halls."

A short time later, he poked his head in and said, "The area's clear. Switch rooms now." When I didn't move fast enough, he chided me, loudly whispering, "Quickly!"

Thirty seconds later I was in the next room. My double looked so much like me that if I had bumped into him in the hall, I would have thought I had found my unknown identical twin. As soon as I was in, my double left to go into my old room. We couldn't be seen in the hallway at the same time. Everything had to look normal when I made my exit. I sat down in a chair beside the bed. I had been told to wait for the nursing assistant to take me to be checked out. I was someone else now—Michael "Mike" Ward. I had to remember that name.

I sat for about five minutes. The longer I sat, the faster my heart beat. I didn't want to be Michael Ward, Mike for short. I wanted to be George Mercy, editor, husband to Jane Mercy. I wanted to go home to my house in Chicago. This was crazy. Why was I here? How could picking up one small book that nobody claimed lead to this?

The door opened. A man in hospital scrubs rolled a wheelchair in. I slipped into the chair to follow hospital protocol. The nursing assistant pushed me down the hallway to the nurses' station where we stopped for a few minutes while he chatted with the nurses behind the desk. He wheeled me to the elevator, and we rode down to the first floor. When the door opened, the nursing assistant pushed me around the corner and toward the main lobby. I saw a woman who appeared to be waiting for me at the front desk in the lobby. She smiled as I approached.

Mrs. Ward, I guess! I thought.

She was a stunningly beautiful brunette wearing a low-cut blouse and a skirt that only reached to about midthigh.

When my nursing assistant stopped, I said, "It's wonderful to see you, my dear." I almost gagged on the words. Nevertheless, I got them past my lips in what I felt was a rather convincing tone, though the beating of my heart caused the words to be a bit shaky.

She smiled broadly. "You're looking good, Mike. I've missed you."

Suddenly, across the room, a man pulled a revolver from his suit coat and began to turn toward me.

I leapt out of the chair onto the floor. As I rolled and looked up, I saw the gun aimed at me. I jumped for the corner of the desk.

I heard a couple of sharp bangs from somewhere in the lobby and the would-be shooter flew across the room, blood spattering from his shoulder and arm.

The front desk nurse screamed and dived behind her desk. "Mrs. Ward" dropped to the floor. I cowered around the corner of the desk, my hands sweaty and shaking, totally stunned.

A moment later, I heard a car spin its wheels and speed off. A couple of shots exploded outside, and tires squealed. I heard a crash.

When I crawled out from behind the desk, two FBI guards were standing by me with guns drawn. Mrs. Ward was sitting on the floor looking deathly scared. The nurse, peeking over the top of her desk, was gasping for air between sobs.

An older couple who had been waiting in the lounge huddled together on a couch, as white as ghosts. A mother held a screaming child in her arms, a second weeping child hiding behind her legs.

One of the FBI agents picked up a gun from the floor, and another agent pressed his hand against the bleeding wounds on the assailant's shoulder and arm. A third agent talked on his phone. Once the lobby was secured, a doctor came to attend to the man's wounds. My would-be murderer looked at me disdainfully as he was being examined.

"Now we go to plan B," one of the agents whispered to me, "and we execute it fast while all the attention is on the lobby."

"Please don't use the word *execute*," I snapped back.

I was rushed out through a side door marked, "PERSONNEL ONLY," down a flight of stairs into an underground parking ramp. Just before we opened the door, we stopped and my double switched places with me again.

The FBI agents who were with me rushed out with him, and I was pulled into a small room by two agents I didn't recognize. One of them handed me a janitor's uniform. He told me to strip off my present disguise and change into the new one as fast as possible. One of the agents also changed into janitor's clothing.

When we walked out through one of the side doors, anyone watching would have seen two janitors get into a car that looked like its next stop should be the junkyard, and drive slowly past the side of the hospital, completely ignored by the police cars, which seemed to be everywhere.

We pulled onto a busy four-lane street. About a mile down the road, we pulled into the parking lot of a small bar. We both got out of the car and walked in like we were regular patrons. We moved to the back of the nearly empty room and slid into a booth. A small bag sat on the floor under the table. The agent handed me the bag and said, "Go into the men's room and change your clothes again. We can't be too careful."

This time I changed into a pair of blue jeans and a plaid shirt. I also put on a light brown wig that I found in the bag. Someone else came in while I was checking myself in the mirror and said, "Give me the clothes you're holding." He had light brown hair and wore blue jeans and a plaid shirt—in the light of the bar we'd pass for twins.

As he changed into my janitor's outfit, he said, "Leave the bar by yourself. Drive straight to Madison. When you get there, check into the TopOne Motel under the name of Fred Nielson." He handed me the keys to a car, and said, "A brown and green Jeep Cherokee with Wisconsin license plates is parked half a block down the street."

I was trying to remember everything he was telling me as he gave me a driver's license with my new name, Fred Nielson, and a picture that looked like him—which meant it matched my current appearance. *How did they do that so fast?* He handed me a credit card with the same name.

"There's a map in the car with instructions on how to get from here to Wisconsin and then to the motel," he said. "Wait in here a few minutes. Then leave immediately." He left wearing my old janitor's clothes, and a wig the color of my hair, before I had a chance to ask him where the "here" I would be driving from was.

With my third disguise of the day, and the gut feeling that it might not be my last, I walked through the bar and stepped out onto the street. I was on my own for the moment. I immediately saw the jeep right where the agent said it would be. I walked to it as casually as I could. I unlocked the door and slid into the driver's seat as if it were my vehicle, trying my best to look like I knew exactly what I was doing. In all honesty, I was so scared I could hardly think.

I decided to put a few miles between myself and this place before taking time to study the map and figure out all of the vehicle's controls. I drove until I found the quiet parking lot of a small grocery store. Only then did I study the dashboard for all the light switches, radio buttons, and heating and cooling controls.

I pulled the map from the glove compartment and quickly recognized from the notes that I was in Rockford, Illinois. I only had to go about a mile to get to the freeway, and then to head northwest to my destination.

Driving gave me time to think about my predicament—and to worry about Jane. Just hours earlier I had been preparing to meet her, but now I was worried I might never see her again. I feared for the worst. Every moment that passed made finding her seem less likely. *Will I ever be able to touch her, hold her, and caress away her hurts?*

Bits and pieces of our mutual terror began to work their way up to the surface and carve themselves into my mind. They were illusory, but like ancient petroglyphs, they wouldn't go away. They were etched deep into my psyche and would either destructively undermine me, or become a constructive part of a new strength, a new resolve for me to draw upon.

I still wasn't able to piece together exactly what had happened in the week before I woke up in the hospital, but it must have been terrible. I tried hard to remember, but while the depths of the horror haunted me, exactly what had happened remained hidden, even more than the scenes from my strange dreams that I now remembered in detail.

As far as I had determined, I had recalled many of the events of the last few weeks, but the ones that linked me most closely to the horror were hidden behind a dense fog. I surmised that Jane and I were bound together by a terror where everything was beyond our control. *How I miss Jane!*

Maybe, when I got to Madison, I would find her at the TopOne Motel. *Maybe, but the way things are going, not likely.*

I had begun to cry so hard that I could barely drive. I pulled off at the next exit and sat there sobbing. I was crying from deep traumas I could only vaguely recall. I wept because of all the horror I had experienced. I wept because I didn't know what had happened to Jane. I wept because of all I had lost, including my very identity. And I wept because I was scared I would experience still more loss and hopelessness. Then I sat back, dried my eyes, and willed myself to drive to Madison. *Maybe Jane will be waiting there.*

I pulled into the TopOne directly off of Interstate 94, parked, and walked to the front desk. The clerk found my reservation, checked my credit card, and asked for the make, model, and license number of my car. She pointed to the motel floor plan, showing me where my room was. "It's on the third floor. The best place to park is right in front of the motel. You can take the elevator around the corner," she said as she pointed in the direction of the hallway.

I asked if anyone had asked for me.

"No. Are you expecting someone?"

"Maybe," I said.

Moments later I struggled into the empty room with the suitcase and carry-on bag I had discovered in the back of the vehicle. It wasn't much, but it was all I had. It reminded me of all I had lost.

Maybe Jane would come tomorrow. "Maybe," I whispered.

16

I flopped onto the bed, exhausted from the turmoil of the day. I cried again; then, miraculously, I slept.

When I woke up, the sun was setting and the clouds reflected a wash of magenta with hues of orange accenting the lacy fringes. I hoped this was an indication that good things would follow, but at the moment my life seemed pretty dismal. I had lost everything. There was nothing I could do to go back. My future hung on the whims of others.

Worst of all, I had lost Jane—and I needed to find her. If she had been lost or killed in the wild transition from the hospital, could I live without her?

I had no choice. I had to rebuild my life, with or without Jane. I wept again at the thought and hoped against all odds we would be reunited soon.

I had to do something to break free from my dismal mood. I looked at the suitcase, and to put my desperation out of my mind, I unzipped it to examine the contents. I lifted the lid and my heart skipped. On the very top of the contents was a five-by-seven photo of Jane. It had obviously been taken recently. She was wearing a nurse's uniform. So that was how they were hiding her.

She looked older than I remembered, and the strain showed in her eyes, but the photo raised my hopes. Perhaps she had escaped. I sat down and stared at her picture until my eyes hurt and my stomach ached from hunger.

I found ten twenty-dollar bills in my new wallet, so I had some spending money. That would be enough to feed me for a few days, but not enough for me to take off on my own. If I tried to sneak away,

I assumed I would eventually have to use the credit card I had been given by the FBI. As soon as I used the card, I would be traced, and it wouldn't take them long to find me.

I drove around until I found a local pizza joint called Hot'N'Zesty, and pulled in. All I wanted was a quick meal, and after that, a good movie that wouldn't tax my mind or remind me of my recent experiences. It also couldn't have a romantic plot. I desperately needed to relax. A harmless comedy would be my best choice. Could I find one like that? I doubted any would be completely harmless.

And what is harmless? I thought.

I looked for a non-threatening escapist plot in the movie guide I had picked up near the front door of the pizza joint. While eating my pizza and downing a large shake, I decided on the movie I wanted to see and asked the waiter how to get to the theater.

Fifteen minutes later I was getting my ticket for the show. For the next two hours I did my best to avoid thoughts about my circumstances. I was only partially successful. Every time I saw some really funny scene, I wanted to laugh with Jane. Every time there was any hint of romance, I wanted to put my arm around her and give her a hug. Nevertheless, the movie was a good break from my hopeless situation.

On my way back to the motel, I stopped at a store and bought a bottle of wine. I've never been much of a drinker, but I thought it would help me sleep. I got back to the motel around eleven o'clock and poured a glass. I took my time drinking it as I stared at Jane's photo.

I finally opened the suitcase again and dug deeper to see what I had. As I moved the clothes around looking for something to sleep in, my fingers wrapped around a solid, oblong case buried in the middle. When I extracted it from the suitcase, I realized it was a laptop computer like the one I had owned, except it didn't have the same dirty keyboard and scratches. That, of course, meant that they must have my original laptop. Could they have hacked the hard drive and found the files of the book? *Our book!*

A note had been slipped between the screen and the keyboard with a password printed on it. The computer screen flashed to life when I pressed the power switch, and I immediately typed the password. I waited anxiously to see what was on the hard drive.

A bright icon was positioned right in the middle of the desktop screen. In capital letters it was labeled "JANE." I quickly clicked on it and saw that it opened a word processing file containing a short note from her. I was overjoyed. It was my first communication from Jane since we had been separated. I read it with some anxiety, hoping to find clues about what had happened and when we might get back together.

The letter said little about either. "Soon," was all it said about when she hoped to see me again.

They were telling her about as much as they were telling me, which was very little. She wrote almost nothing about what had happened, except to tell me she couldn't discuss anything about the ordeal we had gone through, which was probably all that she was allowed to say. The word *ordeal* confirmed all of my dire mental images about what had happened to us, but didn't help fill in any details.

The next paragraph gave me more hope. Jane said she had seen me for a brief moment as I was rushing out of the hospital after the attempt on my life. "I was dressed as a nurse in one of the labs just off the hallway," Jane wrote. "I saw them rush you past, but I didn't dare do anything because I was afraid it would jeopardize both of our lives."

We had been so close, but we could just as well have been a thousand miles apart for all the good it did. If all of this hadn't happened, we would be together now, enjoying each other, loving each other.

The letter gave me a hint of hope. It also made me curse our impossible situation. If I could just start over, I would do it in a second.

———————

Nearly everything I remembered having on my old computer had been copied to this one. Most of my directories and programs were set up just as I remembered them. I was impressed. The entire text of the book was there, as were all of our research notes. They definitely knew everything we had done, and perhaps had examined the files with their own sophisticated programs. They probably knew far more than we did.

As I was shutting down the computer for the night, I hoped for the best. Even so, I once more feared, as I closed the lid on the computer, I might be closing my life with Jane. We had been so near to each other in the hospital, but we hadn't been able to get together.

I poured another glass of wine and this time I drank it quickly. I got ready for bed, turned off the light and tried in vain to shut off my mind like I had shut down the computer. I wished it were that easy.

I tossed around and thought about all the events of the previous two days. I thought about Jane and reached for the other side of the bed only to touch empty sheets.

Finally, I slipped into a troubled sleep. I kept dreaming of gunshots and blood. Always, I was trying to flee around a corner with someone, and we would just about make it when a gun would fire and the other person would violently fall into me. I would keep running and falling, and running and falling.

The nightmare woke me up several times as I lay sweating in a jumble of blankets. Each time I sat up and turned the light on to establish a reality check. And—each time—after about ten minutes, I would lie down again, and eventually fall asleep.

The last dream of the night was the most vivid. Jane's face kept appearing and disappearing, anguish exuding from her every expression. Finally, I saw her in a chair with wires connected to electrodes that were attached to her hands and feet. I saw a demented look flash across a man's face as he threw a switch. Jane's face contorted as excruciating pain shot through her body.

Then I saw a hand reach for the switch again. A gunshot echoed in my ears, and my eyes opened to the morning light—and to new awareness.

All the horrid memories came flooding back as I lay dazed by the sudden recall. I had tried so hard to remember the details, but after realizing the terror we had faced, I wished my mind had kept it all locked up. The memories of the Guild for the Knowledge of Good and Evil, now the Evil Guild in my mind, and those terrible days needed to be processed and dealt with in my conscious mind. Putting these traumatic experiences into perspective wouldn't be easy, but I had to confront them to maintain some level of mental stability.

I now knew why a psychologist had been at my bedside in the hospital. I only wished that he had done more to help me cope with my trauma. I was angry that his first loyalty had been to the FBI and not to my mental health. Still, I was glad that he had been there, and perhaps it was better that I had remembered on my own, in my own time. But how was I going to deal with the horrors that had been inflicted on us?

I looked at Jane's photo with new insight. Her eyes told me they had experienced the same unimaginable terror. She had a right to look worn and sad. Staring at her picture made me want to throw my arms around her and hold on forever. For now, that was impossible. I had no idea where she was—or even if she had escaped from the hospital.

The ringing of the bedside phone shattered my troubled reflections. *Could Jane be calling me?* I wanted to believe that when I picked up the receiver I would hear her say, "Hi, I'm on my way up to your room."

I answered the phone on the third ring. It was another unknown FBI agent. I was devastated. "Are you ready for a couple of visitors?" the agent asked, after introducing himself. "I'm in the parking lot with another agent who goes by the name of Jane."

My hopes soared.

Jane! It has to be my Jane. I responded enthusiastically, "Come up right away, or should I come down?"

"No!" the agent said. "We'll come to your room."

Jumping out of the bed, I scrambled into my clothes and brushed my hair to the side. I straightened the bedspread, covering up my night's torment. I was splashing some water onto my face when there was a knock at the door.

"I'll be there in a moment," I yelled. I quickly wiped with a towel. It would have to do.

"Jane!" I said, swinging the door open.

I stood in shock as I realized my Jane wasn't standing in front of me, but a male agent with some other woman. The agents showed me their badges. The male agent said, "I'm Agent Jackson."

He and the female agent quickly entered the room. I had to admit the female agent looked a lot like my Jane.

"Oh, George, I've missed you so much!" she said.

I was confused. *How was I to react?* I was being called by my real name, and she was pretending she was Jane.

As soon as the door closed, the first agent whispered to me, "Play along here for a bit. This is crucial to seeing your wife."

I didn't see how "playing along here for a bit" would make any difference, but I had been wrong before. Again, what choice did I have?

I told "Agent Jane" how much I missed her, while the other agent wandered around the room with some sort of electronic device he pulled from a small bag. He checked under lamps, around desks, phones, outlets, and any other obvious—and not-so-obvious—places a listening device might have been planted. He didn't find any, and slid into the cheap motel chair. He asked me, as a precaution, to turn on the shower and the television, and then in a quiet voice explained what was happening.

"We need to be certain that you're in a secure location before we can get you and your wife together again," Agent Jackson said.

The female agent added, "The government doesn't want to lose two potential witnesses by bringing Jane into a dangerous situation. I'm a final test to be sure that you aren't being watched."

"Right now, we need you to call the Hunter Hotel in Red Wing, Minnesota, and make a reservation under the name Fred Nielson," Jackson said. "Make the reservation for seven nights for two people, beginning tonight. Check out of this motel as soon as possible, drive to Red Wing with Jane, and check into the Hunter Hotel by this evening."

Pseudo Jane, as I came to think of her, handed me a brochure on the hotel and pointed out the phone number. I made the call. They said they had a few rooms left I could reserve for the entire week. I reserved one on an upper floor overlooking the Mississippi River.

Jackson and Pseudo Jane continued to discuss their plans. I went into the bathroom to finish getting cleaned up and ready to drive across Wisconsin.

After a shower I felt a lot more positive. I put on Fred Nielson's clothes and wig, and was ready to go fairly quickly.

I concentrated on thinking about my Jane because, admittedly, Pseudo Jane looked a lot like her—and she was attractive. I decided that I would keep my distance from her. I didn't want to complicate my real life with a *pseudo affair*. I also didn't want anything I did with Pseudo Jane to hurt my relationship with my real Jane. *I miss her so much. Where is she?*

I did, however, have to make a show of my pseudo-loving relationship with this fake Jane. As we loaded the bags into the back of the jeep, we hugged. She kissed me on the cheek. We laughed.

I had to admit I was beginning to enjoy the playacting, not so much because of the sexual overtones, but because it momentarily took my mind off of the dangers I was facing. I participated in the present drama as an actor might in a mystery play.

After the jeep was loaded, I looked across the parking lot and saw Agent Jackson put his small bag into the back seat of his car. He stood beside the car talking on a cell phone.

Pseudo Jane asked me to check the oil. I thought this was a strange request, but I complied. She looked over my shoulder, not at the dipstick, but instead looking over all of the electrical connections. I speculated she was checking for bombs.

As I walked to the driver's side of the jeep, Pseudo Jane smiled lovingly at me and said, "Give me the keys. I'll drive the first shift. Run into the motel to check out."

I had almost forgotten that small detail.

17

I dropped my keycard on the front desk counter and had turned to leave when an ear-piercing explosion shook the motel and cracked the front window. A blast of heat hit as a fireball soared into the air. My first thought was that Pseudo Jane had been blown up, but to my surprise she came wheeling up to the entrance of the motel in the jeep and yelled, "Quick, get in!"

I gladly obliged, and we swung out of the lot. Pseudo Jane aimed the car in the direction of the freeway. "What happened?" I demanded more than asked.

"Give me a chance to recover, and I'll tell you all I can."

Pseudo Jane didn't say a word for an hour. As soon as we came to the first exit, we turned off the freeway and drove southwest on a side road. She kept checking her rearview mirror. When she seemed confident no one was following us, she pulled off at a gas station in a small town. We filled the jeep with gas that she paid for with cash. She told me, casually, that she was paying for it that way so we couldn't be traced by her credit card. We then had a quick breakfast at a small restaurant, which she, of course, paid for in cash.

As we left the restaurant, she said, "I need to pick up a cheap burner phone, too, so I can make some calls. I don't want to risk having my cell phone traced."

That seemed odd to me. How could anyone possibly trace her phone? I thought all FBI agents would have secure phones, but then, what did I know?

As we continued west across Wisconsin, Pseudo Jane began to talk. She cried a little before she said, "I came to the motel in the car that blew up. I assume Jackson was in the car when it exploded. I barely knew him, but it's a shock when something like that happens."

I saw Pseudo Jane as a fellow human being.

She confided to me that her name really was Jane. *Now how am I going to think of her? I can't call her Pseudo Jane anymore*, I thought. I settled on *Jane Also* as my mental name for her.

As Jane Also drove, she said, "What do you remember from your kidnapping? Did anything stand out?"

I didn't feel secure enough to tell her everything, but I did divulge some details. She certainly understood my memory had returned.

In return, she explained to me why my testimony was so important. "The FBI has been looking for a link to one of the oldest international criminal cults in the world. We know they're involved in a lethal mixture of drug smuggling, terrorism, and spying in the United States, as well as in almost every country on earth."

At first this was more than I could believe, but as I pieced together their ideas of good and evil, it made sense.

"They're sometimes simply called the All-Knowing Guild because of their activities, size, and vast worldwide connections," she said. "They're a sophisticated gang." She started to say something else, but stopped herself. "Sorry. I've already said more than I should."

I tried to pump her for more information, but she absolutely refused to elaborate. All she said was, "You're a potential witness at their trial. I can't tell you any more. Because you've been documented as having had amnesia, even temporary amnesia, their defense could charge you've been manipulated into remembering events to fit the prosecutor's case."

"But I won't tell anyone," I said.

"You'd better not," she said. "I've probably already compromised the case, but you deserved to know why you're so dangerous to them. You're one of the few victims of their abuse who can also identify any of their top leadership. Most of the witnesses who could have testified," she looked away from the road to look me in the eyes, "are dead."

"Not a pleasant thought. So you're going to keep us alive long enough to testify, then let them kill us?"

"Of course not," she said. "We'll do our best to protect you." I wasn't entirely reassured. They didn't seem to be doing too well, so far.

After a pause, Jane Also told me a little more about what had happened at the hospital. "The All-Knowing Guild must have found a weak link in the FBI and recruited one or more agents. That was how they knew your location *and* the details of your escape plan from the hospital. That's also why we can't let you see Jane."

"Is my Jane all right?" I asked, unsure I was ready for the answer.

"I'm truly sorry. Because of the need for secrecy, I have no idea," she replied. "But, also, *because of* the secrecy, that is good news. I'm pretty sure she's fine."

Trees, fields, signs, and the road whisked past. I had no idea where we were until we crossed the freeway again and I saw a sign that read "Minneapolis." I completely missed seeing how many miles away it was.

"Why are we heading north when Red Wing's to the south?" I asked.

"We aren't going to Red Wing now," Jane Also said. "That rendezvous was compromised when they tracked us to the TopOne Motel and blew up our car. We're staying in Wisconsin. I'm taking you to Superior."

We drove down the country roads in silence. We must have driven for another hour while I stared out the window. I had no idea where we were, but Jane Also seemed to know the roads well. She never looked at a map as she turned first one way, then another.

We stopped for lunch in a small-town bar. While we were eating she asked, "Do you remember any details about the book?"

I still wasn't about to discuss our book with anyone, even the FBI, until I had a chance to talk to my Jane, so I feigned ignorance. Jane Also probed me with more questions, but I had already decided that I wasn't going tell her I had a computer in my bag with the text of the book on it. *If she doesn't know, then perhaps she isn't supposed to know*, I reasoned.

Shifting her strategy, she said, "You know, I'm a collector of old books and manuscripts. They fascinate me. What does your mystery book look like?"

She proceeded to launch into a monologue about how a book's age can be determined through close examination, which a lot of counterfeiters don't understand. She explained that whole organizations specialized in not only buying and selling original documents, but in buying and selling certified duplicates of the originals. These duplicates were copied precisely from the originals by talented artisans using a mixture of ancient methods and modern technology.

She laughed when I said, "I guess a photocopy wouldn't qualify."

"I've got thousands of dollars' worth of certified duplicates," Jane said. She asked if I had any other interesting old books or documents, and how the book compared to them. It seemed like she was trying to jar my memory or pry from a different direction to get me to say something that might give her some insights into what I knew about the book.

I laughed and said, "I'm a magazine editor. I have a few old *Time* and *Life* editions that I value. Do they count?" She laughed again, but she didn't seem very sincere.

I began to wonder why she was prying into the book so much. It seemed odd that she had been so careful not to interrogate me about our abduction, but felt like she could ask me any number of questions about the reason for our abduction.

We stopped for a fast food meal and gas in yet another of the small rural towns along the way. She paid for everything in cash and then continued on our drive. Eventually she pulled off onto a gravel road that led to a small cabin by a lake.

"Stay in the cabin while I go into town to get supplies," she said. "We're going to lay low for a couple of days. Here's the key. Lock the door behind you, and stay put. No one, not even the FBI, knows we're here. I want to be sure our 'mole' is caught before I reveal where we are."

Maybe it was just my habit of reading mysteries with Jane, but something about the arrangement seemed strange. Even so, I took the key.

The cabin was remote, but the yard extended around it for about fifty or sixty feet in every direction. The lush grass was so well kept it looked better than many suburban lawns. Flowers of several colors and varieties grew in a bed that ran the length of the sidewalk and across the entire front of the cabin.

I looked back and waved as Jane Also backed out of the drive. Before she left, she stopped and yelled, "Remember to keep the doors locked. Oh—if my brother-in-law Hank shows up, he'll have a key. Don't worry about him. He's okay!"

After she left, I was alone in a pristine wilderness with only the birds to keep me company. On the far side of the lake a lone fisherman I could barely see sat in a small boat and cast an invisible filament out across the water. The sun was sinking and the water was reflecting a red sunset. *Picturesque*, I thought.

Even though it was the second week in July, the weather was unseasonably cool because of a stiff wind coming from the north, and the damp early evening air made me shiver as I unlocked the cabin door. The inside was as neat as the outside. A picture window in the main room overlooked the lake. A large kitchen and bar dominated the left side of the room. There were two bedrooms. One bedroom was furnished; the other was almost empty, except for a couple of sturdy chairs.

There was something about the empty room and the style of construction that bothered me. The door was made of metal. And, like the place where Jane and I had been brutalized, it had no windows. I had flashbacks to the torture we'd received when we were held captive there. Even though this was a totally different place, there were too many stark similarities.

I decided I couldn't stay, in spite of what Jane Also asked me to do. It was too jarring. Something didn't seem right, and I needed to get away from this cabin.

I looked around for a coat and found a camouflage jacket hanging on a hook in a small closet by the entrance, and it was dark enough to blend into the night. I slipped it on and immediately felt warmer.

I didn't know how long I would be outside, so I made a quick side trip to the kitchen. Opening the cupboard, I found a few small boxes of unopened crackers and a bag of cookies. I filled my pockets with as many of them as I could cram in and stepped out the door just in time to hear a car coming up the road.

On the right side of the cabin, dense bushes grew almost up to the edge of the lawn. I rushed for the nearest thicket. If I needed to escape, I hoped I could crawl undetected through the undergrowth and slip around the ridge a short distance away.

I dove into the bushes just seconds before the car approached the driveway. It drove by and I sighed with relief, but only for a few seconds. It stopped a short way up the road, and I heard a second car approaching. That car pulled into the drive. A third car came up the road and must have stopped before it got to the driveway. I could hear its motor running.

I lay flat on the ground behind a tangle of gooseberry bushes, not daring to move. Only one person got out of the car in the driveway. He walked casually to the front door and tried to unlock it, but because I had rushed out without locking it, he appeared to have locked it instead. I could sense his frustration as he uttered a breathy curse. Finally, getting it unlocked, he walked in. A minute later he came running out, waving his arms.

At the end of the driveway, he yelled, "The shithead's not here!"

This did not bode well for me. I kicked into survival mode. Suddenly, everything was happening all over again. I was pretty certain this wasn't Jane's brother-in-law. Were they FBI agents? Jane Also had said they didn't know where I was. If there were sellouts in the FBI, it seemed likely one of them was her.

She's probably the one who planted the bomb that blew up the other agent, I thought. *She dumped me here to be captured by this monstrous cult she calls the All-Knowing Guild.*

Everything was starting to make sense. *That must be why Jane Also asked so many questions about the book. They want our book.*

I remembered my abductors talking about the book. The book was about their cult, about seeking all knowledge of good and evil, but they seemed far more evil than good. Even their definition of *good* seemed more evil than good.

They would soon begin looking for me. I had to figure out what to do. This would be a life-or-death plan.

I had seen hundreds of cop, detective, police, and war shows. In most, the person in my situation—through some clever planning and breathtakingly daring actions—usually escaped relatively unharmed. At worst, you saw the hero or heroine in the bed of some hospital with bullet wounds to the arm or abdomen.

Of course, there were always those tragic movies of superhuman sacrifice where, for some noble cause, the victim dies—or the movie ends in limbo.

The evening news stories were worse. They were full of murders, rapes, and shootings. I didn't want to think of those stories. I wanted to be the kind of hero who made a dramatic escape.

No great plans emerged, except—I realized as I evaluated my situation—they had no idea I was a mere hundred feet from the cabin. If they were familiar with the terrain, I might be safer staying where I was than plunging deeper into the forest.

My guess was they would search the lakefront first, assuming I would simply stay by the shore and walk around the lake.

I decided I didn't dare move. They were far too close, and if someone saw me, it would be over. So I guess my "clever" escape plan was to stay where I was—and remain as quiet as possible.

I looked around and saw a narrow crevice between a couple boulders, hidden from the cabin behind several dense bushes. I thought, *I might just fit into that crack tight enough to evade being seen.*

A number of men had exited the other cars, and everyone was at the edge of the driveway having an animated discussion about what to do. Even from a distance, I heard one of the men talking about Jane Also, and saying something about a complete lakeside search.

I crawled over and carefully slid into the depths of the crevice. I barely fit. I crouched down and stayed as still as I could.

If this were simply a game of hide-and-seek, I would never have chosen the crevice as my hiding place. It was damp and smelled like rotting leaves. No sooner had I settled into its depths than a large daddy longlegs spider crawled up the arm of my jacket. It proceeded up my shoulder and onto my collar. I felt its spiny legs crawl up my neck. I wanted to jump up and slap it off, but I didn't dare move. I froze. The spider was the least of my worries.

I strained to hear what the men were saying. Then one of them shouted, "How the hell should I know where he is?" I was comforted when I heard him say, "He could be several miles down the road or on the other side of the lake by now!" I was also glad it was dark, though the sky was bright on this clear night as the moon traversed across the sky.

I couldn't see how many there were from my small crevice, but I could distinguish at least half a dozen voices. They appeared to have settled on a plan. A couple of them went back to their cars and drove away. Two of them headed down to the lake with flashlights. Two—or maybe three—started walking around the yard looking into the bushes with their flashlights.

The lights swung in my direction and I heard one of the men coming toward me. I hardly dared breathe for fear of being heard. I lowered my head and didn't move, afraid any slight movement of the bushes would be seen, and that would lead him to me.

I was aided in keeping my hideaway secret by my camouflage jacket and a night breeze that rustled the leaves of the trees, masking any slight noises.

The light from the man's flashlight flickered past me, then returned and hovered over me. The steps came closer.

Had he played hide-and-seek here before and known of this hiding place?

He peered into the bushes, and I thought surely he must have heard my heart beating. He rustled through the branches and shined the light where I had been crouching minutes earlier. A moment later, the light swung away, and he moved on around the yard.

Eventually they went into the cabin, and I huddled still in my small crack in the rock as the cold evening dew settled on me. The night sounds echoed inside me as if I were hollow. I crouched in my crack in the rock, wondering if I would be alive in the morning.

18

While the crevice had made me shiver when I crawled in, it provided protection from the chilly night wind. I was also thankful for the jacket. As the night progressed, a hazy mist floated up from the lake, filling in the gaps around me with a frigid dampness that penetrated my bones. About the time I feared I was going to freeze to the side of the rocky hollow—and was so stiff I could hardly move—the wind shifted to a southerly breeze. The mist lifted, and the air began to warm.

I felt like a tree root. Even if I tried to escape during the night, my stiff muscles would have kept me rooted in my crevice. I was sure I wouldn't make it far if I tried. I was too tense. I couldn't sleep. I would doze off and then be jarred awake by a spasm of pain in one of my stiff muscles.

I spent a lot of my time thinking about how much I missed Jane. Where was she? Had she eluded the animals who were so close to killing us? How could they call themselves a guild for the knowledge of good and evil? They were plainly evil. I hoped to the depths of my being that Jane had escaped unharmed, and that no double agents had tripped her up.

I decided the only way to keep my sanity through the night would be to think of our good times together. It would give me a hope to cling to and make death seem further away during my brutal night of hiding in a damp hole that smelled of death.

I had met Jane for the first time at an arts conference sponsored by Great Lakes University. The conference included writing, visual arts, dance, and theater. I had registered for the writing seminars, and Jane had registered for the visual arts.

On the opening night, we had been assigned seats at the same table for dinner. Actually, through some error, we had been given the same seat at table forty-two. We arrived at the table at the same time to find only one empty chair.

From that moment on, we became the closest of friends. Her curly red hair flipped from side to side when she laughed. The bright red-and-purple low-cut blouse she was wearing that night sent daring chills through me. Her gray skirt, cut just a couple of inches above her knees, showed off her slender legs. Hazel eyes held mine in an unblinking stare. But, mostly, we felt right together. We instinctively felt we belonged together. Our paths had crossed and we became intertwined for life.

Neither of us ended up at that table. We had laughed and decided we should just find another place where we could sit together. We wandered around until we saw a couple of empty chairs. About the time we had finished our appetizers, however, the couple assigned to our new table approached. They momentarily looked confused, then moved on without saying anything. We felt a slight twinge of guilt, but that also bound us even closer in a kind of subversive relationship. The remainder of the conference was a blur as we spent all of our free time together.

On the closing night we went to a dance competition. I already knew she was the one I wanted to marry. I think she felt the same way.

We entered the competition for fun. We certainly didn't win. We weren't even close to becoming finalists, but we discovered that we worked well together. We were a team, even if no one else noticed.

After that night, we spent every free moment together. We went to the same activities. We studied together. We took summer jobs in the same neighborhood so we could be together.

In the past couple of months, we had gone through hell together. It had been so refreshing to see her photo and read the note she had sent on the computer. *The computer!* I had totally forgotten about the computer that was in Jane Also's jeep when she left. I hoped there would be nothing on it that would lead our assailants to my Jane.

How we hope for the impossible when we are desperate! I was about as desperate as they came. I feared that by morning my rock crevice would be my grave. I wondered if my body would ever be found. Or would hunters find my bones in this crack in the rock someday, and I would only be identified from my dental records and DNA?

Our book had proven so important to this gang of thugs that they had viciously attacked us. Murder, torture, and betrayal seemed to lurk around every corner. They had even killed the innocent librarian who allowed us to leave the library with their precious book. Having lost hold of the good times with Jane, my mind wandered in many directions, as loosely connected thoughts became links to a chain of terror.

Finally, slender orange shafts of light broke through the branches of the trees. I had made it through the night. In the distance I heard a car approaching and I risked peeking out of my grave to see a black Suburban pull into the driveway. Two men went into the house and came out with a couple of spades. They got back into the SUV and continued down the road.

It didn't take long to figure out what they were planning.

Another car pulled up and two men stepped out of the cabin to meet it. One of the men near the car said, "We found the bitch and took care of her." My first fear was that they had killed my Jane, but I overheard one of them say, "She got what she deserved for double-crossing us."

I realized that they were talking about Jane Also. They probably had no trouble finding her because she had no idea I had escaped their carefully laid snare. She had simply walked into their hands, and they had killed her. Now they were going to bury her in some obscure hole in this remote forest where she might never be found. Though she had betrayed me, I still cringed, thinking of the way she must have died at the hands of these brutes.

As the men disappeared into the cabin, my stomach cried out in agony. And I needed to urinate, but I didn't dare leave my hideaway tomb. The faint aroma of breakfast coming from the warm cabin was a terrible torment. Early morning dew dripped on me from the bushes above, and the dampness penetrated my jacket. The morning cold made me shiver, but the day was bright and clear, promising warmth when the sun rose higher.

Ants, spiders, beetles, mosquitoes, and other miscellaneous bugs didn't make the small cavity I was wedged into any more pleasant. They seemed to know I couldn't move and made me their cozy home in the cold night hours. I had mosquito welts and bug bites all over my body. I itched everywhere and imagined myself swelling up so much I would burst out of my tight hole like a cork under pressure.

After about an hour, two more men came out of the cabin and met a third man walking up the path. I heard the third man say, "We've made arrangements. Hunting dogs are on the way. If he's still around here, we'll track him down."

Once the dogs arrived, I doubted I'd have a remote chance of escaping. It wouldn't even be a fair chase. I could think of only one positive thing: I could get out of this stinking crevice.

I waited in dreaded anticipation for the dogs, as the men went inside again. I decided I had to do something immediately or I was done for. One small kitchen window faced my direction, but I had to risk getting out of my hiding spot.

I built up my courage and slowly crept out of my grave. I shivered in pain, my stiff muscles rebelling as I crawled through the bushes.

The leaves above my head rustled. A crow startled me as it flew off a branch and angled toward the cabin, cawing loudly. I froze. What if the bird alerted them? I stopped and listened for any movement, but I had no choice. I had to keep moving.

I hoped to keep out of sight by crawling along in the thicket until I moved behind a low ridge. Physically, I couldn't go any faster, and—even if I could—any noise I made, or any other birds I scared up, might alert them to my presence. Still, if I moved too slowly, the dogs might show up before I had a chance to escape.

Eventually, the cabin disappeared from view as I crept behind the ridge. I bent down as low as I could while moving toward the lake at an angle so that I could keep the low hill between the cabin and me. As I got closer to the water, the ridge began to drop off. I had to crawl behind another small hill before I dared to stand up.

Now I faced a new dilemma. Should I bolt and run? Or was there some way to fool the dogs? I decided that I had to get down to the water's edge where I might, by some miracle, throw the dogs off my scent by wading through the water.

I still hadn't heard any dogs when I got to the shore, but I expected them any minute. I didn't have a good plan yet. From the stories I had read, the dogs wouldn't be able to track me in the lake. That was the positive side to my logic. The negative side was there were only two directions I could go in the water—right or left. Left led back to the cabin. That meant my only choice was to go to the right.

This wasn't much of a plan. Obviously, they would lead the dogs along the lake. Wherever I got out of the water the dogs would pick up my trail—or the men might just as easily see me wading in the water, or discover my wet tracks.

Suddenly, I had the flash of an idea. It wasn't brilliant, but if I had the time to pull it off, it might just work. I had picked up a pen at the hotel and it was still in my shirt pocket. I found an old receipt in the pocket of the coat I was wearing, and wrote a note to the now-dead FBI agent that said, "Jane, if you get this, I'm taking the boat across the lake. Meet me on the other side. I don't like the looks of the cabin." I signed it "George Mercy" and stuck it in as obvious a place as I could find on a bush near the water. I took a large branch and made a crease in the leaves and mud like the bottom of a boat might make if it slid into the lake. I tromped around, generally upsetting the area as much as possible, all the time thinking, *This will never work!*

But it had to.

I dropped the pen where it could be easily seen near the fake boat launch. It helped that the pen was bright red. I hoped, if they found the note, they wouldn't think too hard about the absurdity of me writing it on a scrap of paper for someone to find in the woods. At any rate, I figured this was my only chance of escaping.

I then backtracked over my trail toward my crevice, hoping I wouldn't encounter any dogs. I was once again counting on the fact that they wouldn't expect me to be only a few feet from the cabin. When they found my trail they would naturally follow it away from my hideaway in the crevice. If this didn't work—if my bizarre plan didn't succeed—I was doomed.

I slipped back along the low ridge just as I heard a vehicle approaching the cabin. I moved faster than I had moved in a long time, still keeping low. All they had to do was catch a glimpse of me to end their hunt before it started.

I was only feet from my hiding place when a van pulled into the driveway. I rolled into my hidden crevice just as its door opened. I heard lots of barking and the sound of several hound dogs springing out. I didn't dare move.

I had spent so much physical and emotional energy on my escape attempt, I lay in my crack in a kind of immobilized terror, worrying that one or all of the dogs would rush straight to me.

Fortunately, they were all leashed when they were led out of the van. One, however, escaped and began to sniff around. Suddenly the hound began to howl as he picked up a scent. I heard it start running in my direction. My instincts told me to bolt and run for my life, but my logic—and fatigue—won out. I didn't move. I didn't even breathe.

I heard his master yell for the dog, "Butch, get over here." He grabbed the leash just as a rabbit bolted sideways out of the bushes about ten feet away. The dog didn't chase the rabbit, but I could hear him still sniffing around as his master stood there for a few moments scanning the brush. Finally, I heard the hound's master pull him back. I took a deep breath and was tempted to peek out of my secret crevice—my personal grave—to see what was happening. Out of fear, I restrained myself.

The door to the cabin slammed close several times. I assumed most of the men had gone inside and were staying long enough to discuss their plans and perhaps have a cup of coffee. I could hear at least two men talking in the driveway as the leashed hounds ran around them.

When the men came outside they were ready for action. I could tell the hounds were being conditioned to my scent. They yelped and howled with anticipation. It would have been fun to watch—if I hadn't been their prey.

One of the men shouted, "Go get 'im!" I crouched as low as possible while the hounds picked up my trail. Then I realized the one flaw in my escape plan. The trail from the cabin led straight to my crevice hideaway.

The dogs started running straight toward me, but one of the men pulled them in the direction of the wooded path that led to the lake, assuming I wouldn't be so close to the cabin. If he hadn't made that faulty assumption, the dogs would have jumped right on me. Instead, the dogs almost immediately picked up my fresh trail that led to the water's edge.

How long would it take them to reach my lakeside deception? It couldn't be more than a minute or two, less if they kept up with the dogs. I could do nothing but wait. The minutes seemed endless, but eventually I heard tramping in the woods again. The moment had arrived. Had they bought my preposterous story, or would their dogs now lead them to me? The dogs yelped as they got closer, but the men must have decided I was gone because they kept them on short leashes and swore vehemently as they jostled their way into the cabin.

I waited in agonizing pain until they all stomped back out again, still cursing at their misfortune. They loaded the barking dogs into the van. And, moments later, they left, their wheels spinning on the loose gravel, kicking up a dust storm.

There were no sounds except the wind in the trees and the buzzing of insects. I figured I was finally alone, but I had a gut feeling this had been too easy. I decided to stay where I was for a while longer, though my physical needs were challenging me to leave sooner rather than later.

19

I waited as long as I could bear my pain before I gingerly rolled back out of my musty crack in the rock. I felt like I was rising from the dead. I stealthily crawled along the ravine again. I didn't stand up until I was on the other side of the ridge and out of sight from the cabin.

I had taken only a few stiff steps when I heard a branch snap not far behind me. I ducked down and froze. Then I heard footsteps rapidly approaching through the rough foliage. I was being followed. I started to run, but I heard the words, "Stop or I'll shoot!" I immediately dropped to the ground and crawled behind a rock. A bullet ricocheted off its surface. My options had run out. There was nothing I could do to save myself. I was too stiff, tired, and hungry to run. I cried out, "Okay, okay, don't shoot!"

I wasn't prepared for what happened next. "Shit, it doesn't matter," he said. "I'm going to kill you anyway. They said they wanted you dead or alive. You'd be a whole lot less trouble dead. I hunt around here all the time, so here's what I'm going to do: I'll give you until I count to one hundred to run for it. Then I'm going to track you down and shoot you in the ass. That'll be more fun than shooting your sorry butt without a good hunt."

The voice started counting. I took a deep breath and started running as fast as my weary legs would propel me. I rounded a ridge just as he reached one hundred. He was crazy, but he was at least giving me a chance, and I was going to take it. It was just a sport to him. I would probably be another trophy kill. I kept running, or at least making the effort to run. My lungs ached and my muscles hurt, but I was moving. I was still alive, even if my hope was dying.

I ran across a road. I jogged up a small hill, and down the other side. Then, half-jogging and half-stumbling with my side aching, I moved sideways away from the lake along a narrow valley. I had no idea where my hunter was. I figured if I could cut back toward the cabin, he might miss me and keep heading away. It wasn't much of a plan, but I was weak and couldn't outrun an experienced hunter, especially in my condition.

When I got to the top of the hill I saw a small opening in the trees that revealed a grassy meadow. I feared running across it, so I skirted along its edge. On the far side of the meadow there was a mound of freshly turned earth. I threw myself over it and dropped from exhaustion into a slight dip in the ground on the other side. I lay motionless on the far side of the low pile of dirt, trying to catch my breath.

"Your time's up!" I heard from about fifty yards across the meadow. Peeking around the mound and through the tall grass, I saw his rifle pointed right at the mound I was behind. I tried to scoot back around the pile of dirt out of his direct line of fire. He laughed while I shook with anxiety.

"How convenient," he said, "now I can shoot you next to that dead FBI agent. Yup, that's where they buried her."

If he meant to shock me, he had succeeded. The mound of dirt I was lying beside was Jane Also's grave.

Out of frustration, and hoping to buy a little more time, I yelled back, "How will that help? Wouldn't it be easier to walk me closer to the road so you won't need to drag me so far?"

My logic seemed to work for a moment. At least he didn't shoot me on the spot, but was I only prolonging the inevitable? There was no way I could crawl away from the mound without being an easy target. I lay behind Jane Also's grave, clinging to my precious life, fearing the time I had left would be measured in seconds.

The dreams I had when my Jane and I were together in Grand Marais were now closer to lethal reality. I was in the bottle and the storm raged around me. The water was coming in around the cork. I was hanging onto the rock for all I was worth but the bottle was sinking. And this time, I would finally go down with it.

I looked up and was startled to see the rifle now pointed just feet from my head.

My hunter said, "I'm not worried about the money. I enjoy the hunt, but they want you dead real bad so I need to give them proof that I've killed you. Anyways, I only need to give them your trophy head. In fact, I think I'll have it mounted first."

He lifted the sight of his rifle to his eye and said, "Run, so I can shoot you in the back."

I ran, expecting to feel my chest explode any second, but the shot I heard didn't come from his rifle—at least the first shot didn't. His rifle fired but the bullet struck a tree several feet to my right. I didn't wait to see what had happened but flung myself back into the woods. I raced down the hill. I would have run back to the cabin and crawled into my crevice to die, but I didn't have the energy to continue—or to watch my step as carefully as I should have. I stumbled awkwardly over a stone and fell forward. As I tried to stop my fall with my right foot, my left foot caught between two rocks. My ankle twisted. I slammed to the ground.

I lay with my face in the dirt trying to comprehend what had happened. Turning my head, I saw three people standing on top of the ridge. I wanted to yell, "Let me die!" All I could do was whimper under my breath, "Let me die." I lay in the grass and wept. I cried for Jane. I cried for myself. I cried just to cry. The release felt so good.

I heard footsteps. I was sure they were moving in for the kill, but the next thing I saw through my tears were faces of concern. A police officer lifted my head and brought a bottle to my lips. A few drops of fresh water touched my parched tongue, and then he poured a little more into my mouth. One of the others was on a cell phone. The third person poured some water onto a cloth and wiped my face. I can't begin to describe how good that felt.

Twice, I had barely escaped death. The thought flitted wistfully through my mind: *All of this could really still end like a happy movie with a storyline finish, "And they lived happily ever after."* That might be hoping for too much, though. Besides, it could only happen if Jane was with me.

Someone unlaced my shoe. My foot was still caught between the rocks. I groaned when he pulled my foot out, but I was relieved to feel a cold compress wrap around my ankle. They threw a blanket over me, and that felt good, too. I had been sweating while I was running, but after falling I had begun to shiver uncontrollably—probably a combination of pain and hunger.

Most of the rest was a blur. I have no idea how long I lay there. The world floated in and out of a fuzzy haze.

Eventually I felt them lift me onto a blanket or stretcher. Searing pains were shooting though my ankle as they carried me up the hill and back onto the grassy meadow.

There was no sign of my hunter when I got there. A few vehicles were parked in the meadow, and as we arrived a van pulled up. Its back doors were thrown open. The outside of the van didn't look like an ambulance, but inside it seemed fully equipped for emergencies. I was lifted onto another cot that was put into the vehicle, and I was immediately connected to an IV line and a monitor.

Someone said, "Hang tight, I'm going to give you a shot." I felt a needle poke me, and I started losing my battle for awareness. The last thing I remembered was the sweet, flowery smell of the meadow.

I didn't know how long I had been under. I kept hearing the coded text from the book being repeated to me in my dreams, *28, 496, 8, 1, 2, 8*. I heard the numbers again and again. I also heard *8,128* as one number. The numbers echoed back and forth like they were being chanted in a cave.

Images of a bottle bobbing carelessly in the waves of an expansive lake appeared and faded. A tree, half with leaves and half with dead branches, stood on a ridge overlooking the lake.

I heard shots fired. The sounds exploded hundreds of times in my head.

As reality began to slowly invade my troubled sleep, Jane became the central image of my thoughts. I dreamed I was looking at her beautiful freckled face, the wind blowing through her red hair, and the light glistening in her deep hazel eyes. I almost felt like she was with me, but then her image faded. I was alone in my world that was at one moment becoming more real, and the next fading away.

A deep foreboding crept over me. Perhaps she had died and she was saying her farewell to me as she floated back into the elements of the world. I was horrified by the possibility. I was equally struck by the possibility that reality was not what I thought it was. If she were saying goodbye to me, how did that fit with the world that I could see and touch, hear and smell, and taste?

Then too, where was she going? Was there something that leapt out of you as you passed back to the elements? *The religious would call it a soul*, I thought. That was what I had learned as a child but long ago given up as a fantasy, along with Santa Claus.

I dozed out of reality again. In my semiconscious state I imagined all kinds of psychotic illusions, but I kept seeing Jane's face and hearing her voice.

Finally, I blinked. My eyes opened and I expected to see Jane, but all I saw was a nurse staring at a monitor by my bed. She looked at me, smiled, and immediately left the room. A moment later the door opened and she walked in again with a woman following close behind.

"Jane!" I tried to yell, but all that came out was a squeaky sound I wasn't sure she would recognize as her name.

Perhaps, too, this was an illusion, more real than the last, but still merely an illusion. I closed my eyes and opened them again. She was still here. I heard her whisper, "George, you're awake!"

She rushed to my bedside and carefully leaned over to avoid upsetting the IV lines and the tube running into my nose. She gently hugged me and kissed my cheek. "I'm here," she said. "We were afraid you wouldn't recover. You were terribly weak. I was so worried. I love you so much."

I tried to smile, but feared it was more of a grimace. We were back together. I wasn't dreaming—and Jane wasn't giving me her graveside farewells. My sense of reality had been shaken, but was still intact. She was real. She was here. She was well. She had been sitting beside me, and I would recover.

On the first day, Jane sat quietly in the chair next to my bed. I was too weak to talk or move, but she held my hand and hugged me occasionally. Within a day or two, I began to feel better. I was able to sit up and started to eat solid food.

As my condition improved, we began getting bolder in our affection. Once or twice when no one was watching, she slipped into bed to snuggle with me for a few minutes.

Jane gave me incentive to recover and get back to living a normal life—whatever that would be like in our new circumstances.

I had a million questions for her, and she probably had as many for me. I would tell her about what had happened to me later, when I felt stronger. For the moment, I simply wanted to know everything that had happened to her while we were separated, so I asked her to tell me her story.

The emotions I would need to confront scared me, but I had to know what she'd struggled with. We faced an uncertain future, and if we were going to move ahead together, we needed to understand how our terrifying experiences would impact our lives.

20

As I tried to lay still and keep my emotions in check, Jane began telling me her story.

"When those idiots from the Evil Guild abducted us, I thought we were done for. I figured as soon as we told them what they wanted, they'd kill us. That's what they did to the librarian, and that's what they'd do to us."

I nodded in agreement. "I was thinking the same thing."

"When they pulled us out of the car and took us in different directions, I was so mad they had to drag me kicking and yelling," Jane said. "They threatened to shoot you if I didn't cooperate. To prove their point they shot a squirrel, blowing it to pieces. I was so scared! I had to at least pretend I was cooperating."

I reached out, touched Jane's arm, and whispered, "I was afraid they'd killed you when I heard the shot. For a long time, they told me you were dead."

"I'm so sorry. It never occurred to me you'd think that," Jane said.

Tears flowed down Jane's cheeks. I wept along with her.

"They shoved and dragged me through the rough underbrush. Finally, we arrived at another car, where they pushed me into the back seat.

"They drove for about an hour before turning onto a gravel road. After driving for another couple of miles they turned onto a narrow dirt road. They didn't drive far before they stopped and dragged me from the car. They pushed me into what I found out later was an old farmhouse, up a flight of stairs, and into a small, dark room.

"They forced me to sit on a wooden chair where I was bound, blindfolded, and left alone. The room was so quiet I began to imagine what death must be like. The thought that death would be blackness without pain went through my mind.

"I started to think that perhaps death wouldn't be so bad," Jane said with a hint of sadness in her voice. She closed her eyes and added, "But there would be no awareness of life or of anything, would there? All would be lost, gone forever."

I tensed my fists. *How could they do this to my Jane?*

"I clung to the hope that somehow we would come through this alive, but there was always the nagging dread that maybe our luck had run out," Jane said.

"I was pretty sure it had, too."

"When they came back," Jane whispered, almost like she feared they were still listening, "they removed my blindfold. The room I was in looked like an upper-story bedroom. They threw a couple of loops of rope around my arms before ripping the duct tape from my mouth. I screamed. My lips felt like they were being torn off my face. I yelled at them, telling them what kind of SOBs they were.

"They told me they wouldn't return until I quit yelling, and left me alone again. I screamed curses at them for a long time before I gave up and began looking around to see how I might escape.

"The windows were covered with boards and heavy metal strapping. A small gap near the top let in barely enough light to see. Chunks of paint were peeling from the woodwork, but the door looked like it was made from metal.

"About a half hour later they came back and untied me, but kept my wrists taped together in front of me. They left some water and a cheese sandwich on a small end table before locking me in again.

"If the room was designed to isolate and depress me, they succeeded. I wanted them to knock on the door, open it, and say, 'Oh, sorry, we made a big mistake. We'll take you home now.' Of course that wouldn't happen, but it gave me a little peace thinking about the absurdity."

Jane stood up and walked to the window, staring at the sky. The light created a halo around her hair. I watched quietly, allowing myself to enjoy the effect. I knew she needed a little space.

She turned to face me, and continued.

"I was hungry and exhausted. As the sun began to set, I became more claustrophobic. All I could do to relieve my tension was close my eyes and dream about some of the good times we've had. I thought about our honeymoon as we walked out onto the balcony of our suite in the early morning mist and looked across the valley of Yosemite National Park. I remembered the photo you took of me with wet hair in my white bathrobe while I watched a mule deer grazing below.

"I wondered at the time if our love could last, but it did—even when our schedules became hectic as we both finished our master's degrees. I remembered how the crazy pace threatened to tear us apart, but how we always took time to keep our love fresh. You were so cute."

I gave her a big smile and rolled my eyes. Jane returned the smile and winked. Then she looked down and continued her account.

"I finally lay down on a flimsy mattress and pulled the sheet over my head. I didn't sleep long before they woke me in the middle of the night to begin what I'm going to call the 'First Inquisition.'

"I think their goal was to keep me on edge—to keep me guessing. They threatened to rape me, and to kill you, but they mostly asked questions about why we had taken 'their' book from the library.

"I refused to admit we'd taken any book. They hated that answer. They questioned me again and again, trying to get me to admit we had their book. They kept saying, 'If you tell us where our book is, we'll let you go.'

"After grilling me for what felt like two hours, they left. I was exhausted, but I hurt so much that I couldn't sleep. My wrists were still taped and my hands felt like they were going to fall off. I tried to tear at the masking tape with my teeth, but they had used so much of it and had done such a twisted job, I only succeeded in making my wrists hurt more. To add to my distress, my attempt had also made my lips raw.

"I was so scared. I considered telling them everything, but we had made a pact on the shore of Lake Superior to hide our book. I still might have given in, but two thoughts stopped me.

"First, after all they had done to capture us, I wasn't convinced they had any intention of letting us go. I wish we'd let them find the book when we had a chance, but we didn't. Of course we felt so attracted to the book we couldn't, but I wish we had given it to them.

"You know, I still don't understand its hold on us. Could they be right? Does the book have some kind of evil connection to the human desire to become a god?"

"That's their perverted opinion," I said. "After all, it is supposed to be the *Book of the Knowledge of Good and Evil*."

"I guess. This is a pretty ruthless gang we're dealing with. At any rate, my second thought was, 'If the book is so valuable to their evil schemes, how many others might be hurt or killed if they get it back?' Maybe none, but I fumed and worried about their plans every time I had to face them."

"You were probably right," I said. "I also assumed they wouldn't let us go even if we told them where the book was. They didn't seem like the type I could trust to keep their word."

Jane stroked my arm. After a few moments, she said, "I was so afraid. By that point I was sure I'd never see you again. I sat in the corner for a long time wanting you to hold me in your arms and tell me everything would be all right. But I knew our lives would never be the same again. Could we pick up our jobs? Could we drive to work every morning and live normal lives? If they raped me, could you still love me?"

I smiled and reached out a hand to her. "I've always wanted you—and always will."

"I know," Jane said, taking my hand in hers, "but I felt horrible and didn't know what they'd do next. I still clung to the hope that we might get out of this mess. I hung onto the notion that every minute they didn't kill one of us, we had a chance. I still grasped onto a misguided notion that, in the end, the book might change our lives for the better. Now, of course, I know that it *will* change our lives forever, but into something terrible."

"I'm so sorry," I said. "If this is too hard for you, you don't have to tell me any more right now."

"I have to while I have the courage," Jane said. "I hurt every-where. There were no openings for air to circulate, so the room was hot and suffocating. I felt like I was breathing through cotton stuck up my nose. My tongue was so dry that it didn't feel like it belonged in my mouth. It was the longest night of my life.

"I kept hoping that the next time I opened my eyes, morning would come, and the nightmare would end. But every time I opened my eyes, it was still dark.

"Once I dreamed I saw your face with a look of terror on it. Your features were so vivid I gasped, and I realized you were probably struggling through the night like I was. The thought frightened me. There was the chance that even if I made it through my ordeal, you might not. Life would be so empty without you.

"When I woke the next time, I saw bright light streaming through the slits in the boarded-up windows. I had survived the night from hell. The thin shafts of light brought hope, however small.

"A couple of pieces of dry toast and a glass of juice were sitting near the door. For a while I felt better, but I was still locked in an oppressive room.

"When my abductors finally showed up, they immediately set the chair in the middle of the room and told me to sit down. I hesitated for only a moment before one of them grabbed me and slammed me down into the chair so hard I thought my back was going to break! Then they tied me up for my next torture session.

"The first thing they did was grab the front of my blouse and rip it open. I flung myself against my restraints and screamed at them with all my strength. I was so disgusted—and so mad. In the end, all I could do was sit and cry. That, unfortunately, seemed to give them confidence that they could make me crack."

Jane just stared at me as I leaned forward and cried out, "I'll kill the bastards!" I was so mad I was shaking.

"Don't," Jane said. "Please, don't. That's exactly the kind of reaction they want. They did it to show me how weak I was; at least that's what Dr. Frank told me."

I leaned back again, exhausted. We were both trying to sort out our emotions.

Television and movie heroes made it through these kinds of adventures so easily. I remembered hearing a writer at a seminar say that whenever she used violence in her novels, she always had to remember to deal with the consequences.

Modern movies and television seldom confront the consequences of their violent scenes. The dead are just dead. They have no relatives who grieve, no children who cry themselves to sleep at night because they've lost their parents, and no friends who mourn. And the heroes charge through their own scenes with no personal consequences. They confront violence with more violence. They shoot and kill to uphold an image of justice that too often translates into a reign of vengeance.

I had to fight that desire. I recognized that to return violence to achieve some kind of balance of suffering would destroy me. *Where is the balance in that?*

Jane finally whispered, "They never physically raped me. But they emotionally raped me."

I was so angry that my face burned with rage. My hands tensed into fists. I think my reaction scared Jane but also helped her understand how much I cared for her.

She bent down and hugged me. "All that's behind us now. We need to look to the future."

It may be in the past, but it will always color our future, I thought. *The nightmares will always be there. The shame will confront us again in a hundred ways as we rebuild our relationship. Our trust in people will always be tentative. Our belief in ourselves will never again be absolute.*

———

"I need to rest for a while. I can't take any more," I whispered to Jane.

I still wanted to hear her story, but I had to escape for a while to digest what I had heard, and to sleep. I needed to make sense out of how all the loose threads of our torn lives could be rewoven.

I recalled a new suit I had received when I was in high school. The first time I wore it, I caught the sleeve on a nail in the garage as I was getting into our car. That nail had been there for years and had never snagged anything before, but this time it dug into my coat and pulled a great L-shaped piece of fabric loose. We took the jacket to a fabric shop to be fixed. It looked pretty good when we got it back, but there would always be a rough edge where it had been woven back together.

Our lives would be like that. We would always have places that had been patched together. Nevertheless, the stitches on my coat were strong and had held firm through the years. I hoped our lives could do the same.

I closed my eyes, exhausted from the emotion of Jane's experiences and my own reactions. We could resolve more of our issues in the days, and years, to come.

21

When I woke up the next morning, the light in the room seemed psychedelic. I couldn't focus on anything. Dripping wet sweat oozed from every pore in my body—I felt like I was being roasted over burning coals. My eyes rebelled against the light streaming through the window.

I struggled to reach over and ring the buzzer attached to my bed. A nurse came and asked what I needed, but my mouth didn't work. All that came out were a few unrecognizable words, and she saw I was in physical distress. She checked my pulse and blood pressure, took my temperature, filled in some information on a computer, and left. Moments later, she rushed back into the room with a doctor.

The doctor looked at my stats on the computer, and then at me, and said, "You may have a serious infection. As a precaution, we're going to put you in isolation."

He followed the nurse out the door and returned wearing a gown, mask, and gloves. He did a standard eye, ear, nose, throat, and lymph node check. He ordered blood samples to be taken. Meanwhile, I lay semiconscious but aware enough to know the doctor was concerned I might not survive whatever was happening to me. I was too weak to object. Every time the doctor touched me, I wanted to scream. I heard the words *septic shock*.

After they left the room, the nurse came back with an IV bag. When she inserted the IV catheter into my arm, all I could do was shiver from the pain. She attached other things to my body, but I was too groggy to see what they were.

Finally, I was alone. I vaguely remembered seeing Jane come into the room wearing the same kind of protective clothing as the nurse. I heard her soothing voice tell me through her face mask, "George, you can survive this. You have to live. Please fight this infection with all you've got. Please, please, please."

The last thing I remember hearing before I went into a coma was Jane's voice pleading, "God, please help him get through this!"

I remember thinking, *God, I hope I make it through this!* I repeated it as an unbeliever's prayer. I didn't believe in God—unless God was the mindless order of nature or something like that. Still, invoking the name comforted me. Perhaps it was an emotional reaction dredged up from my childhood, or a vague hope in what I wanted to believe but couldn't.

———————

Was I having another dream, a vision, or a hallucination? I couldn't tell. Maybe it was caused by my high fever, or the infection. I didn't know.

Like my previous dreams, I started out in my bottle floating in the lake, unable to do anything to save myself from the storm. I lost track of time as I hung onto the rock and watched the ferocious waves threaten my life. Suddenly everything changed.

The clear glass of the bottle turned gray. The air became murky. At first I assumed the bottle was filling with water, but I didn't feel the liquid death dragging me under. Instead, the glass turned into formless haze. I looked around. I was sitting on a chair in the midst of the fog looking at a red door in a dismal, gray wall. I sat staring at it for a long time. When I say that the door was red, I mean that it was a dusty red, not evenly painted, the kind of door you would expect to see on an old barn with weathered wood showing through.

I dreamed for a brief moment of the old barns I had seen in rural Illinois, when the color of the door began undulating, shifting in color, shape, and brightness.

I speculated about what this might mean, as the color changed to the hot red of burning embers in a fire, or a burner on an electric stove. The heat patterns rippled off its surface with such intensity I feared I would be severely burned if I touched it. A smell of scorched flesh filled the air. The wall around the door glowed like hot charcoal. I was so captivated, I couldn't move. I kept staring at the red heat emanating from its surface.

The door stayed that way for so long my eyes watered from the searing heat.

Then, the door began to gradually change again. It turned the brownish-red color of dried blood. The cold from the new door hung in the air like dry ice evaporating into cold steam, the kind of cold that sucks the life out of you—cold as death itself. Frost expanded outward on the wall around the door. Time seemed to stand still while I sat shivering in a chilled trance.

Just when I imagined the steam from my breath was about to turn into icicles, the door changed once more. This time it looked like the petals on a bright-red tulip, alive and responding to the breeze. I could almost feel the flower opening to the sunshine. The previously frosty wall around the door glowed with a lively greenish hue. The door radiated vitality, drawing me to it like the outdoors would on a summer day when the sky is a brilliant blue and the trees are lush with green leaves rustling in the breeze.

I sat staring at the doors as their colors cycled through their transformations. I was mesmerized, hypnotized by their ever-changing power.

At times I wanted to throw one of the doors open and race through to whatever experience waited for me on the other side.

At other times I was deathly afraid of what would happen if I got too close. The door could kill me, change me, or perhaps give me new life. I didn't know the answer, but in my dream I sensed the power of each door.

Whenever the surface changed into the flesh-burning red door, I would shudder from the emotional blast of its heat. I sensed the door wanted to consume me in a fiery blast. I thought of this as the "Door of Flesh-Burning Death." If I stepped through it, I was sure it would be into a fiery furnace, but death would come quickly.

After the door shifted color again and became the door exuding the bitterly cold aura of dried blood, I described it as the "Door of

Frigid Death." This version represented absolute death to me—firm and final. I would freeze to death instantly as I stepped across its threshold. I wanted to run from its icy morbidity, but I couldn't. I forced myself to remain seated, but the Door of Frigid Death compelled me to keep staring at it, as if in a frozen daze.

Finally, when I couldn't stand the pain of frigid death any longer, the door shifted to the inviting flower-blossom red, the "Door to Refreshing Life." I sensed that I could never live and be healed of my disease unless I walked through this door. It called me to step through and experience total and complete healing. I would be renewed the moment I opened the door to whatever future was waiting for me on the other side.

For some reason, even in those moments when I was sure I would be healed, I was afraid of going through the door, thinking it might deceive me. If I stepped through it when it felt like life and healing, I might realize too late that it still meant death. So, even as the door beckoned me to open it and walk through, I stayed seated.

In my dream, I struggled to look around to see where I was, and I couldn't spot anything that would give me even a clue. In every direction, except where the door stood before me, a murky atmosphere hid everything around me. I couldn't tell if I was looking at the gray walls of a dingy room, or at an impenetrable evening fog hiding an eternal void.

Gradually, the color of the door began to undulate again, turning into the fiery shimmering surface that looked like red-hot iron pulled from a forge. I could feel the blistering heat radiating from the door.

I reflected on how my fifth-grade Sunday school teacher, Mrs. Jones, would say, "Accept Jesus Christ so you will know today that you won't burn in hell for all eternity." If I believed in a hell, this door would certainly be the entrance—but I didn't believe in a hell or a heaven. The heat of the door appeared to promise me a death that would be agonizing but quick.

When the cold, blood-red door suddenly returned, I felt the chill of death surround me again, tempting me to open it and step through.

As my bones and muscles froze under its frigid atmosphere, the door's color and hue rippled back to the image of life and the inviting flower-blossom red that was so glorious to behold. This time, as I compared the Door to Refreshing Life to the fiery door and the frigid door, it looked smaller, not measurably smaller, but slightly diminished in size. Or maybe it only felt smaller because I had perceived that both the fiery hot door and the chilling door of death were bigger.

The doors undulated through their changes several more cycles. Each time the doors I thought of as leading to my death appeared, they grew a little bigger. *Were they also moving closer?*

I sat perfectly still until I suddenly felt compelled to turn my head to the right. A golden key was hanging from a string attached to the ceiling. At least, I rationalized that it must have been hanging from the ceiling. I couldn't see the end of the cord it was hanging from. It disappeared deep into the brackish haze.

I looked back at the door again, now the Door of Flesh-Burning Death. It looked a lot bigger than it had originally, and it had moved even closer. The heat beat against my body. The door was so close I had to hold my hand over my face to ward off the hot energy it was generating. It repulsed me, making me fear the pain of burning to death, while simultaneously inviting me to step through and be done with the agony in a flash of scorching flesh. I cried out in my delirium, "Stop! How much more can I endure?"

I looked to the right, and then to the left for any sign of hope. I saw a small tree with a round fruit hanging from one of its branches. It wasn't any fruit I recognized, but it looked refreshing. A voice said to me, "Take the fruit and eat it. Then you will have the knowledge you desire, and you will be refreshed with a new understanding of how powerful you are." I looked for the source of the voice. All I could see was a snake wrapped around the base of the tree. "Yessss, eat of the fruit," the snake hissed.

I looked at the fruit again. It looked attractive. I stretched my arm up to reach it. Pulling it off the branch, I bit through its skin. It was juicy and sweet, and it immediately quenched my thirst. I took another bite. I couldn't resist its robust taste.

I felt powerful, like I could handle anything.

Suddenly anger and hate overwhelmed me. *Aren't I right? Isn't everyone else always wrong? Isn't killing justified if it gives me power—and aren't sexual exploits desirable if they satisfy? Aren't lying and stealing justified if they help me control the world?* I decided I was most important, and I needed all the knowledge of the world to control it. I had to trust in my own strength to succeed. I had to survive to fulfill my ambitions, to fulfill all of my compulsions. I could stand on top of the tallest mountain and rule the world.

Then I began to question my new insights. *Wasn't this the message of the Guild for the Knowledge of Good and Evil?* This was their goal. They wanted to have all the knowledge of evil, as well as good. That knowledge would make them into gods. *Would it make me into a god, as well?*

Could this be me? I asked myself. I knew it was. I had eaten the fruit. I was guilty.

I looked back at the red-hot door. For the first time, I saw the image of the tree from our book's cover emblazoned on its surface—except now the round symbol of the fruit was missing. *Of course it's gone*, I thought. *I've just eaten the forbidden fruit.*

The tree blazed with the same burning intensity as the door. It smelled of burning wood as its heat scorched my face.

My guilt tempted me to step through the door to realize my need for control, and then to die. This would be just retribution for following my wicked heart. I resisted the temptation by gripping my chair so hard my fingers bled.

I had almost lost my courage to resist when the door finally shifted to the color of frigid death. It was even colder and more revolting than before, but there was still a powerful invitation to walk through and end my suffering.

This door also had the symbol from the book carved into its cold surface, except that this tree had no leaves on any of its boughs. With angular branches that were cracked and broken, the tree itself looked frozen and dead. As the bone-chilling emotion tried to draw me toward its finality, I futilely attempted to rise from my chair and flee, but I couldn't move away from it.

Eventually, when I had reached the edge of total desperation that could only end by opening the door, it changed once again. Almost before I knew what was happening the Door of Frigid Death dissolved into the Door to Refreshing Life. But the door was now smaller than ever and had moved still farther away. It too, had a tree on it, but this one looked like a cherry tree in full bloom. The leaves were bright green.

This door called to me, "Come. Enter, and you will live!" It exuded friendly warmth, beckoning me, but somehow I knew that it wouldn't allow me to control my own destiny. I didn't trust it. As long as I sat where I was, I remained alive—though I didn't know how long I could continue in this state of indecision.

Eventually, I would have to choose, but I wasn't ready to make that fateful decision. Too much was at stake, and I wasn't prepared to take the risk.

I looked to the right to see if the key was still hanging on the string. It looked farther away, but the gold key still glowed in the dim light as it spun around on its string, dangling from the unseen source.

For a long time I just stared at the key, wondering why it was there, and why it appeared only when the door to life appeared. I looked carefully at the distant door and realized for the first time that there was a keyhole in it. I wondered if the other doors had keyholes, or if I had missed that detail. For the first time, I looked forward to confronting the doors that had come to mean certain death to me. I had to see if they needed a key too.

To my horror, I watched the Door to Refreshing Life move farther away, and I felt the transition to the next door before I saw it. The Door of Flesh-Burning Death cast its rays of terrible heat, and I opened my eyes to its awful presence only feet away. I feared my clothes would catch fire. I pushed myself against the back of my chair as hard as I could, but questioned whether it would be better to fling myself through the doorway to end my agony. The red heat burned my eyes. My skin dripped sweat, not only from the heat, but from the intensity of the hate and anger I felt attacking me. The door challenged all of my senses in a barrage of self-loathing, commanding me to quickly end my worthless life. Once I opened the door and jumped through, my self-deprecation would be over.

Against my better judgment, I found myself rising from my chair with my hand extending toward the knob. My fingers blistered from the heat as I reached forward. I sensed the moment I touched the doorknob all of my free will would be gone, but—after the initial blast of searing heat—so would the pain.

As I looked at the knob, I saw no keyhole. *No keyhole—no key.* I focused on the key, and it was the key that saved me from taking hold of the fiery knob. I stood only feet from the blazing door, enduring its vitreous heat. My face burned. My hands blistered. I kept visualizing the key and finally the heat subsided. I opened my eyes and moved my hand away.

The door started to change again. The Door of Frigid Death morphed into view. Its size amazed me as it appeared right in front of me. I could easily touch the door from where I stood. An awesome force dared me to pull it open and jump through. It beckoned me, enticing me with the reward of a quick, frozen death.

I felt like an alcoholic walking by a liquor store; no, more like an alcoholic walking past a bar that had a neon sign out front advertising free drinks. The urge to enter was overwhelming, but I again looked for the keyhole. This door didn't need a key either, but promised to open freely. *It might open too freely.* I resolved that I wouldn't willingly go through this door either.

Yet, perhaps like a drunk in a bar, no amount of resolve could keep me from acting against my base impulses.

It took all of my determination to sit back down in the chair. I focused on the beauty of the key. I closed my eyes and forced the image of the key's golden glitter to surface. I gritted my teeth and held onto the sides of the chair to keep my body from leaping into the door. "Change!" I cried. "Change your color, or I'm lost!"

Immediately, the door began shifting back to the Door to Refreshing Life.

I rejoiced and vowed to rush through the door as soon as I was certain the shift was complete. I looked again to my right. The key once again materialized out of the haze, but it was now hanging almost out of reach. I would need the key to go through this door, but before I tried to get it, I took another look at the door to make sure it had the hopeful flower-blossom color.

My heart sank. I saw the door was indeed the right one, but it had become small and distant. How was I ever going to make it through? It was now no larger than a pet door. Had I waited too long and lost my chance to choose healing and life? Still, the door was there. I had hope. As small as the door was, it invited me to enter.

I turned and focused intently on the key. I began to move ever so slightly toward it. I found that only by concentrating on the key could I make any progress, so I completely filled my mind with its image. I envisioned holding the key in my hand and how it would save me. Finally, amazingly, I stretched as far as I could, reaching across the impossible chasm and grasped the golden key. I had it in my hand, and I felt instantly revitalized. I held *hope* in my hand.

I started to move back to the door of life. I passed the chair I had been sitting on, but I had no idea how I would get through the small opening of the door. The key I held didn't look like it could possibly fit into the tiny keyhole. Doubts began to eat away at the hope I had that I could unlock the small door and pass through. It seemed totally illogical, and—as soon as I doubted the possibility—the door began to change back to the Door of Flesh-Burning Death.

So this is it! This is the end, I thought as the door began to emit the hot glow of death, threatening me with a burning desire to end my life.

I struggled with the temptation. I would never have been able to restrain myself from the urge by my own will, but I looked once more at the golden key, and—resisting the urge to throw it aside as useless—I began to gain strength from some power in the key itself.

When I looked back at the door, I was surprised to see that while I had been concentrating on the key, it had changed again to the warm glow of the Door to Refreshing Life. This time the door had again become full size, and the key looked like it would easily fit.

I rushed forward. I lifted the key and effortlessly inserted it into the precious lock. I unlocked the door as quickly as I could and grabbed the handle. The door swung freely open, and I jumped across the threshold before it could change back again. As I did so, I heard doves cooing overhead and rushing streams of water flowing over waterfalls. The air smelled fresh, like it had when I was standing on the shore of Lake Superior after the storm had passed. I shivered with new life. The key had freed me.

22

I opened my eyes and stared at my new life. For a while, I couldn't comprehend where I was. The images of the doors still filled my thoughts—burning death, frozen extinction, and the hope for new life. I was having trouble connecting with my new reality.

In my hallucinations, I had stepped—or maybe fallen—through the door of life, but this seemed a strange place for the door to open into. It appeared almost as dim and dreary as the surreal environment I had come from. I didn't know what to expect next.

Slowly, the pieces began to fall into place. I remembered what had happened and why I was in the hospital, but where was everyone? The nurse? The doctor? Where was Jane?

I could feel that several tubes and wires were attached to my body. Exhausted, I lay as still as possible. Maybe I couldn't move. My body was cool, but the sheet over me felt damp and clammy. I wanted to call out, but could feel something in my throat and nose—more tubes.

The door to my room opened, and I had a flashback to my dream. Bright hallway light pierced the dismal darkness, and I saw the outlined image of Jane. When she entered, I saw she was wearing a mask.

It must have taken some time for her eyes to adjust to the darkened room. She stepped closer. First, a look of surprise, then one of joy, electrified her face, followed by an expression I couldn't quite understand. She appeared to be uncertain about what she was seeing.

Hesitantly, she said, "George, if you know who I am, please do something to show me you hear me!"

I was so weak that I could hardly imagine what to do; I couldn't speak, but my eyes were open so I blinked twice and then smiled weakly.

She gasped and exclaimed, "George, you're alive. You're not brain dead. You know me. I thought I'd lost you. I didn't know what I was going to do! Oh, George!"

Tears streamed down her face. She laughed and cried as she fumbled for something beside my bed. In less than a minute a nurse came rushing into the room. I realized Jane must have pressed a call button.

By the look on the nurse's face when she entered, she had expected some new crisis, or, perhaps, even my death. The nurse paused, then looked ecstatic when she saw I was awake. She immediately began taking my temperature, checking my pulse and blood pressure, and examining all of my wires and tubes.

Then she hugged Jane, and I watched in amazement as they both laughed and cried. I was too weak to do anything other than manage a feeble smile.

The nurse left and, through her tears, said, "I'd better go and report you're awake." On her way out I heard her say, "Praise the Lord for an amazing miracle."

Strange, I thought.

We were alone. Jane still had her mask on, but she bent her face close to mine, tears streaming freely down her face. She touched my hand, whispering, "I love you." Over and over again, she whispered, "I love you."

With great effort, I smiled and blinked.

The nurse returned with someone to help her. They deftly rolled me to one side of the bed, then to the other, as they worked at changing my sweaty sheets and gown. The nurse gave me some more medications and then left me alone again with Jane.

Jane looked completely worn out, like she hadn't slept in days. I wanted to tell her how glad I was to see her, but I was too weak—and the tubes running into my nose and mouth made speaking impossible. After only moments of doing my best to respond to Jane's affection, I was already exhausted. She smiled softly, then sat down on a chair in the corner and gave in to sleep.

Moments later I also dozed off. This time, I slept quietly, with no nightmarish dreams or hallucinations to interrupt my rest.

I didn't wake up until a doctor came into my room on what I guessed was early the next morning. "Your vitals look better than they have since you entered the hospital, and you appear to be breathing without difficulty.

"Follow the light," he said, as he moved his penlight back and forth, up and down. I couldn't move my head, but I followed the light with my eyes. He nodded in appreciation.

"Can you move your fingers or toes?"

I tried. Amazingly, I was able to get both my fingers and toes to respond. He was delighted, but I was shocked at the amount of concentration such a small exercise took.

"I don't know how you did it, but you've beaten the odds," he said. "Several times, I thought you were at death's door."

You have no idea how true that is, I thought.

"You're on the way to recovery from a highly drug-resistant infection." He smiled reassuringly. "But, today, I believe you're going to make it."

In just two days, I was sitting up in bed and looking forward to my first walk. I hadn't understood how close to death I'd been until Jane told me the details of my infection.

With relief in her voice, she quietly explained how, after I had gone into a coma, I had gone through various stages of illness.

"For the first couple of hours you looked like you were in severe pain. You had a fever that climbed to 107 degrees. After that, your temperature dropped below normal, and you started to shiver uncontrollably. Finally, you seemed to relax for a while. Your temp returned to normal, and you appeared to improve. But just when you looked like you might recover, it would start all over again.

"They drew blood several times. The lab results showed you had an infection that was highly resistant to antibiotics and attacking your entire body.

"Every time the cycle repeated, you seemed to grow weaker."

I recognized the pattern as the same sequence of events I had experienced in my hallucinations. My body had gone through every stage my dreams had gone through, conversely, my mind had experienced every stage that my body had gone through. *Which was in control?*

I wondered if I would have recovered faster if I had trusted the door of life sooner. If I had gone through that door right away, would I have been healed almost immediately? And if I hadn't gone through it when I did, would I have died?

I smiled at Jane. "That's amazing," I said. "In my hallucination, I was experiencing the same things. I saw three doors, one for each diagnosis."

"What do you mean?" she asked.

"I'll explain later," I said, "but for now I'd like to know what happened while I was in my coma."

"The doctors were really worried," she said. "A team of specialists worked day and night to find an antibiotic that would work. They needed to find something to destroy the bacterial strain attacking your body before it killed you. They explained to me that if they found a mix that worked . . . well, they weren't very hopeful. They even notified the Centers for Disease Control to tell them that they had discovered a dangerous, unidentified infection.

"Every time you went through the cycle of high fever and shivering pain, you grew weaker. Before the last attack, the doctor tried to prepare me for the worst-case scenario, telling me that the next episode would probably be your last.

"He told me your body had used up all of its reserves. Even if you came out of your coma and lived, your chances of recovering physically and mentally would be nearly impossible. He said your fever was so high it had almost certainly caused brain damage and, depending on the severity of the damage, it might actually be better for you to die than be comatose for the rest of your life." She paused and squeezed my hand, looking into my eyes. "In other words, he was telling me I might need to give them permission to let you die."

I thought it was harsh of my doctor to discuss those options with Jane while I still had any chance of recovery. He must have been pretty certain I wouldn't survive and was doing his best to prepare Jane for the worst. When I first regained consciousness, I'd had no idea Jane might be thinking I was dead.

"When your last attack of fever struck, it was worse than all the others. I rushed into the lounge and cried."

She looked like she was going to cry again. I reached over and touched her fingers.

"I came back into the room for what I feared would be my last look at you before they removed your body," Jane said. "When I first saw you, you were lying perfectly still, and my eyes still weren't adjusted to the light after coming from the bright waiting room. I didn't see you open your eyes."

Tears flowed down her cheek. This time, I cried with her. Jane had gone through her own kind of hell watching me fight my infection.

"When I saw you blink, I didn't know how to react. How could a dead person blink? Maybe it was some kind of strange muscle contraction. Maybe I was just imagining what I thought I saw. It was only when you did it again that I realized you must be alive.

"The word of warning from the doctor haunted me. He was so sure that even if you lived, you would never be normal again. So even though I was happy to see you alive, I never expected you to have a chance to live a normal life again." Jane closed her eyes. "I cried for a long time after the doctor told me you probably wouldn't recover."

I smiled at Jane and said, "But I did survive. We'll be okay."

I had read about the correlation between healing and having a positive mental attitude, and with the relationship between my dreams and me overcoming my condition—it all verged on incredible.

We would need time to process everything we'd both been through.

———

After taking some time to simply enjoy being together, I decided to let Jane know about what had happened while I was in my coma. First, I explained the whole sequence of doors I had seen. Then I told her about the fruit, and how good it had looked.

"I had to eat it," I said. "After I did, I felt filled with energy at first, but soon it changed me. I felt the power of the knowledge of evil. I wanted all knowledge, like the Guild for the Knowledge of Good and Evil told us they wanted. At the same time that I desired all of that knowledge, I had the overwhelming sense that it would destroy me.

"I saw the same image of the tree from our book on all of the doors. Well . . . It was the same tree, but it had different effects on each door. On the first door, it burned with the intensity of death by fire, and the fruit was gone. On the second door the tree was icy cold and leafless, like it was calling me to the death of a corpse.

"But," I said, "while the third door also had a tree on it, I had a different feeling about it. It didn't feel like death lurked behind that door. The leaves on its tree were bright green; it was filled with flowers, and I was sure the door would open to a new chance at life."

As I told her about seeing the key and trusting in it to open the door to life, she stared at me in silence. When I told her how I had finally opened the door with the key and stepped across its threshold to open my eyes in the dark hospital room, she let out a sigh of relief, like she had been holding her breath.

"For being in a coma, you remember an awful lot," Jane said.

"It surprises me, too," I agreed. "Even so, somehow I feel like I finally ended up choosing life—and that choice saved me from dying of the infection."

"That's a little strange," Jane said, "but I agree, there had to be some relationship between your dreams and your healing. I think you must have wanted to overcome the infection so much that you finally won the battle. Maybe your decision to choose the key reflected your renewed desire to live, but I don't see how choosing the key and walking through the door caused your healing. That's a little too, well, weird."

"The most amazing part of the illusion really was the key," I said. "It was so vivid. And I couldn't go through the door to life without it. I can still remember what it felt like to hold it in my hand. I knew that it held healing energy. I felt alive and full of love, the opposite of how I felt after I ate the fruit. The fruit made me want to control everything, to react in seething anger, and dominate the world through hate. But, in the end, when the door started to change back to the door of death, the key gave me hope, and it was that hope that gave me my last chance at life."

While I had a feeling the key held some deeper meaning, I knew we wouldn't be able to solve the puzzle in that hospital room. It seemed like the number of puzzles confounding me was growing. The more I tried to solve them, the more they multiplied.

Although I couldn't explain it, I planned to hold fast to the hope I felt in the key. I was sure it would give me mental and emotional strength as we continued our quest for a new life.

———————

Later on, we discussed the image of the tree carved onto the surface of the doors from my recent hallucination, which led to trying to figure out what we should do about the book.

My immediate feelings were mixed. I wanted to get rid of the book I now associated with the Guild for the Knowledge of Good and Evil. I was, however, still drawn to the secret knowledge hidden in its dusty pages. I was also intrigued by the prospect of discovering the codes to open those meanings to us.

At the same time, I associated our book with how I felt after eating of the fruit in my nightmare. I was both attracted and repelled. I was nauseated by the insights into my evil intentions, but the book still held its power over me. I wanted to explore the knowledge it contained. A part of me still wanted the feeling of power it had given me.

It was, after all, our book. And my nightmares were, after all, only dreams.

We kept coming back to one question: Should we turn the book over to the police, or should we continue to hide it?

"For now, let's *not* tell them. We can change our minds. We can give them the book whenever we want to, on our terms."

"I agree. Let's live dangerously," Jane said, laughing. Her laugh rang hollow, as we both realized that, in the past few weeks, we had learned just how dangerous our lives could become.

As I was agreeing, I remembered the key in my hallucination had saved me from my near-death experiences. Was I replaying the dream now? Would I someday reach for that key to give me hope and save me from the power of the *Book of the Knowledge of Good and Evil*?

Several medical tests were done because my sudden recovery was unexplainable. I was told that the doctors would have considered my recovery a miracle even if I'd had severe brain damage. At a minimum, I was told, at the stage of the infection I had, I should have faced several months of recovery—and maybe years of physical and mental therapy. Yet I would walk away with no more ill effects than if I had recovered from a bad case of the flu.

One morning, my doctor, Dr. Peterson, came into my room followed by another man. Jane was with me when Dr. Peterson introduced the new FBI agent in charge of our security. Agent Arnold Berglund then introduced us to his assistant, Agent Jeannette Christie. They didn't stay long, but scheduled a briefing on our case for the next day in the hospital conference room. We had been so focused on my recovery that we hadn't thought about how much we were still in danger.

After Dr. Peterson and the agents left, Jane and I stared at each other for a long time. Finally, Jane sighed. "Here we go again. We just recover from one adventure and we begin another one."

We had spent so much time talking about my hallucinations that I still had not heard the rest of Jane's story, but I felt like I needed to before we met with the FBI. I hoped I would be able to handle her pain.

I don't exactly know why, but distancing myself in time certainly had helped me overcome my fears, and the image of the key from my hallucination had also given me more courage to face whatever had happened. Jane and I could look to the future with hope. I assumed the amazing optimism I had sensed when I grasped the key was nothing more than an emotion, but it would do for now.

23

I asked the FBI guard at my door if we could go outside for a while. Apparently the question surprised him; he snapped to attention and said, "I'll check." He immediately called his office. "I need to speak to Arnold Berglund." He held the phone to his ear for several minutes before he said, "Sir, I have a situation here." He went on to describe our request and waited for several more minutes.

Finally, he said, "Yes sir," and disconnected the call. "They decided allowing you to go outdoors would be good for you. The hospital has a gazebo in the back that's well hidden by the trees. You can be alone there, but you must stay in the gazebo. Wait in your room for fifteen minutes so we can set up a perimeter in the garden to protect you. Then I'll come in and take you there."

Twenty minutes later we walked out a back door. As we approached the gazebo, our guard handed me what looked like a small plastic remote control and said, "Under no circumstances are you to wander around. When you want to come back in, push the button on the remote and a buzzer will go off in the office. One of us will come to escort you back."

"Okay," I said, not entirely sure I understood all that was going on. "Thanks."

The gazebo was in the middle of a small lawn, hidden in the midst of lush bushes and tall trees. It had a classic round roof with green shingles. The deep green supporting posts were arched at the top, with light green trim on the inside of the arch. Several steps led up to the floor of the gazebo, and benches lined the inside of a railing. Around the base of the gazebo, bright red, purple, and yellow flowers were in full bloom. Under other circumstances, it would have been incredibly romantic.

We walked up the steps and sat down.

"This may seem strange, but I . . . I just realized that I have no idea where we are," I said.

Of course, I knew we were in a hospital. There were a lot of military personnel around so I guessed it was some kind of a military center, but I had no idea *where*.

Jane said, "We're at 'a high security military base in the central part of the United States.' Each time I ask, that's all they tell me."

In a voice just above a whisper, I told Jane, "I guess that eliminates just wandering away, doesn't it!"

Our guard overheard our conversation as he was leaving and, laughing, said, "I'm supposed to protect you—don't make me have to shoot you."

"Don't worry; I'm not ready for any new life-threatening adventures," I said.

Once Jane and I were alone in the gazebo, I asked her to tell me more about what had happened to her. She began by asking me a few questions about what I remembered, and was pleased that I recalled almost everything, even after my narrow escape from death.

She took my hand and proceeded to tell me more details of her story.

"The second day those creeps from the Evil Guild bound me to a chair again. They kept threatening to rape me if I didn't tell them where 'their book' was. I would have given in a hundred times, but I continued to believe that if I told them, they would rape me anyway. And what was to stop them from killing me after that?

"Once, only once, did they break their pattern of abuse and let me shower. Then they told me if I talked, I could walk out as a free person. I told them I didn't believe them, and even if I knew where their book was, I would never tell.

"That was when they told me you were dead, and said, 'So why not just give up and tell us where our book is?'

"I yelled at them, letting them know where they could go. I told them what kind of slime they came from, and—no, I couldn't tell them where their book was."

I hugged Jane, and whispered in her ear, "I'm so sorry you had to go through so much crap."

"But we're together now," Jane said. "We need to go on from here."

I hugged her, and said, "I can't wait, but I still need to hear what happened."

Jane looked down, took a deep breath, and continued.

"After my screaming episode, they changed their tactics again. Now their story was that you were actually alive, but if I didn't talk, they would torture you to death.

"I wasn't sure what to do, but I figured that, if you had talked, they wouldn't need to threaten me. My only defense was to play dumb. They might have had complete control over me, but I wasn't going to give in. I wouldn't tell them about our book.

"They seemed to be getting ready to begin some nasty sessions, when all of a sudden they told me to get ready to leave. Before I realized what was happening, they threw me into the back of a Suburban. An hour later, I was at the cabin where you had been taken. I think they decided that if we saw each other being tortured, we would talk."

I interrupted. "It's because I told them I wouldn't talk unless I saw you alive."

Jane stopped and smiled before she said, "That demand probably saved my life."

I had the feeling there was more Jane wasn't telling me, and I was glad she hadn't given me these details before my illness. I would have been so angry and upset, I probably would have gone insane with rage. In my coma, I might have walked through the red-hot door in my anger. Would I have died? I didn't know, but I was glad I had chosen the key and the door that led me out of my illness.

I focused on the idea of the key in my dream. Simply thinking about it calmed me and gave me hope everything could work out between us, and that our situation would soon improve.

Jane continued, "When I was pulled into the room where they had you tied up, it was hard to think of you looking at me. I didn't want you to see how awful I looked. They had humiliated me, and I felt ashamed. Later, in the hospital, Dr. Frank worked hard to help me sort out my feelings. He helped me put the blame back on the criminals.

"My dreams are still terrible, but I think I'm over the worst. I can accept myself again, though sometimes I don't want to go to sleep because I still have nightmares about lying under that sheet, half naked and in pain. Sometimes, in my nightmares, I still hear them calling me a whore and leering at me."

I pulled Jane into my arms and held her tight, not daring to let go, not saying anything, and longing for our lives to be normal again.

Finally she let out a long sigh. "That helps. I need a lot more of your hugs."

"I still don't understand one thing," I said as we sat back. "How did the police find out where to rescue us? I didn't think we had a chance."

"My FBI guard told me they'd found a slip of paper with a license number written on it on the floor in our house. They traced that to a front for the Guild for the Knowledge of Good and Evil. From that, they found a connection to the purchase of the property where you were being held.

"They had just staked out the perimeters of the property when the car I was in drove past. If I hadn't been in the car, they wouldn't have found me, and the Guild would've killed me, or worse."

"But why—and how—did the FBI even get into our house?" I asked.

"Apparently they decided the events surrounding the book in your office's computer system were suspicious, but they couldn't tell why. They decided to stake out our house in the morning, right after we were kidnapped. When they checked our doors, they saw the house had been broken into. They pushed the front door open and announced their presence before rushing in—and finding us gone."

I didn't remember writing down any license number, but I must have done it before I went back to the bedroom. I was amazed at how a series of small actions could change the direction of a whole chain of events. The FBI had found the license plate number in our house, and their research then led them to the gang holding us in some obscure house in the middle of the woods. We were now hiding from that same evil guild so we could testify against some of their leaders at a trial. And all of this started because we had picked up a strange little leather book in the library.

Somehow, after all that, we were finally together again. We had been physically and emotionally wounded, but were still alive.

"So, what happened to you after we were rescued?"

Jane closed her eyes before answering.

"I kept waking up at night thinking I was still locked in that horrible room, shivering under a thin sheet. In my crazed dreams, I relived what it was like to have my pillow wet from the tears I shed for you, for us, and for what we had lost. In those moments I would yell at my persecutors. When I woke up, my pillow would be really wet—and the nurses were concerned about my mental condition. The medical staff had to sedate me so I could sleep.

"At first, the stress of everything I had gone through made me paranoid that all men could become my tormentors, and for a few days I hated every man I saw for what he could do to me. Fortunately, the hospital assigned me a female doctor. I don't think I could have endured a male doctor touching me. If you and I hadn't had such a good relationship before all of this began, I don't know if I could ever have found balance in my life again. I don't know how women who are continually abused endure their pain."

I didn't know how to respond. Both of us just stared into the bushes across from the gazebo. I was digesting Jane's nightmares by comparing them to my own. Mine were based on threats and fear. Hers were based on an invasion of her whole being. I marveled that she could even discuss her experiences with me.

I worried that her abuse would become part of my fears and nightmares, and that I would be left feeling ashamed that I couldn't protect her.

Jane broke the silence. "Did you get my message on your computer explaining that I saw you when you were escaping from the hospital?"

I smiled. "I can't tell you how happy that made me. What happened at the hospital while I was escaping? Where were you?"

"Fortunately, they dressed me in a nurse's uniform," Jane said. "I can thank my FBI agent, Brenda, for that last-minute idea. No one but Brenda, a nurse, and I knew about the disguise. It was also Brenda's idea to fluff up the sheets to look like I was still sleeping. She even added a couple bags of real blood under the covers, so if someone tried to shoot me, they would think they succeeded.

"She also decided that probably the best place for me to hide would be right out in the open. I spent my time working—with my back to the lobby to minimize the chance someone might recognize me, especially you. It was a big risk. When all the commotion began, I was scared senseless that you'd be killed."

"You were that close?" I said.

"Yes." I could tell she was disappointed that we had been so near each other but hadn't been able to get together. "After your escape, one of the FBI agents checked my room. My bed had been shot up. He said blood was everywhere. At first, he was sure I was dead. I can't thank Brenda enough for her idea. As she kept me safe, she said someone inside the hospital must have squealed on us, telling the terrorists from the Evil Guild where we were and how we were planning to escape."

"After what the Guild told us, that doesn't surprise me," I said. "They seem to have members everywhere. Maybe one of them even worked at the hospital."

"Only the chief hospital administrator, a couple of nurses, and the doctors were supposed to know our real identities," Jane said. "Only the chief administrator and the agents were supposed to know where we were. There was, of course, the possibility the Evil Guild had searched all of the hospitals in the area and walked all the halls, observing what rooms FBI agents appeared to be guarding."

"That's why they were trying to keep us apart," I said. "We've both seen the faces of our kidnappers, and either of our testimonies could put them behind bars for life—or worse. The Guild was willing to do almost anything to eliminate us."

"Oh, George, when I heard that they kidnapped you a second time in Rockford, I was sure I'd never see you again. Then when I heard that they found you alive, I could hardly believe you survived. I was thrilled when one of the FBI agents said the government was going to find a more secure location for us so we could be together again."

"I hope that's possible," I said. "The guild seems to have spies everywhere. This must be a huge case. The government seems to be working extra hard to protect us."

"But . . . what will happen to us after we've testified?"

"I don't know. We'll just have to face that when we're done."

Jane and I talked into the evening. Our guard was replaced and we kept talking, hugging, and refocusing on being together. We had lost our *nothing can happen to us* invincibility. We knew that we could lose each other forever.

We were facing a much more dangerous life than we'd had before we found our book. We had to deal with the knowledge that there were people who wanted us dead. We had to trust our agents to protect us, but I had already dealt with an agent who had sold herself out to the Evil Guild. I didn't want to trust anyone after my experiences with that betrayal, but I did trust Jane completely. She was the one person I truly believed in.

Yet, as I listened to her story, I understood that we were incredibly vulnerable. Either of us could have given in and talked under the extreme pressure we faced. Although we'd been together for years, we knew more about each other's strengths and weaknesses after the past few weeks. We knew we could trust one another more completely because we had gone through more than most couples must ever endure to prove their loyalty. We weren't invincible, but we were committed to each other. If we failed, it wouldn't be because we lacked commitment. We had already maintained that under severe pain. If we succumbed, it would be because we were human. And even the strongest human can be worn down and destroyed.

Deciding which other people we could trust would be harder. Learning to have faith in others takes time and going through difficult circumstances with them. Then, too, sometimes learning to trust is learning to know *when* to trust. I might trust our guards to protect us in the hospital, but could they be trusted when their lives were at stake? They would watch us as we sat in the gazebo, but would they jump in front of a loaded gun to protect us? Would they risk their lives for ours? And, for that matter, whom would I risk my life for?

Dusk was falling as I considered that I had risked my life over a fancy old book. Yes, I had suspected at the time that the book might have great value, but would I do it again? It certainly had proven to be valuable to the guild that claimed all knowledge of good and evil. Though they claimed the knowledge of good, I was certain they were really all evil. Good was only a cover for their self-centered evil.

Jane and I were stuck in an impossible situation. We knew too much and could never go back. I had a feeling we would be tested in new ways. To survive, we would need to believe in each other completely—and be careful about trusting anyone else too much.

———

I pressed the button to let the guards know we were ready to go back inside. A guard escorted us into the hospital so that we could quickly stop by our rooms to wash up and then get some dinner.

As we approached my room, we were met by both of the agents assigned to us. Berglund said, "Pack your things. We're going to leave in thirty minutes. I don't have time to explain. You'll be briefed on the way about what's happening and why we're departing so suddenly."

My first reaction was, *We're civilians, not military. What gives this guy the right to order us around?* My second, more reliable reaction was, *They've saved our lives and now they're only doing their jobs. We'd better follow them.*

I heard Jane's stomach growling. I could tell Berglund was determined to leave on a firm schedule, but I screwed up my courage and said, "Could someone at least get us some dinner to eat on the way?" I added for emphasis, "We haven't eaten all day—and I've got to keep up my strength."

I was happy they took my request in good humor. Agent Berglund told one of the guards to pick up some sandwiches and sodas from the lunchroom. Then he escorted me to my room, and Agent Christie went with Jane.

We were in a United States Air Force car and on the road in almost exactly thirty minutes. The agents didn't say much as the car moved across the base in the direction of an airstrip, where a government jet was waiting for us.

Moments later, we were rushed aboard the plane, buckled in, and airborne, still holding our hastily packed meals. Once again, we were heading from one mysterious location to another.

24

All of the window shades were closed in the plane. As we adjusted to the half-light, Agent Christie turned to us and said, "As you know, you're officially under the protection of the United States government. When you get to Washington, DC, you'll be testifying against the gang which calls itself the Guild for the Knowledge of Good and Evil."

"I prefer to call them the Evil Guild," I said.

They told us the Guild was involved in everything from drugs to stealing top-level military and government secrets. Jane and I looked at each other. We both knew the Guild was far more dangerous than that.

Christie said, "The Guild has been around for centuries, if not longer, but their notorious activities have been recognized as a threat to our national security only recently. They've been shipping guns and explosives into and around the country and, even more troubling, they've been attempting to gain access to our nuclear research centers."

That sounded more like the Guild.

"As much as we know about their nefarious activities," Berglund added, "very few of their members have ever been caught and tried in court. Even fewer have been convicted. We arrested two of the top figures from their US branch near the house where we rescued you."

Berglund held up a dozen photos, and Christie asked if we recognized any of them.

Both Jane and I immediately pointed out three of the people who had been in the room when we were interrogated.

Berglund nodded and explained what we somehow already knew. "You've both seen their faces and could testify against them.

I must warn you that most witnesses have never made it to court. There's no easy way to put this. Your lives are at risk. I'd say you're on a red-alert status. Even if you choose not to testify, there's a good chance they'll kill you just to make sure they'll never be compromised. We will, of course, make every effort to keep you alive."

That wasn't news we wanted to hear, but it wasn't exactly a surprise. *What chance do we have?*

I whispered to Jane, "I feel like we've just been told we have an advanced case of cancer and our odds aren't good."

Jane whispered back, "I don't know how I feel. Right now, I'm kind of numb."

"We know the Guild has spies in a lot of major corporations, and even within the government and its related agencies," Christie said. "They already sacrificed one of their inside agents when they attempted to capture and kill you in Wisconsin. They would do that again in a second to protect their leaders."

"When we get to our destination, we expect you to identify the suspects in a police lineup," Berglund explained. "This will then become part of the prosecutor's evidence in the pretrial hearings.

"As an added protection, we're planning on having a couple of decoys leave the plane first, in case, if by some new subterfuge, they've found you're on this plane."

"Would you like to meet your decoys?" Christie said.

When we answered, "Sure," she told us to look behind us.

A couple of agents who were dressed exactly like us were seated there. At a glance, I would have said they were our twins. *Are we so typical that it's easy to find duplicates at a moment's notice?*

Agent Berglund handed us bulletproof vests and light jackets. "Put the vests on first, under the jackets."

"The police will take you to a prison, where you'll be instructed what to do," Christie said. "You'll have an FBI car behind you and one in front of you all the way, to protect you from any unexpected confrontations."

Then, with obvious concern for how we'd take the information, Berglund explained the rest of the shocking news. The words hit us like a flash of light exploding in front of our eyes on a dark night—the kind that leaves a disconcerting impression of what you've just seen and reappears every time you blink.

Berglund's steely eyes were penetrating as he said, "You'll never be able to return to your old life. Consider it history. After the trial, we'll stage a fake death for you before the Guild for the Knowledge of Good and Evil has a chance to kill you." There it was—our future with no past. He blinked twice, cleared his throat, and then continued. "If you were to go back to your previous jobs and home, they'd find you. You'd probably be tortured. You would certainly be killed within days. The history of this cult is brutal, as you already know. They've been known to do some pretty nasty stuff to informants."

"So," I began, then paused out of frustration before saying, "how did we get in the middle of all this mess, and how do we ever get back to normal once this is over? We'll have no family, no friends, and nothing—absolutely nothing familiar to build our lives around, except each other." Jane squeezed my hand as we each took a deep breath of our new reality.

"To answer the first question, well . . . let's be honest: you stole one of their books," Agent Christie said. Jane and I exchanged a glance, which the agents obviously recognized. "Of course you didn't know it belonged to such a dangerous gang. You probably assumed you just found a stray old book on a library shelf.

"While the book itself has significant archival value, to the Guild for the Knowledge of Good and Evil, its apparent worth goes far beyond its contents. They believe that it contains ancient secrets going back hundreds, and maybe even thousands, of years. The book is sacred to their guild, but—because of their beliefs—certainly not holy.

"We also know the Guild was using it as a resource for passwords for their encrypted secret messages. That you were attempting to figure out the book's meaning was, I'm sure, troubling to them. It also explains why they put so much effort into destroying all your research." Agent Christie nodded to her partner, who picked up the story.

"We figure they were able to track you down from library records of everyone who checked out during the window between when the book was left and when it was to be picked up," Berglund said. "We suspect they got access to the library's surveillance videos.

"We know a checkout librarian who was working at that time was kidnapped and killed. We're certain there's a connection. We also assume that's how they narrowed down the list of possible targets to you."

"That pretty much agrees with what the Guild told us," I said.

Jane put her head on my shoulder. "How could this happen? It's our fault she's dead. It's all our fault."

"I'm sorry," Berglund said. "But you need to know what kind of people you're up against. It's important that they're brought to justice."

"We already knew about the librarian. The Evil Guild told us they killed her when we were being tortured. But to be reminded so bluntly that she was murdered *because of what we did*, well, it's a shock," I said, my arm around Jane's shoulders.

"I understand," Christie said, "But we have to move on from here. Remember, they are the murderers—and they must be stopped."

"Why didn't they try to kill us right away?" I said.

"We believe they first tried to get the book by watching and waiting for a chance to steal it back without attracting attention. You were apparently too clever for that, so they finally abducted you. If you had just left the book on a coffee table, they probably would have simply broken into your house and taken it. You protected the book so well you almost got yourself killed because of it." She shrugged. "You still might."

"By the way," Agent Berglund said, "we now have the book. We got a search warrant and found it in your safety deposit box. You could have saved us a lot of trouble by telling us where it was. So tell me what you thought you saw in the book that made you hide it—even from us."

I began by telling him how I discovered the book in the mystery section of the Harrison Library and immediately fell in love with its elegant antique beauty. I told him how much we adored the marbled paper on the inside of the cover; the soft, aged fibrous pages; and the gold-leaf edge.

"I sensed that the book would somehow change our lives forever," I said.

Both of the agents' eyes rolled up.

"Well, I guess it changed your lives all right," Berglund agreed.

"How could this happen? It's our fault she's dead. What will happen to us?" Jane whispered through the onset of tears.

Berglund and Christie looked at each other, and then looked back at Jane like they wanted to help, but didn't know how. For the next fifteen minutes, no one said anything, and I held Jane in my arms. I wanted to cry, too, but I was also angry. I was angry with myself for taking the book. I was angry at the Guild for what they had done. And I was angry because we had already lost so much.

Suddenly, Jane looked up. She wiped her tears and said, "Sorry, okay, let's get on with what we must do next."

I nodded in agreement.

Both agents were silent for about a minute. Finally Berglund said, "We want to know more about what happened so we can get a better picture of how the Guild operates."

I described how we got the book from the library. Then I described the man in the dark suit and the limousine we saw when we were getting ready to leave.

"He looked suspicious," Jane interjected.

"Actually, we know about that incident," Berglund said. "We have the police report. Please continue."

"When we had a chance to study the book, we discovered that the text didn't look like any language we could imagine. It looked like it was filled with random letters," I said. "At first glance, the letter combinations appeared almost discernible as words, and their combinations as sentences. Every sentence began with capitals and was punctuated, but nothing made any sense. Nothing was readable.

"I contemplated the idea that the book was simply a design mock-up for another book, but that didn't make any sense because the pages looked like they were printed with a vintage letterpress. It would take way too much effort to do a random book design with that technology. We figured the book had to have some hidden meaning, and we had a nagging feeling that there must be a code we needed to find in the text to discover its secrets."

"The text looked like it had recognizable patterns. We assumed they must contain keys for understanding the book," Jane said.

"That seems likely," Berglund said. "We're also working under that assumption."

I continued. "We decided that the book was too fragile to work on, so I scanned it to a file and Jane took it to work to run a program that would convert it to text. While we were both gone, our house was broken into and our first research notes on the book were stolen."

"We also know about the break-in," Christie said.

We didn't say anything to Berglund or Christie about the deep emotional attraction we felt for the book, *our* book the government now possessed. I wondered if they would be just as dangerously attracted to the *Book of the Knowledge of Good and Evil*?

We were surprised when the pilot announced that we were approaching Washington, DC, and were cleared for landing.

Agent Berglund quickly switched the discussion back to the issue of our safety. He established a list of rules that would have made my conservative mother sound positively tolerant. Basically, the rules boiled down to one primary directive: "Don't look at anyone. Stay close to us, but don't look like you know who we are."

In light of my experience, I was beginning to get nervous about our chances of making it in and out of the jail to identify the crooks without seriously risking our lives. I wondered if we would be safer following Agent Berglund's rules or if we might be better off ducking our agents at the airport, getting a hotel room on our own, and then showing up at the jail unannounced.

As I pondered the second option, I realized it didn't seem like a reasonable—or even possible—scenario. The agents would be watching us to prevent us from attempting such a daring plan, and even if we did get away, someone from that nutcase guild might figure out who we were and follow us as we slipped away. *What good would freedom be with no protection?*

Besides, where would we go with nothing and no options? A homeless shelter? It didn't seem desirable or feasible, but I needed to spend some time thinking through some worst-case scenarios to make plans for our survival in case the worst actually happened to us—again.

My thoughts of alternative options were interrupted when Agent Berglund said, "As soon as we leave the plane, you are to go directly to the gate scheduled for Flight 204 to Atlanta. You will wait there for two agents who will lead you down secured stairs into a service area in a restricted zone. Their names are Tim Lorsay and Isaac France. They'll lead you to a car that will take you to your hotel. Your reservation at the hotel is under an alias to avoid detection. They'll provide you with the necessary credentials on your way to the car. There will be agents in the hotel. You should be safe there."

25

Our plane landed. Christie helped us into our bulletproof vests and jackets, which we put on while our look-alike decoys left the plane with two other agents who had been at the back of the plane. We stood inside the plane, but out of sight near the airplane door for several frustrating minutes. Both Berglund and Christie had earpieces in. As I watched, I noticed tension building on their faces. Suddenly there was a lot of animated talking between them and whoever was on the other end of the transmission.

Personally, I was ready to leave. I desperately wanted to get out of the plane, but Agent Christie frantically pulled the door shut and quickly secured it. The plane immediately revved its engines, turned, and taxied toward a hangar.

I glanced at Jane; then I looked at the agents. "Don't worry. The agents who left first simply decided that the plane was too exposed for you to get out at the terminal," Christie said calmly. "We've decided we should let you out in the hangar instead."

Seeing the surprise on Jane's face, I could tell she didn't like this change of plans any more than I did. Something was obviously wrong. This seemed too much like our previous unplanned diversions, but we had no other options.

As we got closer to the hangar, the plane suddenly turned again, just missing the building with its wing. The turn was so sharp Jane was thrown into a seat and I bounced off the wall. I saw Jane strap on her seat belt. Berglund, Christie, and I quickly sat down and strapped ours on, too. At the edge of the building, we made another sharp turn as we all gripped our chairs. As soon as we were around the side of the hangar so that we could no longer see the terminal building, Agent Berglund yelled, "Everybody out—now!"

The door swung open and Christie threw a rope ladder out of the door. We were out of the plane in less than a minute. Berglund pointed and yelled, "Run for that dark blue car. Hurry."

Christie and Berglund drew their guns as we made a dash for the car. Jane, Christie, and I flung the door open and jumped into the back seat. Berglund slid into the passenger seat. The agents looked so tense I knew this was serious. The driver accelerated away from the hangar and sped down a service road.

———

We had driven about a mile from the airport when Agent Christie said, "One of your doubles and one of the accompanying agents have been killed. They were shot as soon as they exited the security zone in the airport. Two of the hit men have also been killed and a third was seriously wounded. The airport is on lockdown."

Jane looked horrified. I was numb. We could have been there. One or both of us could have been killed.

Those agents had risked and lost their lives for us; they didn't even know us, yet two of them had died in our place. Of course, they didn't die *just* for us. They died for the cause of freedom and for a way of life. *They died doing their duty*, I rationalized, trying to make sense of it all. They died for us as part of their job, and it's possible they died because they enjoyed a life of danger and intrigue. Nevertheless, they died, and we were alive to wonder about their motives for risking their lives for us.

A few miles down the road, we pulled into a garage, where we quickly switched cars before driving to a small hotel about an hour away.

———

"This hotel may seem like it's in a quiet neighborhood, but don't let your first impression fool you," Berglund said. "It's not safe, even though, at this time of the day, it might look like it is."

"And don't go out at night," Christie cautioned, as if she were speaking to children. "The nightlife around here is wild; not the kind of place you'd want to hang around. This hotel caters to an . . . *adult* crowd with dubious motives. It rents rooms by the hour, and several drug busts have been made here in the past few months."

"We're staying here precisely because of all of that. The guests usually keep their mouths shut," Berglund said. "Few want to advertise they've been here, but even fewer would ever expect us to hide out in this kind of place."

The car we had arrived in left as soon as we got out. "We don't want the car to attract attention," Berglund said.

I glanced around and saw that the neighborhood had several XXX-rated dance bars and adult stores. It certainly wasn't the kind of place I wanted to stay, and especially wasn't a place I wanted to bring my wife.

After we checked into the Hot Spot Hotel around 7:00 p.m., Berglund said, "Stay in your rooms until you can be outfitted to blend into the neighborhood better. Otherwise, all our advantage in hiding here might be blown."

Our room was small and decorated in baroque gaudiness. A mirror with a gold frame and two gold cherubs adorned one wall. The bed had a silky gold-and-red bedspread, and a golden headboard. The drapes were a flaming red with gold trim. A medium-sized flat-screen television sat in the corner. It looked out of place in this egregiously decorated room.

Even though it was fairly early, Jane and I both dropped onto the bed, completely exhausted. I didn't think I could sleep, but in moments I was oblivious to the world. Neither of us woke up until late the next morning. I thought about what had happened the day before. Jane apparently was thinking the same thing. As I was saying, "It's about time we check the news," she was already moving toward the television set.

"With everything that happened in the airport, this must be an active news day," Jane said.

When we turned the set on we had to change channels quickly to keep from being assaulted by the blatant sex of a pornographic station. We clicked past two similar channels before we figured out the remote and quickly found the menu for the regular cable. I had been in hotels before that *offered* such stations, but I had never been in a hotel where the set was tuned to one as the primary option.

When we found the news station, we discovered we were right. The airport was crawling with reporters who gave extended accounts of what had happened, along with endless speculations about why.

"During one of the busiest times of the day, a government-owned plane landed. Four people left the plane and walked a short distance across the tarmac to the terminal entrance. They climbed the stairs to the main floor and followed the concourse to the terminal building. Upon entering the terminal's lobby, several gunshots exploded, echoing up and down the corridor," the reporter stated.

The television screen shifted to another reporter positioned outside the airport, who said, "Two FBI agents were killed instantly and one was severely wounded. He is paralyzed. One unknown person was killed, along with two of the gunmen. One shooter was wounded and captured by the authorities."

After shifting the view to show the buzz of ambulances, police cars, and people running in and out of the terminal, the reporter said, "Several other passengers waiting for flights were injured trying to escape the area. One passenger is in the hospital, but will be released after a period of observation."

The reporter went on to describe a counseling program that was being set up to deal with the trauma of the day's events. People were asking how children would be impacted. There was already an outcry about how so many guns could have made it into the terminal, and why the shootout had occurred with the FBI.

It had been a dumb plan. If the FBI had assumed there was such a great risk that they needed their elaborate strategies—including decoy look-alikes for us—then they should never have been planned for a peak time in a busy terminal.

Of course, if the Guild for the Knowledge of Good and Evil was behind this, which was the only scenario I could imagine, they were ultimately responsible for the disaster. Once again they were defining good as for *their* own good.

The reporters kept looking for people to interview to get fresh insights into any causes, excuses, and excesses that might explain how and why a disaster of these proportions could occur.

I usually found watching such reports gripping for about ten minutes. After that, it seemed that reporters usually ran out of updates or new details, so they spent most of their time looking for heart-wrenching angles. Usually they either failed or imposed on people who should have been left to suffer and grieve silently.

That day, however, the reports were troubling for personal reasons. We were part of the wild act of terrorism being reported. We didn't cause it, but it occurred because of all the events swirling around us.

We weren't mentioned in the morning's news. In the future, we might be. We could easily have been the center of every story. We could have been the ones who were killed.

I was pretty certain the news media would eventually track down the source of the disaster. Maybe they would even find us. I certainly didn't want to be on the news, but it was also troubling to see that the real reasons behind the story were being covered up. As we discussed the events of the previous day, Jane and I came to the conclusion that the cover-up was probably designed to hide the source of the agency's bad decisions as much as it was to protect us.

My journalistic training made me want to tell everything to a reporter. I was tempted to rush out and call one of the news services to announce the facts, but then everyone who was hurt or injured might blame us. We were, after all, the reason behind all of the events. We had stolen the *Book of the Knowledge of Good and Evil*, and as a result, we were at least partly responsible. It wasn't our fault that a wicked guild was attempting to destroy us, but that didn't mean we had no guilt. I guess we had a sense that we all share the blame for some things.

I looked at Jane and could see she was deep in thought. We both stared at the screen, mesmerized at the events being reported. Jane looked horrified. I probably did, too.

When Jane couldn't stand the silence, she blurted out, "Isn't there anything we can do to stop this?"

"I don't like it any more than you. We didn't start it, but we could easily end up being its next victims."

"I wonder how well they're protecting us," Jane said. "It seems everyone trying to protect us becomes a magnet, drawing danger to themselves—and to us. Maybe we could do just as well on our own."

"I've been thinking the same thing for a while."

Jane's eyes opened wide. "Okay, what's your idea?"

"We might be able to get away by living on the street until things cool down, but I have no clue how to do that."

"It doesn't seem to be a particularly attractive solution," Jane said. "Living on the street might be a way to escape, but it would also be dangerous, and definitely unpleasant."

"You're right. The more I thought about the idea, the more I figured we couldn't pull it off. We'd have no money and would never be able to use any identification because it could be traced. We're in an unsafe neighborhood and don't have any way to get out of here. We would also be traveling together, which would make finding us easier.

"On the plus side," I said, "the FBI can't put us on the *Ten Most Wanted* list. We haven't done anything wrong."

Jane flopped down on the bed laughing. I dropped down beside her and laughed, too. Realizing neither of us had done anything seriously criminal was therapeutic.

A knock on the door brought us back to our new, immediate reality. With some trepidation, I asked, "Who's there?"

"I've got clothes and food. Let me in before I drop your tacos," Christie said.

I jumped up and swung the door open, trying not to look guilty for the treasonous talk Jane and I had just been having. Christie and Berglund were both pretty decent people, as well as careful agents. We thought of them as both our liberators and protectors.

Christie carried a beat-up suitcase in one hand, a bag of tacos in the other, and an old duffel bag hung from her shoulder. Berglund stood beside her with two large drinks and another duffel bag. In spite of our conversation, I was happy to see them. Jane and I hadn't thought much about food, but we were ravenous. We greedily consumed everything, leaving only the greasy bags as evidence of our feast.

While we ate, Christie said, "We're checked into the rooms on either side of you in case you need anything." She and Berglund also told us there was another agent on our floor and two more in the hotel—but they wouldn't tell us who they were or where they would be watching us.

"It's better you don't know some things," Berglund said. "They're hidden backup in case there's trouble."

Jane and I looked at each other. "Thanks. Let's hope we don't have any," Jane said.

As soon as Berglund and Christie left, Jane and I tried on our clothes. To say they fit perfectly would be a dramatic overstatement, but they were comfortable. The small imperfections in material and the slight fading indicated they were probably purchased at a secondhand clothing store. We were getting used to putting on other people's clothes, and Jane and I actually had fun trying on the outfits and laughing at some of the combinations. We felt like kids again.

After our dress-up time, Jane and I still felt the weight of the previous day's ordeals and snuggled together for a long nap. We didn't wake up until Christie knocked on our door. According to the clock, we'd been asleep for much of the day.

Once inside, she told us, "The proceedings at the jail have been put off because the agency wants to let things cool down before you're brought in to identify the Guild's leaders."

I thought, *And protect yourselves from an investigation if people figure out the connection between what happened at the airport and the real reasons for this disaster.*

No matter how much they tried to cover it up, I expected sooner or later the pieces would come together. The prosecutors were really trying to hold their case together for the trial. They didn't want the airport incident to upset their witnesses' testimonies.

Berglund eventually showed up, bringing a dinner of cheap brats and greasy fries from a local street vendor. Jane and I were hungry enough to be glad for even such cholesterol-laden food. Christie and Berglund joined us, pulling the room's two chairs closer to the bed, which was both extra seating and our dining table.

We turned on the television while we ate. All four of us wanted to see what the evening news was reporting. Not much had changed, except now there was a complete listing of everyone who had been killed or injured. The only fresh news was that one of the bystanders had died from heart complications related to a previous heart attack.

New angles had, of course, been found to try to keep viewers tuned in. Someone who arrived at the airport just moments after the shooting had missed his taxi and otherwise would have been standing in line at the terminal. He thanked God he hadn't been there.

I wondered about those who had been caught in the crossfire. Who did they thank? And what about the guy who had a heart attack? He never had a chance to thank anyone.

After Christie and Berglund left, Jane continued to sit quietly on the side of the bed while I got up and sat on the chair vacated by Berglund. Neither of us spoke for several minutes.

Jane finally broke the silence. "Honey, why don't we change the way we look even more? I don't think the clothes are enough. We could dye our hair. You could grow a shaggy beard. Let's not make it easy to figure out who we are."

I didn't need to ponder the idea for long. The plan sounded fantastic to me. It gave me a sense of relief and the feeling of regaining some piece of control. Maybe we could do something more to keep ourselves safe. Jane and I had a hundred dollars Christie and Berglund had left as "emergency money."

They were here to protect us, and if changing our appearance would help them, why not?

We had seen a drugstore two or three blocks from the hotel when we had arrived. We figured it must sell hair dye and makeup, so we decided to slip out and see if the store was open.

Christie and Berglund, of course, would never have allowed this. The sun had set, and from the sounds we were hearing, they were at least partly right about the neighborhood. Since it was dark, we suspected the drugstore might be closed, but we had been cooped up in our gaudy room too long, so we decided to risk the dangers and potential disappointment. We grabbed our jackets, leaving our cumbersome bulletproof vests behind, then opened our door just wide enough to peek up and down the hall.

A couple was slipping into a room a few doors down, but they didn't notice us. We stepped out and walked to the stairs as quickly as we could. We didn't want Christie or Berglund to know we had left. We would also need to slip past the undisclosed agents who were there to guard and protect us. We hoped that these agents were focusing their attention in other directions—looking for intruders coming into the hotel, not for people leaving.

Jane and I decided that the best way to escape was to boldly exit through the front door. We figured all of the hotel's side and back entrances would be watched more carefully. We would simply walk out like we had paid for the room in advance and were leaving before we were caught in our indiscriminate act of adultery.

When we got to the stairs leading down to the lobby, we took a moment to observe the area. We looked around the corner and over the stair rail. Someone was sitting in the lounge chair looking half asleep, but he was obviously glancing up occasionally to check out anyone entering. Two couples were paying for rooms at the front desk, making a clean escape impossible.

We had turned to go back to our room when a couple half-fell out of a room a few doors down. They were obviously drunk—or something—and looked like they had just used up the hour they had paid for in the room.

"I have an idea," I told Jane.

Walking up to them I said, "Someone's watching for us. Mind if we leave with you?" They looked at each other nervously, but then burst out laughing, as if we'd just told the best joke of the evening. "Sure, why not?"

"Let's go for it," I whispered to Jane.

We staggered along with the couple, and didn't look at anyone as we joked and stumbled out the door like we had known them for years. Soon we were standing on the sidewalk. We turned immediately and walked unsteadily toward where we remembered seeing the drugstore. A block away, we burst out laughing as well, feeling like we had just won Oscars for acting.

The street was crowded with people. Neon signs seduced passersby with garish reds, yellows, blues, purples, and oranges. As we meandered down the blocks of bars and adult stores, we held each other tight, feeling like we were rescuing ourselves from the storm of humanity's vices.

After we got a few blocks away from our hotel, the businesses thinned out and those remaining were closed, with barred doors and windows. We had remembered the drugstore as being only a few blocks away, but realized we must have miscalculated the actual distance because we were unfamiliar with the area. Finally, about nine blocks from the hotel, we found it as locked up and barred as all the other legitimate businesses we'd passed.

"I can't believe we went to all this trouble to find it closed," Jane said.

We turned to retrace our steps back to the hotel, worried about our future. We were disappointed by our failure to increase our chances of escape.

26

We had walked about a block on our way back to the hotel and were a couple of steps from crossing an alley between two buildings when I heard a scuffling sound coming from its depths.

We immediately stopped and looked nervously at each other. Over the dull street noises echoing down the alley, we heard a man confronting someone in the dim light from a doorway.

The man yelled, "Give me the money. I'll shoot. Hurry up. I haven't got all night!"

The other man said, "Calm down, I haven't got any money on me."

Not long before we would have raced back to the hotel as fast as our lungs and our legs would have allowed. Instead, I pushed Jane back and peeked around the corner again, ready to bolt and run if necessary.

The man holding the gun was facing the other direction. I took Jane's hand and we crept past the alley. I wanted to be as close as possible to the hotel in case we had to flee for our lives, but before we bolted I thought of an idea that might also save the life of the man being held up.

I picked up a small piece of broken concrete from where the sidewalk and alley met. I flung it deep into the alley to make the robber aware there was some activity around him, hoping that he wouldn't know where it came from.

The chunk of concrete clanged against some trash cans close to the robber. He turned and shot his gun in that direction. Before I could react, the two men struggled for the weapon. I ducked back around the corner of the building, not wanting any stray bullets penetrating my body. I heard the gun clatter to the ground and moments later loud footsteps pounded toward us accompanied by swearing. The thwarted robber was obviously on his way in our direction.

Jane flattened herself into the shadows of a shop doorway. I dropped to one knee as tight to the building as I could get.

I don't know what gave me the courage to make my next move. Perhaps it was my instinct to protect Jane, or maybe it was fear or frustration at being put into this position, but as the gunman came around the corner, I tackled him. We fell with a thump and his head impacted the pavement with a loud cracking sound that reverberated off the buildings. He groaned with a heavy, gurgling sound.

I jumped up in dread from where he lay. Jane ran up to me and threw her arms around me, shaking with fear and relief. We were holding onto each other in shock when a man wearing a blue dress shirt and dark trousers walked up to us. He gave us a huge smile and brushed a hand through his dark brown hair.

"Thanks for saving my hide. Name's Blake." He looked up and down the street before he extended his hand to us. He crouched down, lifted the limp arm of the robber, and felt for his pulse. He put his hand in front of the robber's nose and flatly announced, "He's dead."

"He's what?" I cried.

"He's definitely dead," he said, "but keep your voice down. Do you want the whole city to know what happened?"

"Dead? How can that be?" I said.

"His bad luck." Blake shrugged his shoulders. "He's dead—you . . . you saved my life."

"Dead? It can't be. I had no intention of killing him. How could that be? Dead?" I tried to find some way to wrap my head around what had just happened. It had all been so fast. I never intended to kill the guy—just slow him down.

"Do you want to get involved with the police?" Blake asked.

I didn't know how to answer.

Jane responded for us, "Of course not, but what will happen? Shouldn't we call someone?"

"Probably, but I'm sure he has connections," Blake said. "After all of this, I don't want one of his buddies coming after me. Keep me out of the conversation, if you do call—and I suggest you don't let anyone know you were the ones calling."

"Do you have a cell phone we can use? We could just say we found someone dead on this block, and hang up?" Jane said.

"Cell phones are too easy to trace."

Blake, with more composure than I would have had, rolled the dead man over, pulled a phone from his pocket, and turned it on. "Great, it's not password protected," he said. He handed us the phone. "You can use this to call, but make the call as fast as you can."

We dialed 911 and told the emergency center about finding a dead body and approximately where we had found it.

As soon as we hung up, Blake grabbed the phone from us and wiped it down with a handkerchief. "We don't want to leave any evidence."

At first I thought he was being ridiculous, but I recognized the wisdom in being slightly paranoid. I didn't want any new people after us.

————————

We walked in the direction of the busy X-rated strip as police sirens grew louder. With Blake's help, we blended into the activities of the night.

Our new friend led us into a club where a jazz musician was wailing on his saxophone from a corner stage while another was keeping beat with a drum set. The room was dark, with purple spotlights reflecting off brick walls. It smelled of fried food and old booze.

The atmosphere was both celebrative and meditative as many patrons listened intently to the jazz while others talked above the clanking of silverware against plates.

We found a table in a side room off to the right of the main lounge. It was quieter there and we could talk without raising our voices. We sat on padded chairs by tables covered with black cloth and clear plastic, a lame attempt to appear elegant while being practical. Blake flagged down a waitress and ordered a round of drinks, asking her to put anything else we wanted on his tab.

I asked Blake what he did for a living and he said, "Oh, a little of this and a little of that—I run a pawnshop a block over. I should be smarter than going down dark alleys at night in this neighborhood." He leaned back and looked at Jane and me. "Now, who are you, and what are you doing in this dive?"

"We're just tourists," I said. "We do a little of this and a little of that."

Blake smirked. "So, what do you have to hide?"

I tried to be noncommittal. "No more and no less than anybody else around here."

"That much?" he said, grinning first at me and then at Jane.

I didn't really know what to say. Almost on cue, the saxophone and drum went silent. The constant jazz beat stopped, I presumed, for a much-needed break. Friendly chatter continued, and sounds of the restaurant and bar clattered in the background, but that only made our silence even more obvious.

Then, as if Blake clearly saw our dilemma, he leaned across the table. "Do you need to get a fresh start?" He took a quick glance to see if anyone was within earshot. "Maybe some new IDs?"

Are we that transparent? Or is Blake that intuitive? I thought.

Defensively, I said, "No, of course not!" He held my gaze, and after a few seconds I added, "Well, maybe."

Jane arched an eyebrow at me, grabbing my hand beneath the table. The gesture didn't go unnoticed by Blake, who looked at us intently. "Face it. You two look like a couple of scared rabbits. Tell me if I'm wrong. My guess is that you're a typical young couple who got caught up in something bigger than you can handle. It might be gambling, or drugs, or any number of things. Whatever it is, you need a fresh start."

I tried to determine what Jane was thinking. She was looking at me like she was attempting to do the same thing.

I looked back at Blake and said, "Even if we wanted to, we have no way to start over."

He just smiled. After a moment, he said, "You just saved my life, didn't you? But, anyway, it would cost your life savings to get two new identities of the quality I can work up for you."

"Who said anything about new identities?" Jane asked, speaking up for the first time since we'd sat down.

"Doing it right isn't just faking some papers, you know. It's having contacts to get John Does or, er, *Jane* Does to fit personality profiles. And if that isn't possible, then fresh profiles must be created, and that often costs even more to myriad government agencies, businesses, credit bureaus, and financial institutions. There are payoffs, and inside people who need to be nurtured."

"Okay, okay," I said. "So you can make really good fake identities."

"I'm one of the best in the business," he said.

Jane looked momentarily horrified and asked, "You . . . you don't kill anyone to get their identity, do you?"

Blake laughed. "Of course not. That would unnecessarily complicate my life. Not to mention make it much more dangerous."

After thinking about what he said, I replied, "It all sounds terribly illegal. We may be in trouble, but we haven't done anything *really* illegal."

I thought about the dead guy in the alley, but Blake just shrugged. "Suit yourself."

"I hope we don't need to do anything so extreme," Jane said. "But could we have a little time to think about the implications of taking such a huge step?"

We hardly know this guy. What is Jane thinking?

The jazz duo started to play again, something mellow this time. The mix of the light jazz, and the noise of the people eating and talking, was a distracting background as I tried to sort out the ramifications of such a bold move. This was more than just hair dye. It was not the kind of step we could back off from.

And yet, how different was it from the offer the FBI was making—and what real choice did we have? Should we trust our safety to the FBI, which had already compromised our protection, or to this guy we had only met an hour ago when we saved his life? In my mind, I guessed the odds were probably about even.

Blake didn't say a word. He reached into his shirt pocket and handed us a business card for his pawnshop. Standing, he started to leave, then he stopped and said, "By the way, thanks again for saving my life."

As soon as he left, Jane let out a long sigh. "I'm glad that's over. What a terrible night."

"I'm still shaking," I whispered. "Criminal or not, I feel awful. I never intended to kill anyone."

"But you *saved* someone else's life," Jane whispered back.

"Now all we need to do is figure out who was the bigger criminal: the one I killed, or the one I saved."

We sat quietly and listened to the music, wishing we had never left the hotel. If we had stayed in our room, none of this would have happened. Our situation was becoming increasingly precarious.

We had left the hotel because we wanted to find a better way to disguise ourselves. We wanted to improve our chances of escaping from the Guild for the Knowledge of Good and Evil. Our very lives depended on not being recognized by this gang that wanted our book so desperately it was willing to kill for it.

As the evening progressed, I rehashed over and over how I had become responsible for someone's death. Our escape into the night had far greater consequences than I could have ever imagined. A man died because I tackled him. Even though he had clearly indicated he intended to murder Blake, I felt terrible about having caused his death. How do you reconcile doing such a thing? Of course, if he had seen us, he probably would have shot us just as quickly.

We sat in the bar until around two in the morning, when the musicians quit playing.

———————

Nothing could change what I had done. We had to move on. Our survival depended on not getting mired down.

"I guess it's about time to sneak back into the hotel."

Jane smiled warmly, as if to say, "Yes, dear, I'm resigned to my fate." We got up to leave, weaving around the now-empty tables, and were ready to open the door when someone tapped Jane on the shoulder.

"You two don't want to go out there by yourself this time of night," a young woman said.

"Why?" Jane asked. "What choice do we have?"

"Not enough people out there now to keep you from getting mugged, or worse. It's too easy for someone to sneak up on you without being seen."

Based on our earlier experiences, we weren't going to argue the point with her, but we were stuck. What else could we do? Seeing our concern, our unknown protector said, "I can tell you're new around here. I'm kind of new myself. If I were you, I would get one of them rooms upstairs an' wait 'til morning to leave."

I considered what she said, but wasn't sure if we could trust her. Maybe we would get the room, and then she would contact a friend or two to attack us.

She continued, obviously sensing my concern, "I saw you come in with Blake. Don't worry. His friends are my friends."

I pulled Jane a step away and whispered, "Can we trust her? After all, if she was going to rob us, she could just as well do it when we were on our way back to the hotel."

Jane nodded and turned back to the young woman. "So how do we go about getting a room? Ah, what did you say your name was?"

"Name's Cookie." She offered her hand, then turned to walk away. "Follow me."

Cookie led us up a flight of stairs and into a room with a heavily stuffed couch and several upholstered chairs. A middle-aged woman who was underdressed and overly made up came into the room. She stared at us quizzically as she asked Cookie if she was bringing in some business.

"Not your usual kind, Ruby," Cookie said, quickly adding, "I'm just trying to keep them safe."

The woman asked us if we had any money, and I told her truthfully, "We've only got a hundred dollars between us."

Ruby said, "Give me fifty and the room's yours for the night—out by seven."

Stupidly I protested, "But . . . that's half of everything we have."
A few months ago I wouldn't have blinked at three times that per

night for a room, and probably would have forked over a lot more in some hotels at a convention.

"I usually make that much in an hour," she said. "Okay. Tonight it's yours. But if you tell a soul, I'll kill you myself." She winked at Cookie and said, "What is it with the strays you bring in?"

Ruby led us down a hall past several rooms. From the sounds coming through the doors, they were obviously occupied by passionately involved couples. Finally, at the end of the hall, she opened the door to a small but clean room. There was a typical hotel bathroom to the left of the entrance. The room was decorated atrociously with a flowered pattern on the wallpaper that matched the bed covering. The bed was king sized and nearly filled the room, leaving no space for chairs.

"Stay here until morning, and don't worry about the seven o'clock thing," she said. "When you leave, pay me whatever you can. But don't worry, the room's yours 'til you go."

"Thanks," Jane and I said in unison.

"I don't know how to thank you enough," I added.

When Ruby left, Jane and I flopped down in the middle of the bed with our clothes on. Jane snuggled her head into my shoulder. I chuckled and commented about the kind of place we were spending the night. Jane turned her head so she could see me, and giggled like a schoolgirl. We laughed again when we saw our reflections in the mirrored tiles above the bed. With a "when in Rome" attitude, we made love. Minutes later, we were sound asleep.

27

When we woke, the curtains were glowing brightly from morning light. I poked Jane and asked what time it was.

She had no idea, but we figured we must be in serious trouble. We had planned on getting up at dawn and sneaking back into our hotel room. I was pretty certain that one of our agents would have checked on us by now and found we were missing. The FBI had probably started a full search, with other agents quietly scouring the area.

That thought both encouraged and worried me.

"They must really be upset with us by now, but what can they do?" Jane said. "We haven't really broken any laws. It's not like we were under arrest."

"And I can't imagine they've connected us to the death of the man who threatened to kill Blake," I said.

Jane was already up and getting dressed. "Let's hope not. But, by now, the agents must know we've sneaked out of the hotel—or they'll think the Guild broke into our room and kidnapped us."

"If they assume the latter, they'll probably widen the search area," I said.

Jane and I got ready to leave as fast as we could. On our way down the stairs we discussed how much we should pay our host. We decided to pay the full fifty dollars she had asked for, even if it wasn't the wisest thing to do given our financial situation. She had been kind enough to give us the room, and we'd had a much better night's sleep than we would have at the hotel. We stopped at the desk and paid, noticing the clock on the back wall—it was almost eleven o'clock. We were in more trouble than I thought.

Jane and I rushed back along the street. As we approached the block of the Hot Spot Hotel, we saw police cars parked in front of the building with their lights flashing. Several ambulances were in the small parking lot, along with other official-looking cars.

We immediately stopped. I looked at Jane and said what we were both thinking: "Either they've assumed the worst about our disappearance, or something awful has happened."

We ducked into the only open restaurant. We sat down at a booth near a corner window where we could see the activity. The window was heavily tinted so, if the activity related to us, we were pretty confident we wouldn't be spotted. Still, we knew we were in a pretty wild neighborhood. It was entirely possible the police presence had nothing to do with us.

We couldn't imagine why Berglund and Christie would have called out so many reinforcements to find us. That would have been counterproductive to their attempt to keep our location secret. We were, according to them, the only witnesses the FBI had to testify against some of the top leaders of the Evil Guild.

As Jane ordered a cup of coffee and a caramel roll, she noticed a television set above the bar. She asked the waitress, "Could you turn the television to a news channel to see what's happening across the street?"

The waitress shrugged. "Sure; go ahead and turn the set to any station you want, but don't expect to find any coverage about what's happening down here." She told us that kind of police activity happened a lot in the neighborhood. "You might get a couple of sentences on the six o'clock news," she said, "but that's all."

I started surfing channels. We were amazed to see that several stations had broken into their regular broadcasting to show images of the same hotel we were looking at. One camera angle even caught a corner of the very restaurant where we were now hiding.

As the television cameras zoomed in, stretchers were carried from the building while the news anchor commented that three FBI agents had been gunned down early that morning. The anchor speculated about a possible relationship between the airport terrorist attack the day before and the agents' death. "The FBI agents may have been protecting two people due to testify against several dangerous members of a secret criminal cult. The same cult may have perpetrated the attack yesterday at the airport." He concluded asking, "And where are these two individuals now?"

"How are they getting the information for these reports?" I asked Jane. "Are they leaks from the FBI—or has the FBI decided to be more open about the case?"

I saw a flash cross Jane's face, and she whispered, "What better way could the Evil Guild use to track us down? They become a source of information to the press, expecting that someone will eventually recognize us and find us for them."

"If that's true, we're in serious trouble," I agreed.

The camera panned the scene again, settling on another reporter who stated, "The names of the dead agents haven't been released yet." The reporter turned the microphone to a hotel employee. "One of our guests said he heard some popping noises around three this morning when he left. Two people, a man and a woman, rushed from the lobby shortly after that."

Jane and I looked at each other. We were both getting the same uneasy feeling. "Are we being set up?" I asked. "The agents who were killed must've been Christie, Berglund, and one we didn't know. We probably saved our lives by going out into the *dangerous* streets."

"At the very least," Jane said, "we're probably in no more danger now than we were under government protection."

We had nearly been killed several times. Somehow the Guild always seemed able to find out where we were and plot our deaths. Now Christie and Berglund were most likely dead. We grieved for them—and for everyone who had given their lives to protect us. It all seemed so unfair.

We continued watching the news, trying to figure out our next move. We evaluated our resources. They were meager: the clothes we were wearing, and now after buying coffee, only about forty dollars. We couldn't survive long on that.

We contemplated giving ourselves up to the FBI and asking for protection, again. But, after everything that had happened in the last twenty-four hours, we didn't seriously consider that a viable or safe option.

Jane pushed the last piece of her caramel roll around her plate, becoming more tense as we watched the news. I felt absolutely alone and hopeless, wondering how things could possibly get worse when we were shocked by the next news flash.

First, a newsroom commentator confirmed what we had already guessed. "The names of the murdered agents have been released. They are Jeannette Christie, Arnold Berglund, and Larry Travis. We are attempting to find out more about their backgrounds. Back to you, Kyle, on location."

A young man standing in front of the Hot Spot's lobby sign nodded as the camera focused on him. He glanced down at a piece of paper in his hand. "From an undisclosed source, we have learned the names of the two missing persons that those three brave agents were protecting. They are George and Jane Mercy, both from the Chicago area. Due to their sudden disappearance corresponding to the time of the agents' deaths, they are currently suspects in the murders. They are considered dangerous."

So the search for us was on. Now both the law *and* the Evil Guild were after us. I was pretty sure that one or both would eventually track us down, and that would be the end of our story. After all, we were sitting in a restaurant directly across the street—we could actually see Kyle from our booth.

"It won't be long and they'll have our photos circulating around the nation. They've already fingerprinted us, so the prints will be available to the police," I said.

"I assume they'll keep following up every lead to find us," Jane said.

Our situation had gone from frustrating to depressing—and deadly. If we eluded the federal manhunt, the Guild would probably find us and torture us to death. If the authorities found us, the Guild would make sure we didn't survive.

We had finished our coffee, but it was a quiet morning so the waitress didn't seem to mind that we were overstaying our service. In fact, she seemed to sense our emotional stress and came around with a second refill. She stayed for a few minutes, watching the news as she leaned against the back of the booth. Casually, she said, "I hope they catch those nutcases. You don't murder three FBI agents and get away with it."

The comment cut deeply. I could tell Jane was seething inside. I decided to subtly object to her quick conclusions. "What if they didn't do it?"

Our waitress gave me a quizzical look and, for a few seconds, I worried that she had seen through us, but her image of two crazed killers must not have matched our appearance. All she said was, "Nah, not likely! They must've done it."

I was amazed at how quickly the assumptions of the news broadcast had been believed. And I was nervous about any gun-happy police officers who might be just as quick to jump to that same conclusion. I was afraid this meant any evidence found from now on would tend toward convicting us—and any evidence to the contrary would be ignored or "missed."

I wasn't blaming the police. It just seemed like, if the news broadcast was correct, their assumptions had been set—and they would focus their energies on finding us guilty. I could only hope that someone from the police force might see through the charade.

I had one other hope, but it was no more likely to be believed. Maybe the FBI would have confidence in us and decide that the Guild for the Knowledge of Good and Evil had committed the murders. They would then look for the right kind of evidence. I wanted to believe there was at least a chance they might consider the Guild to be behind the murders and that we had either escaped or went missing because they captured us.

I felt trapped sitting in the restaurant but where could we turn? I had a quick flashback to my Grand Marais dreams. This time I imagined Jane and I were both in the bottle crashing in the waves of Lake Superior, and the cork looked like it was coming loose. Water was beginning to seep in around the neck. The bottle would soon sink. We were hopelessly doomed.

But then I recalled the key in my more recent dream—the key to the Door to Refreshing Life. I reflected on how I felt it had saved me in the hospital, and I remembered feeling such great hope when I held it.

Where is that key now? Could I grasp its hope again and live through this crisis?

———————

Jane touched my arm, breaking me from my reverie. The waitress had walked far enough away that Jane was able to whisper, "We'd better leave before they televise our photos. Once they do, we won't have a chance of getting out of the area. I think our only hope is to find Blake. We'll just have to trust him. We've nowhere else to go."

"Blake!" I gasped. In all of the excitement, I had forgotten about Blake. Maybe we did have one last chance of escaping.

Jane and I left a two-dollar tip for our waitress in the improbable hope that she would believe our version of the story if she decided we were good tippers, and therefore, good people. The rationale sounded dumb as I looked at our rapidly diminishing funds, but when you have little hope, sometimes you try to create small symbols to stand against the tide of fear threatening to drown you.

We mustered our courage and walked out the front door and down the street in the direction of Blake's pawnshop. As we passed the jazz bar, Cookie whistled from the door and waved at us to come in. We hesitated a moment, but then ducked through the door into the quiet bar. She pulled on Jane's arm, drawing us both up the stairs to the "hotel" where we had stayed. We followed her quickly, walking quietly up the plush steps. At the top, we stepped into a side room.

"You're the couple they're talking about on the television, aren't you?" she said.

"Are we that obvious?" Jane asked as she glanced nervously around.

"No," Cookie said. "But they just showed your pictures on the news—and then I saw you walking down the street."

Jane and I looked at each other as if to say, "So this is it!"

Cookie saw our hopeless looks and said, "I know you didn't do it 'cause you both were here in the bar when it happened. I can testify to that."

Jane and I couldn't help but smile at Cookie's sincerity.

"Cookie, if you decided to testify on our behalf, it might help us—but you might end up dead along with us," I said. "There are some really nasty people trying to kill us. This is just their latest attempt. They've even convinced those trying to keep us safe into believing we're murderers."

"Well, even so, you can't just go out there like nothing's happened. They'll find you!" Cookie said in exasperation.

"Can you get us in touch with Blake? He said he could help us." Jane looked at me like I was crazy, but I couldn't think of anything else we could do but cut straight to the chase.

"I know where to find him," she said. "I'll get him over here."

Cookie led us down the hallway into another small room—her private quarters. "You can stay here for now, but be quiet. I don't want anybody thinking I have someone living with me. If Ruby thought I had a boarder, she'd kick me out."

Jane and I nodded. We settled in while Cookie went out looking for Blake.

About an hour later, Cookie came back into the room with a bag full of supplies, including hair dye, scissors, a fake hairpiece, and several other makeup items you might find in a theater company's dressing room. She had far more makeup than we had ever planned on buying when we left the hotel the night before.

"Blake gave me all of this stuff so you could get out of here undetected."

Jane looked relieved. "So you met up with Blake? How can we ever thank the two of you enough?"

"You're not through this yet," Cookie said. "It was the least I could do. Now get busy and make yourselves look like you belong here."

"When do we meet Blake?" I asked.

"Not 'til dark. Then you're supposed to go down to the bar and wait. Blake'll meet you there."

We had quickly learned that evenings in this neighborhood brought out people who dressed on the eccentric side. With the help of Cookie's supplies we would be able to meet Blake without being noticed.

"I'll leave you two for now to get ready," Cookie said. With her hand on the doorknob to leave, she paused. "I'll be back after awhile. I'll knock before coming in."

The fake, but very real looking, tattoos on the back of my neck and on my arm would make my middle-class identity less apparent. When we were done, if I hadn't seen Jane get ready, I wouldn't have recognized her. Her red hair had turned black. A small cheek tattoo and a fake lip ring made her look pretty tough. After we were made up, dressed up, and had practiced how to act, we sat on the side of the bed and waited.

When Cookie finally came back, she instructed us on how to walk with the kind of casual, self-assured gait that would make us fit in. Cookie's last advice was, "Don't talk much; that's harder t' fake."

Jane seemed to adapt well, but as apprehensive as I was, I wasn't sure I could pull it off. Cookie waved my fears away and assured me, "Don't worry. You'll do jus' fine. You'll hardly be noticed."

"It's the *hardly* part that worries me," I said.

Cookie hesitated. "When I tap on the door three times, come out right away, and go straight down to the bar. Find a table and order something. You might have to wait a while. Blake likes to pick his own time. He might be here quickly, or not 'til closing."

We would have to be careful not to bump into any customers on our way down so that Cookie's part in our makeover and escape was kept hidden. We had to keep her safe.

As we waited for Cookie to scope out the scene, Jane put her head on my shoulder and we held hands. Once again, we faced the possibility of death together. Even more, I feared being arrested and separated from her again. After all, if a jury found us guilty, we would each face death alone.

When the three taps came, I jumped up like I was spring-loaded with anticipation and fear. Jane gave me a quick kiss. She looked like a "tough chick," but her kiss reminded me of all of our good times.

We opened the door to an empty hall and hurried down the three flights of stairs to the jazz bar. The neon sign on the door flashed the words *Jack's Jazzy Jazz*. I tried to remember the right way to casually, but assertively, walk into the bar without attracting attention. We were faking our parts, playing life-or-death roles.

We sat down at a table in the corner and tried to look natural. Jane reminded me of what Cookie had said. "If you're a little scared, but look like you're trying not to show it, you'll probably fit in."

"I guess a tough act is really an attempt to hide fears, prejudices, or suppressed anger," I whispered, leaning close to Jane. All of those qualities were being shown around us in the club. Basically, we tried to blend into the wall, pretending to listen to the jazz, even though my beating heart interrupted the rhythm.

I ordered a drink for myself, and one for Jane. We were getting close to the end of our meager allowance and had eaten nothing all day except for the roll we shared in the restaurant. Our hunger exacerbated our plight. During the rest of the day we had been so active and under stress we had ignored our basic needs. Now we faced the possibility of sitting here for hours. I whispered to Jane, "I'm so hungry I'm afraid my growling stomach will upset the musicians."

The couple at the table next to us left half a small loaf of bread when they got up to leave. Before the wait staff came to clear the table, I grabbed it.

Jane whispered, "Good move."

I split it in two so we each had a little. We had just taken our first bite when the waiter came over to our table, followed by a well-built man. He bent low and told us in a subdued voice "This establishment doesn't allow snitching food from other tables." He apologized, but said this policy was necessary for a "high-class establishment."

I could see the mixture of humiliation and hunger in Jane's face, but I didn't dare blow my tough-guy cover. I wanted to say, "We'll put it back if we can stay," but I didn't figure that line would work.

Instead, I said, "Let's get outta here!" I tried to sound indignant and streetwise, but not so much that the burly bouncer would physically throw us out.

We couldn't alert Cookie of what had happened, because the bouncer followed us all the way out the door and told us he didn't want to see us hanging around. Then he went back in, slamming the door behind him.

Outside on the street, I worried that Blake wouldn't find us.

"At least we hung onto the pieces of bread." Jane smiled, holding up the remnants of her measly dinner.

I was too worried to return her smile.

The street looked scarier than it had the night before, but I hugged Jane in what I thought would look like a kind of tough way and told her, "Let's watch for Blake from the corner."

I wanted more than anything to hold her and comfort her, but I didn't dare show any signs of weakness. We sat on the sidewalk with our backs against a dark brick building and waited.

28

The humid air enveloped us as we tried to blend into the night. I was thankful for our disguises—and for the fact that it wasn't raining. Jane and I took turns watching while the other rested. The bar closed, and we never saw Blake.

"Blake probably has a closet full of disguises of his own, and we didn't recognize him," Jane suggested.

"I think you're right. After all, Cookie got all this stuff from him."

We were alone on the night streets, in a tough neighborhood, with just about everyone searching for us. This wasn't a good time to begin learning how to live as vagabonds. But then, was there ever a good time?

I woke up just as the street lamps were going out and the yellow hues of morning light were casting long shadows down the street. Jane was leaning against a small recess in the building's wall, still asleep. I had slid sideways and was lying on the sidewalk with my head on her lap. Eventually she would wake up, and we would face our first full day among the homeless.

When I shifted slowly and began to stand up, I noticed a burly-looking character in a filthy coat casually walking toward us. Jane was just beginning to open her eyes when he approached and said, "Get off my block while you still can." Jane jumped with a start.

Apparently we were invading his panhandling turf.

He held up a long knife to prove his point. I begged for a couple of minutes to get ourselves together, promising him we didn't want to hang around any longer than we had to. He glared at us, but didn't intrude further as we struggled to adjust ourselves and wander down the street. I think that even he pitied us a little.

After we rounded the corner and were well away from the aggressive beggar, I felt my pocket for my wallet. It was gone! Where the pocket had been, I only felt flapping cloth. Someone must have cut it in the night to steal my wallet. We were now not only homeless, but penniless, and our hunger was becoming unbearable.

When I told Jane my wallet was missing, she cried, "How could you let that happen? How could you?"

I turned my back to her and showed her how my pocket had been neatly sliced open with a sharp blade. Then she realized how dangerous our situation was. Jane grabbed me in her arms. Shaking from emotion and a lack of food, I gained enough composure to whisper to her, "I think we need to find a homeless shelter before tonight."

We continued down the sidewalk with the slow gait of refugees.

After walking around the neighborhood for most of an hour, we saw Cookie across the street. She avoided looking at us as she spoke to a young man who glanced in our direction before he turned and jogged around the corner.

We had walked about two blocks when the same man suddenly popped out of an alley right in front of us, looked up and down the street, and quickly whispered, "Blake sent me. Keep walking until you get to the alley two blocks up. Turn left and walk down it." Then he strode briskly past us.

The command was strange, but Jane and I were relieved that someone was watching out for us. We had been found and, with a little luck, might yet survive our ordeal.

We looked at each other, shrugged our shoulders, and laughed nervously. Satisfied that we once again had hope, we picked up our pace.

Even in daylight, the alley looked dark and foreboding, but hope carried us into its cavernous depths. We continued down the smelly alley until a door swung open in front of us. I was so surprised that I jumped away, pulling Jane after me.

Blake shook his head and chuckled at my fright. He stood in the door with a big toothy grin.

"Come into my office," he said.

We stepped into what appeared to be a dismal warehouse—or the set of a horror movie.

"Nice office," I said.

The space inside looked to be about three stories from floor to ceiling, and stretched the length of the block. A long track with a suspended crane ran down the middle of the building from one end to the other. Several truck bays were visible along the adjacent wall to our right. There were no windows on the side of the building we had entered but, about halfway down, on the side facing the street, large windows filled with dirty glass covered the top half of the wall. Their stark light cast ominous shadows behind the rows of large crates, which filled much of the floor space. At the same time, the light pouring down in dusty streams chased back the darkness, leaving the impression that the light itself had dimension.

Blake didn't say anything else as he led us behind a stack of crates. He walked to an old radio bolted to a heavy support timber. He twisted the knob back and forth until he found a noisy rock station. Then he turned on a fan, which added to the noise level. I had the distinct feeling he didn't want our discussion to be overheard. I could easily believe spies might be hiding in the mysterious shadows, waiting to discover our deep secrets.

Blake offered us a couple of small wooden crates to sit on. Jane and I were thankful for the rustic courtesy, but our greatest need was a bathroom.

Blake must have noticed that we were uncomfortable. Before I could ask, he said, "There's a bathroom along the wall, about ten yards to your right. You can't miss it."

Jane and I rushed in the direction he was pointing.

The bathroom was built out from the wall, and we found it easily. It wasn't much, just a small room with a musty old toilet and a tiny sink, which the door just missed when it opened. While it wasn't particularly clean, I had seen worse in gas stations. A single bare lightbulb hung from a cord.

Jane went in first. I stood outside looking around the dusty old warehouse as I waited. After a couple of minutes, I heard a shocked groan from inside. I asked through the door if there was a problem.

"The water's cold!" Jane shouted.

I laughed. "Quit complaining. A few minutes ago we didn't have *any* water."

Finally, it was my turn to sit on the crusty old stool with my knees only inches from the chipped pastel-green wall. Afterward, I tried to clean up as much as I could with the icy water.

Feeling a bit better and marginally cleaner, we walked back to where Blake was patiently waiting.

As soon as we sat down, Blake handed each of us a can of juice and a couple of granola bars. "Here's breakfast. I figured you'd be pretty hungry by now." Jane and I wasted no time in devouring the meager fare.

"It's time to get down to business," Blake said after giving us time to eat our breakfast. "First, do you have any money to cover the costs of your new identities?"

Panic set in. We had nothing, absolutely nothing. We were back to where we had been before Blake had tracked us down, except now we were a little cleaner and not as hungry. Our momentary delusion of a new future had been shattered.

Jane and I responded in almost perfect unison, "No! Nothing."

I shrugged. "Everything we had was stolen last night while we slept."

I could tell Jane was doing her best to look calm, but I knew she was close to breaking down. I probably looked the same.

Sensing our obvious agitation, Blake said, "I didn't mean to frighten you. I was just checking. I mean . . . I owe you my life. That's worth a lot to me, so don't worry, we'll make this work. I also know you're innocent. You deserve a break."

I grasped Jane's hand and squeezed it.

Blake said, "I don't have any identities in my bag right now. It could easily take several weeks to put together something credible enough to stand up to the scrutiny you'll face. You're in serious trouble, and that demands *verifiable* aliases.

"Then again, with lots of luck, it might take as little as a few days, but I don't want to get your hopes up. It'll more likely take a month."

"A month?" I gasped.

Blake shook his head and added, "Well, as I've said, sometimes an identity will fall into place, but I can't promise anything. For now, you'll have to keep living on the street. It won't be easy, but you can do it."

This time Jane squeezed my hand before she spoke. "How? How can we? For how long?"

"I'll do what I can to help," Blake said. "I should be able to move you somewhere safer in a week or so. Today, you'll need to get to the mission in time for their evening meal and then go right to the homeless shelter if you're going to have a place to sleep tonight. I'll get you some temporary names—of missing homeless people that can't easily be traced. As long as you don't get into any trouble, the names should work."

Jane and I had already experienced one scary night. I looked around the warehouse and asked, "Isn't there somewhere you can keep us?"

"Not for a few days, and not that's as safe as the streets, but I'll find a place soon," he said.

When I had thought of living on the street as a way to escape a few days ago, it seemed impossible. Now, after our recent experiences, we were scared to death—but what could we do? We had no choice but to accept Blake's offer—it was either that or turn ourselves in and take our chances with the FBI. At this point, I figured the FBI was the more dangerous option. They were, after all, still looking for us as the main suspects for the murders of their three agents. There was always a chance they would figure out we couldn't have committed the crime and put together another protection program for us.

But that was a risk I wasn't ready to take at the moment. Plus, their protection hadn't been too successful so far.

"Okay. What do we need to do?"

———

Blake seemed to understand our fears and the difficulties we were facing. It was almost as if he knew from experience what was going through our minds.

"First, you'll have to give up just about everything," Blake said. "You no longer exist. Where you came from and all contacts with your past are terminated as of right now. When I say terminated, I mean *done*—you can't have contact with *anyone* from your past. All your energy must be directed to surviving in the future. You need to constantly watch out for yourselves. Never carry a wallet. Never end up on Crazy Clide's block again. I heard how you got chased away from there." He looked up and saw the questions on our faces. "Don't ask me how I heard. The streets are full of ears and mouths. The stories spread quickly."

Blake continued, "I recommend not drinking alcohol, but always have just a hint of the smell on you. Remember, you're supposed to be down on your luck, with too few skills, and too many problems to keep you from finding regular work."

"On the plus side," he said, "it's summer, so the weather is decent for being outside. And the mission is a few blocks from here. You'll be able to eat one good meal a day."

Jane looked just as scared as I felt. How would our relationship fare under the stress of living on the street, spending our nights in a homeless shelter, and eating only one meal a day?

I reached over and clasped Jane's hand to reassure her how much I cared for her. "We can do this. Okay?"

Jane nodded. "We'll have to, won't we?"

Blake stopped briefly and stared around the warehouse.

Pointing to his left he said, "The Blessed Hope for the Homeless Mission—everyone calls it the "Be Hop" for short—is three blocks that way, but you'll have to listen to a little preaching and gospel singing before you get to eat. Sometimes the singing is pretty good. Most just tolerate the preaching, but a few always seem to respond by converting to their beliefs, or as they call it, 'being born again.'"

I asked, "Isn't there any other place to eat? Can't we go to a restaurant?"

"No," Blake said. "You have to get immersed into street life right away. After you eat at the Be Hop, you can go to the shelter for the night. The Caring Friends Homeless Shelter is six blocks east of the Be Hop and has accommodations for married couples and families. The rooms are small and the walls paper thin, but if you get there early enough, you should be able to stay together."

He added, "I know this won't be easy. You'll be told to leave the shelter every morning unless the weather is really awful. You'll never have quite enough to eat, and you'll have to share a community bathroom with dozens of other people. During the day you'll need to take care of yourselves however you can. But I'm confident the two of you will manage."

Blake lectured us for a half hour on how to survive; then he began asking questions. He wanted to know our strengths and weaknesses. He wanted to know what we liked to do—and what we absolutely hated. In short, he wanted to know everything he could about our personal lives.

"I need to know each of you well enough to make new identities to fit so perfectly you'll be able to transition into your new life with ease," Blake said. "On the other hand, we also have to construct your identities in new and different directions so you won't turn up in journals or go to conventions where people from your past could recognize you."

I was impressed with his thoroughness.

"Your jobs must be absolutely unpretentious," he said. "You don't want any publicity and you can't do anything that might call attention to yourselves. At the same time, I want to make your identities fit you well enough to be interesting and challenging so you won't accidentally slip back into your old patterns and habits."

He stopped and thought for a moment.

Jane whispered to me, "How will we ever get through this?"

Almost like he understood our fear, Blake said, "I know this will be hard. I never said it would be easy, but I want you to be as happy as possible—and not be afraid of making new friends.

"On the other hand—and I cannot tell you this enough times: you'll never again be able to contact any of your old friends or even mention your previous lives. Even harder, you must never contact your relatives—especially not your parents. Whoever you're running from will constantly monitor them."

We had heard this from Agent Berglund, but the implications hit even harder this time. Jane and I looked at each other, too shocked to respond.

I envisioned my dad, with his graying hair and my mom, with her black hair curling over her shoulders. My parents were almost always dressed up. They were both professionals who had worked in downtown Milwaukee. They saw their morning objective as getting my brother Douglas and me off to school moments before they rushed to their respective offices downtown.

I recalled lots of evening meals together, nighttime hugs, and prayers before bed. I had never been close to them, but to be told I could never contact them again was a blow. I had always thought of my life in contrast to theirs, but I now realized how much I still loved them. Even though I hadn't talked to them in months, I realized how much I would miss them.

I looked at Jane. She had the same blank stare as I did. I assumed she was thinking the same things about her parents. This was probably even harder for her because she had always enjoyed visiting them whenever she got the chance.

And it wasn't just family. We would be losing all of our friends, too. Yet, it dawned on me, we had most likely already lost them when the news went national. Most of them were probably saying: "They seemed like such a friendly couple. We had no idea they would turn into such brazen murderers. What made them snap?" Inside, they might be saying, "Boy, I hope I never snap like that!" At the same time they would sound condescendingly righteous, letting the world know this would never happen to them.

Blake asked question after question, but never wrote anything down. "What isn't written down can't be traced," he explained.

He not only asked questions about *what* we liked and disliked, he followed up with questions about *why* we liked or didn't like those things. When he asked about hobbies, he wanted to know if we were members of any groups that pursued that hobby, if we had friends with the same hobby, and how we felt when we couldn't do that hobby.

I told Blake, "I love photography, but I'm not a member of any photo clubs or organizations."

"Good," Blake said.

"I love to paint," Jane said, "and I've had a couple of shows at the university where I teach; I mean where I taught."

"We'll work on that," Blake said, "but that might pose a greater problem. Future shows could be monitored for paintings that look like yours. Computers can now find styles that match. If you decide to keep painting, you'll either need to change your style or avoid shows."

Blake continued with his interview. "What restaurants do you like? Why do you like them? Did you go there alone or with friends? What did you usually order? Are there other restaurants you don't like? Why?"

The range of questions included jobs, friends, vacations, what we did in our spare time, and even how we met.

Finally he said, "You'd better hit the streets for the night so you can make it to dinner at the mission and find a place at the shelter."

Before we left, he gave us each a shot glass of whiskey, telling us, "Take a sip and spill the rest on your clothes so you have an odor of alcohol on you." We did as we were told, none-too-happy about the taste—or the smell.

He gave us ten one-dollar bills each and said, "Always keep the money in various parts of your clothing." Before he opened the door, he gave us a couple of energy bars for some quick calories and said, "Plan to come back here in two days to answer more questions."

Then he sent us out to face our uncertain life on the street.

"Well, I guess this is it," I whispered to Jane, hugging her before we exited the alley.

"We can do this," Jane whispered in my ear.

"Yes, let's get on with it."

We walked at a steady, unhurried, pace down the street in the direction of the mission, following the advice Blake had given us: "Don't look too determined. You need to look like you've done this before."

29

Jane and I barely got through the doors of the Be Hop Mission before they were closed behind us. I whispered to Jane, "It looks like we can leave anytime, but we can't come back in after we leave."

We would be forced to sit through a church service before eating, which in itself didn't make us feel very good about our situation—or ourselves.

We stank. We were stiff and tired. We were hungry. And now we were going to be subjected to singing and preaching before we could eat our first real meal in two days. And we would have to go through this every night before we got our free dinner. Somehow, the meal didn't seem quite so free anymore.

There were no seats left, so we stood in a back corner of the room. At first I was pleased we could slip in unobtrusively, but then I overheard someone complain that by the time we got through the food line there would only be the "scuz crap" left on the bottom of the kettle. I felt nauseated just thinking about *scuz crap*. Would I sit through the whole program and still not get a decent meal?

The service started quickly with a kind of religious pop music, sort of a mix of gospel and jazz. I was surprised by how much it mirrored what we had heard in the jazz club. I hadn't attended church since high school and had pretty much tuned out years before that. I wondered if the singers were sincere, or if this was more of a show. I looked around and decided these people wouldn't come down to a mission like this to impress anyone like us.

I had to admit, the program wasn't as boring as I thought it might be, and we found out there wasn't going to be any preaching that night. Instead, they announced that a couple of people who had survived homelessness would share their testimonies about becoming Christians and moving on to successful lives.

While walking back and forth across the narrow stage, the first speaker talked at length about having built a successful career in finance—and his misplaced faith in money and wealth. He cried as he explained his loss of self-control. Gambling, drinking, and drugs had become his life. He said, "There was a depressing moment when I realized I'd completely ruined myself. I'd lost everything, including my home, my family, my friends, and all the wealth and fortune I had acquired. I ended up sleeping in an alley.

"When I'd hit absolute bottom with nowhere to turn, I thought seriously about suicide," he said. "I was trying to figure out how to make my death dramatic enough to get on the news. Then I heard the message of the love of Jesus. It didn't matter how low I'd sunk. Jesus loved me and would forgive me. I could begin again, guilt free."

He continued, his voice rising, "My born again experience began when I accepted Jesus. With Christ as my savior, and the Bible as my guide, I've rebuilt my life. Through God's grace, I am saved. I can testify to the saving love of Jesus Christ."

"One down," I whispered to Jane, "and one to go."

The second speaker told how Christ had redeemed her from the guilt of being a sexually abusive parent's victim. She told us more details than I would have liked about how she had struggled because of what her dad did to her. She said, "I quit school at sixteen and ended up living on the streets. A guy who seemed really nice offered me a place to stay if I would work for him. He convinced me to become a prostitute to pay rent and keep myself off the streets." She described how demeaned and scared she was.

"Then, one day," she said, "I heard a story of how Jesus had forgiven a prostitute." She explained how she had, over time, dealt with her sexual issues through the love of Jesus. She had gone back to school with the help of someone she had met at the mission. Now she was working as a nursing assistant in a hospital where she ministered to women who had been abused.

Their testimonies were compelling. I was truly amazed at how their conversions had changed their lives. I couldn't argue with their success, unless I called them liars. They seemed sincere and were likely telling the truth, but I still couldn't believe there was a God who cared for each one of us. The power and scale of such a God seemed impossible to me.

If they believed so strongly in their religious experiences that they changed their lives, I couldn't blame them for wanting to tell the world. Their "conversions" must have had tremendous impacts, but I thought the experience of the whole mission meeting was sort of like watching a patent medicine show. There was always the chance that some people would be cured if they believed strongly enough that tea and spice were medicines. I just couldn't buy the medicine these folks were offering.

———————

After the meeting, I looked around the room at the men and women, and even saw a few children. Some looked like they hadn't bathed in a month. I felt dirty, itchy, and sticky because I hadn't showered in three days. I whispered to Jane, "Are we too clean to eat here?"

Jane glared at me and said, "Shut up. Get into the line and hope the food isn't gone before we get there."

As I watched Jane, I sensed the depth of her despair. We had no choice but to face the indignities of being fed as homeless people. Our only hope was to stay unnoticed street people for now and wait for our new identities.

Finally, we reached the front of the line and our plates were filled with some kind of goulash. We were also handed a dinner roll and a glass of milk. The meal wasn't much, but it looked to us like a feast in a five-star restaurant.

Jane and I sat facing each other in the cafeteria-style room. Jane ate everything on her plate but still looked distraught. I didn't need to ask her what was wrong—just about everything was. I touched her hand and she smiled back with only the slightest hint of the old spark she'd had when we were living in our own house, driving two cars, and going to jobs we liked. *If I had only overlooked that elegant little book in the library . . .*

I began to think about what we had left behind. *What will happen to our cars, our house, and our jobs?* I suppose the bank would repossess the house and cars—if they hadn't already. Someone else was probably editing *my* manuscripts.

I was saved from my depressing self-pity by an announcement that the dining room would close in ten minutes. When I looked around, I saw only one homeless family and a few other people left. A couple of them were asleep. One of the mission staff was waking them. He had an imposing presence that was hard to challenge. I wouldn't want to tangle with him, but he also appeared to have a gentle personality. He would sit down beside those who were sleeping before shaking them awake. It was almost like he considered them important customers, or even friends. Maybe they were.

Jane and I were encouraged by his kindness, and we left the mission with a hint of optimism.

Our optimism would last only a few minutes. As we stepped onto the street, the same burly mission worker approached us. "You don't quite fit here, do you?"

"What do you mean?" Jane asked.

"Well, you look like a lot of the people here, but you're too polite, for one. Second, you're too clean."

Too clean? I felt too dirty.

He continued, "Then, too, you look like you're going somewhere. At least you act like you're hungry all right, and homeless for now, but you don't look like you fit on the street scene. You got something going for you. You're not gonna be lifers here, are you?"

I suppose the comment should have encouraged me, but it showed that our act wasn't good enough. We were too transparent. If the wrong person saw through our facade, we were done for. It was only a matter of time; would it be hours or days?

I smiled at him weakly, and he only nodded a farewell as we stepped into the dim light of the street and turned in the direction of the homeless shelter. He yelled at us as we walked down the street, "I have a feeling that God's looking for you, and he will find you!"

The only words that stood out to me were *will find you*. They were terrifying words, a pronouncement of doom.

Who will find us? I thought.

Did this man know about us? Could he even be a friend of Blake's who was trying to communicate a message to be extra careful? Or was he just an evangelistic missionary trying to sell his religion?

Or should I add God to the list of those who are trying to find us? So now the police, the FBI, the Guild, and God, are searching for Jane and me?

Whatever he meant, I decided to be more careful. I also tried to shuffle and stagger a little more. Jane and I decided that we shouldn't walk together because they were looking for the two of us. We split up, but kept within sight of each other, as we hobbled down the street to the "homeless hotel."

Jane arrived at the shelter a few minutes ahead of me and was let in. As I approached, I had a nightmarish thought that I had lost her. I wished that we had decided to stay together, but I knew that if we were confronted by any of our pursuers, we would have wished otherwise. It was a cruel choice. I had to force myself to keep shuffling along like the world had pushed me down and I had no future.

The door to the shelter was less than half a block away. I felt like it would take a lifetime to get there, as I concentrated on taking the next step, then the next.

Then, I caught my toe on a crack in the sidewalk as I approached the entrance and, for a moment, my shuffling act looked real. In a moment of despair, I felt myself plummeting forward. I hit the sidewalk with a thud, and I was sure I must have broken something. I had a momentary flashback to the robber I had tackled a couple of nights earlier. While his fall had been fatal, I was able to roll over and sit up.

I wanted to check all of my limbs, but I decided that I shouldn't act too quickly or look too concerned. I was supposed to be somewhat inebriated and anesthetized by alcohol. I did feel my face, my fingers edging around a major sidewalk burn on my cheek, and when I felt my nose, it was bleeding. I mustered all of my courage to stand up. Now I was legitimately more than a little wobbly on my feet.

The door was right in front of me. I pushed it open and stumbled in.

I scanned the room for Jane, but Cookie was the only person I recognized. I was surprised and relieved to see her there. She came over, and said, "I'm so sorry, but the place is full. You'll have to leave."

I whispered, verging on a whine, "But . . . Jane?"

Cookie hushed me and nodded her head toward two police officers who were questioning one of the workers.

She smiled sadly and whispered, "She's fine. Don't worry, but you better get out of here! It's a warm night and there's an abandoned office building three blocks from here." She nodded in the direction. "You should be able to find some shelter there, but don't tell anyone I told you."

I was stunned. I wanted to protest, but knew I couldn't cause a disturbance because of the police, so I said nothing. My momentary hesitation gave Cookie a chance to look at my face and she gave a slight gasp.

"Wait a minute," she said as she briskly walked into an office. She came out with some sterile wipes and gave them to me. She also gave me a small pack of about a dozen aspirin that she said came from a supply donated to the shelter. "Sorry, this is the best I can do. You've got to go."

To emphasize the point, a large security guard opened the door for me, and Cookie turned her attention to another of the many lost street people who were seeking shelter.

I didn't need to pretend to stagger any more. As I was exiting, a police officer was also leaving. He looked at my scraped cheek and bloody nose. Even though it hurt like hell, it also disfigured my face, and he didn't appear to recognize me as one of the wanted persons he was probably looking for.

His distraction, however, caused me to stumble on the first step. He caught my arm and helped me maneuver the rest of the way down to the sidewalk. I started to stagger away from him, but he took me firmly by the arm, leading me to his police car.

I shook with fear, worried that he had identified me. My mind was telling me to bolt and run, but just possibly, he had some other reason for his actions. Trying to get away would alert him that I feared being arrested and probably wasn't as drunk as I appeared. He would then investigate me more thoroughly, and I would be doomed.

He frisked me for I don't know what: weapons, booze, drugs? With surprising care, he helped me into the back of the patrol car. I dreaded every moment, but I had to continue to play the part. I feared that he might test my alcohol level, but he seemed convinced that I was inebriated.

The ten-minute drive to the police station was agonizing. I wasn't sure I would get out alive. He had to have a photo of me. As soon as we got into the light, I feared he would recognize my face. However, when the cell door locked, all he said was, "You're lucky, you get a free night at Sobriety Inn."

A couple of other vagrants in my cell laughed—either at his comment or at me. I went to the corner bunk and sat down. My face still burned from the fall, so I wasn't in any mood for conversation. I lay down and rolled over with my face to the wall, my injured cheek exposed to air. I tried not to move because every time I twisted my neck or opened my mouth I wanted to scream.

I lay there for probably an hour, unable to sleep because of the pain before I remembered the aspirin and sterile wipes Cookie had given me. I didn't remember the policeman taking them from me when he frisked me. *Are they still in my pocket?*

By some luck and carelessness—or compassion—they hadn't been removed during the search. Perhaps the police officer had seen Cookie give them to me, and thought I needed them. I don't know why, but I hoped they might bring a little relief from my agony.

When I dabbed my scrape with the wipe, it stung, but the coolness was also refreshing. I was too thirsty to swallow the aspirin without water so I looked around. I saw a sink in the corner and paper cups in a dispenser. I filled one with water. I had just popped an aspirin into my mouth and swallowed it when one of the prisoners grabbed me by the throat. He flung me against the wall. I froze in panic.

"Give me the drugs!" he demanded.

I held out my hand, and he took the aspirin, stared at it, and said, "Aspirin? Who the shit tries to smuggle aspirin into jail?"

The other prisoner stuck up his middle finger at me to emphasize his disappointment, but then said, "Let him go. He's not worth getting in trouble over."

The thug who was holding me threw me aside, slapping my bruised cheek.

I yelled in pain, and he grabbed me again saying, "If you scream one more time, we'll all be in trouble! Now shut up."

I quickly lay down and remained quiet in spite of the pain. It would be a long night.

30

I woke early the next morning to the sound of a police officer checking the cells. My body was so stiff that I could hardly bend my knees. My face felt like a sledgehammer had hit it broadside.

The cocky officer told me it was time to leave and I should be thankful for the free lodging. He jostled me out of the cell and through the door of the station, laughing when I tripped over the door ledge on my way out.

"Still not sober?" he jeered.

He was the antithesis of the policeman who had brought me in. On the positive side, he also hadn't recognized me as the fugitive they were looking for, and after my confrontation with my cellmates, I had slept some. Maybe the pain from the slap I received, while intolerable at first, had numbed me to the milder pain later.

In the morning light, my face throbbed with every beat of my heart. Looking in a dark window, I stared at my reflection and barely recognized myself. *No wonder the police couldn't identify me!*

As much as I hurt, the pain had probably been worth it. The scrape, the large area of black and blue skin, and the puffiness of both cheeks disguised me more effectively than my makeup. My red nose probably helped, too.

I shuffled down the street toward the homeless shelter, hoping to find Jane. I no longer needed to act my homeless part. My face and body hurt so much that I could hardly walk. Every step was agonizing, but I had to keep moving to limber up. I was nearing the shelter and still hadn't seen Jane. I worried about what she would think when she saw me, but first, I had to find her. I needed her comfort, and I wanted to snuggle up to her in some quiet corner of a park.

I saw Cookie emerge from behind the shelter. I wasn't sure she would recognize me, but she walked in my direction. As she passed, she slipped me a small note taped to the back of a fifty-cent coin. She smiled indifferently, but whispered, "Leave here now, and read the note later."

I felt a cold fear descend. *Could something have happened to Jane?*

My life now revolved around a small note taped to the back of a coin. I wanted to run, but my body and fear kept my shuffle slow and deliberate. I desperately wanted to know what the note said, but worried the words might crush me under a weight of despair. On the other hand, they might tell me where Jane was hiding. I shuffled toward an alley that looked like it harbored doom in its narrow depths.

When I had hobbled a short distance into its dreariness, I gingerly sat down beside a garbage dumpster. I turned the coin over and carefully removed the note. It could be the last touch point I had with Jane, or it could tell me she was just around the corner. I held my breath. Once I opened the note, I faced a new crisis. I had walked from a bright street into a dark alley, but as my eyes adjusted the small precise handwriting slowly became readable.

"Police searching everywhere. Jane OK. Don't be seen together. Couples searched, questioned. Don't attend meeting tonight. Contact you soon. Destroy note!!!"

I was alone again; so terribly alone. I felt like I was a yo-yo and Jane was the hand. I would be snapped up to her. Then, just when we thought we could make a new life together, I would be flung away. My only hope lay in the power of the string to snap me back to her when I had reached the distant end.

I read the note again before I tore it into tiny pieces. When I was done tearing and tossing pieces here and there, I had only one word left in my hand. On a tiny scrap of paper the word *together* remained intact. I stared at the word for a long time. Finally, I held that piece up to the wind and it was gone, but its image lingered like an etching on my brain.

An hour or more passed before I decided I would walk back to the mission. I might at least see Jane from a distance, but if the note was true—and I had little doubt it was—I would hardly even dare glance at her. A more immediate reason for returning was to see if they could give me any medical help.

Though I was beginning to feel a little more limber, I continued to move slowly with a slight stagger. As I approached the mission, I saw a police car in front of the entrance. I wasn't sure what to do because Jane and I had been there earlier—together. Would anyone remember seeing us? Dare I tempt fate by walking into the mission and asking for medical help for my face, when my injuries were my best disguise?

I decided to wait until the police left, but I couldn't just stand here. That would be asking for attention, so I shuffled on past.

I still had the ten dollars Blake had given me hidden in my shoes. It was almost noon, and I was incredibly hungry, so I walked toward a small corner grocery store. Then I reminded myself that I was supposed to be an alcoholic and decided to visit a liquor store instead. I walked along the street watching several store entrances to see if my fellow wanderers went into any of them. Most went into a liquor store on the next block and came out carrying bottles of, I assumed, cheap wines and whiskeys. I decided that I should go there and buy a bottle. If nothing else, the contents would help ease the pain in my face.

The store, in fact, did have a lot of inexpensive liquors. I settled on a flask of whiskey, made my purchase, and left. The store gave me an uneasy feeling. I had the impression that the clerk believed I was worth no more than the cheap whiskey I had purchased.

A police officer watched me as I walked out of the store. I felt that I had made the right decision to buy the whiskey, although it meant I was nearly broke, with only four dollars and some loose change in my pocket. I walked slowly down the street to an alley that led away from the mission. I had little hope of getting a place for the night, but I remembered the old warehouse Cookie had told me about. That would have to do.

I took a sip of the whiskey to look the part of a bum as I slipped into the alley.

While my scraped and swollen face was keeping me from being identified as George Mercy, I was scared it might become infected. I remembered old war movies where whiskey had been used as an antiseptic, so as soon as I got into the alley, I poured some of the whiskey into my hand and rubbed it on my injured face. It burned like hell when it touched the raw scrapes, and it took a lot of willpower not to scream in pain.

After all that, it better work.

I hadn't shaved in days, and the last time I had washed my face was in the warehouse. My whole body itched, I wanted a bath, and the day looked like it might be hot and steamy.

I took another shot of the cheap whiskey to feel its warmth slide down my throat. It was a false feeling, but it provided some comfort from the pain, both physically and emotionally. This was a dangerous way to deal with reality. I began to understand how easily I could lose my equilibrium and give in to this fake substitute for hope.

I started walking in the direction of the mission when I saw a police officer approaching. I thought about turning around and walking away, but decided such a move might look suspicious. I kept moving forward with a stagger that was only slightly exaggerated, and I hoped he would let me continue past without recognizing me. There were far too many cops around, even for such a rough neighborhood. I was pretty certain that Cookie was right: if Jane and I were seen together, we wouldn't stand a chance.

I didn't look up as he approached. I concentrated on continuing my unsteady pace, acting my part now with a lot of stiff muscles to help me be convincing. Seeing his feet approach right in front of me, I tried to sidestep him. In the process, I stumbled sideways. The police officer reached out to help steady me. Once I was solidly on my feet, he pulled a couple of photos out of his shirt pocket.

I feared this was going to be the end. All he had to do was see my photo to identify me. I was sure I was done for.

Instead, he held the two photos out for me to examine. "Have you seen either of these people?" he asked.

I stared at the pictures, taking time to squint at each one. Could those photos really have been Jane and me? The people in the photo looked so clean and healthy.

I remembered the spring day only a couple of years earlier when a photographer friend from the office came with Jane and me for a Saturday picnic beside Lake Michigan. He brought his camera and spent the better part of an hour taking photos of us in the park and along the lake. Some were mystical soft-focus ones. Others were adventuresome and fun shots of Jane and me running along the beach or climbing rocks. A few were perfectly focused head and shoulder photos with the lake behind us. These photos were from that series, and mine would have been an excellent photo to use to identify me, except that now I looked like I had been on the street for years because of my injured face.

I tried to stay calm.

"Nope, haven't seen 'em," I said with a slur.

"Has there been anyone new in the neighborhood?" he asked.

"Don't know. Always somebody new and somebody disappearing," I replied. I hoped this answer would end my interrogation and I could leave quickly.

"What I'm asking is this: Have you seen anybody strange or different around here in the last couple of days?" he continued, attempting to press me for information.

I felt like he sensed he was close to getting some answers, almost like he subconsciously recognized me and was trying to keep me talking until he figured out he was looking right at his suspect.

All I said was, "Sorry," as I shrugged my shoulders.

He studied me for a while longer, like he was trying to match the photo up with my swollen face. Then he continued down the street.

I couldn't stay hidden in plain sight much longer. In a few days my face would start to heal. The swelling would go down and my natural disguise would begin to disappear.

I reflected on the man who had stopped me at the mission. If he were asked, he could immediately point me out as someone new—someone who didn't fit in. I decided that I didn't dare go back, but I knew I needed to eat at least one meal a day or I would starve.

Jane didn't have my natural injured disguise, so I was worried they might have already found her. I was reassured, however, because the police had asked if I recognized *either* of the people, meaning she must still be free. I wanted to walk around the neighborhood to try to see her, but reasoned her best chance of surviving this mad hunt for us would be for me to put some distance between us. I turned and walked away. Our whole world was shattered. Nothing remained but despair.

———————

As the day wore on, I realized there was nowhere I could just sit down for a while and relax. All I could do was walk. I walked past the jazz bar where Jane and I had waited for Blake. I continued on past the hotel where the agents were murdered. I must have looked absolutely forlorn and pathetic because, as I stumbled along, a man stopped me and handed me five bucks. In my old life, I would never have given a bum on the street five dollars. I had always assumed they would just drink the money away. My sense of pride took over, and I turned to my generous patron and said, "Thanks, I don't deserve this."

The man turned and faced me. "That's exactly why I gave it to you."

I realized it was the same person I had talked to at the mission. *How can this be happening? I stayed away from the mission to avoid him.*

I had no choice but to go along with him, so I asked, "What do you mean by, 'That's exactly why I gave it to you?'" It was a dumb question. I knew that as soon as I had said it. I should never have asked an open-ended question. It could only lead to a discussion, and all I wanted to do was to run and hide.

"Because, that's what someone else did for me—and it changed my life," he explained.

"What do you mean?" I said, realizing I had again asked a leading question—and instantly regretted it. Perhaps there was something interesting about this guy. Or maybe it was my journalistic background. Whatever it was, it was pulling me into a deeper discussion than I wanted.

"Jesus died for me so that I might live," he replied. "I didn't deserve it but . . ."

I cut him off, saying, "Quit the religious talk. I grew up going to church. I know that most people who say they're Christians aren't exactly looking reality in the face." Reaching out my hand with the five dollars, I said, "Here, take your money. I don't want to owe you anything."

"Keep it," he said. "You don't owe me anything, but if you ever want to talk, you can get a hold of me at the mission. Just ask for Buddy. Everyone knows who I am. And don't worry, I haven't— and won't—tell the cops you're new around here. I'm a pretty good judge of character after working here twenty years. Even if you were the one they were looking for, you probably didn't murder anyone. Course I'm not saying I think you're the one they're looking for, only that you're new and don't fit in with most of the people who come to the mission; though you fit better today than you did yesterday."

He turned and walked briskly away in the direction of the mission, while I folded the bill and stuck it in my shoe.

31

I continued walking away from the mission, the homeless shelter—and Jane. My body hurt, and my head felt like it was going to explode. My stomach was so empty I imagined a black hole was sucking the life out of me, but I had five dollars again, plus the four dollars left from the liquor store. This time I was going to use it to get something to eat. There was a small storefront sub sandwich shop across the street that looked inviting. *A sub and a soft drink would taste great about now.*

I spent everything I had on the sandwich and drank water. I was broke again, after eating what would likely be the only meal I would have all day.

Eating alone in a bustling fast-food restaurant can be extraordinarily depressing. I missed having Jane to talk to—or even just having her sitting next to me.

While I was eating, I watched the noon news and saw our photos being broadcast. How could I continue to hide with the kind of search they were doing—even as well disguised as I was by my injuries? I was shocked when a reporter announced a $5,000 reward for information leading to our arrest. She concluded her story by saying, "If you spot either of these people, call the police immediately. Do not confront them. They are considered armed and dangerous."

That, of course, was preposterous. Jane and I had planned to purchase a gun after our house was broken into, but I wasn't the kind of person who would shoot anyone except in self-defense.

I reflected on the implications of owning a handgun in my present situation. What if I were caught with one? I might be in even greater danger. Anyone would assume I was the dangerous murderer being shown on the news and shoot first.

Still, I couldn't deny I had killed a man. I couldn't argue that I would never take any actions leading to someone's death, though I could point out it had been a defensive move. I could say it wasn't intentional and explain that I wasn't trying to kill him. I might even state emphatically that it was justified given the circumstances. On the other hand, I could never again say I was free from the weight of having ended someone's life.

I experienced the same anguish for the hundredth time, wishing I could go back in time and replace the book, walk away from the library, and re-enter a normal life with Jane. No matter how hard I tried, sooner or later, I had to face up to my actions and move on.

But could I? I still felt the draw of the book and a sense of anger at being separated from its power in my life.

I finished my meal, hoping no one was watching the television too closely. As I was leaving, I noticed the clerk staring at me for a fraction of a second longer than she had to. She was probably only shocked by my injuries, but all someone had to do was think, "Isn't that the person the police are trying to find?" and my life would be over.

I was ready to bolt from the restaurant, but I mustered all of my courage and walked out as casually as possible. I even maintained my street-person slow shuffle. Once out of sight of the window, I increased my pace, still trying not to draw attention to myself.

I turned into the first alley I saw, expecting to hear police sirens any minute. The shadows of the alley looked like inviting places to hide, but I wanted to put more space between the restaurant and myself.

I kept moving. I shuffled across streets and hurried through alleys. I occasionally walked up a street so that I wouldn't be traveling in a straight line.

The scenery changed. I didn't recognize where I was. The apartments and shops began to look more upscale. I felt safer, but at the same time became more nervous because I felt like I stood out. I still needed to move on, so I began to weave a path at an angle from the route I had come. I was thoroughly lost, hoping only to find a neighborhood where I could blend in.

As I went forward, I realized I looked even more out of place in an even nicer neighborhood. I was afraid that sooner or later someone would notice me, and that would trigger my arrest.

I began to move back in the general direction from where I assumed I came. I hoped no one would call the cops on me before I got out of the neighborhood. Gradually, I found myself in a locale where I didn't look so out of place, but I still didn't recognize any landmarks.

I stumbled behind a row of small shops and rested. As I sat in my secluded spot, I could hear police sirens. I doubted they were blowing the sirens in search of me, but their incessant noise reminded me that I was being hunted. My only hope for eluding them was how disfigured, bloated, and scraped my face looked. The photo they had shown on the news broadcast—while I would rather they hadn't broadcast any picture at all—was actually an asset. I looked so young and wholesome. The past months had aged my appearance, and my present predicament made me look like crap.

———————

I don't know how long I slept, but when I opened my eyes, it was night. I was startled when I heard noises in the garbage can next to me. My fears were confirmed when a large fuzzy shape ran across my hand. I jumped, knocking the lid off the can, causing a loud clanging of metal, first against the building, and then on the pavement. I heard more scurrying all around me, driving me into a kind of frenzy.

I would have run away if I could have seen where I was going. Instead, I froze and didn't move a muscle for several minutes. My neck felt like it was going to crack. The scrape on my face was pulling against my healthy skin, causing an itching and burning sensation. I was shaky, both because I had slept in an awkward position on the unyielding pavement and because my stomach ached for food. The stifling heat didn't help, and my already-stiff muscles kept tensing up, threatening to knot into painful cramps.

After the piercing sound of the bouncing garbage can lid stopped echoing in my ears and the rats had found new hiding places, the alley became deathly quiet again. I could still hear traffic in the distance, and again heard a siren wailing.

I tried to decide my next move. Should I stay in the alley and just move away from the garbage cans, or should I find a more comfortable place for the rest of the night? I had no idea what time it was.

A mist began to blow into my face. That convinced me I had to find some shelter to protect myself from the weather, and I needed to get away from this rat-infested alley.

I had never felt so alone. Even when I was in the bleak Wisconsin wilderness, I didn't feel like I was far from civilization. Yet, here I was in the middle of a huge city, feeling absolutely destitute, isolated from the humanity around me.

I remembered the myths about Hades and the underworld, where dead spirits supposedly roamed. Although I didn't believe in such things, death and spirits suddenly seemed to haunt the alley. Another rat moved against the cans, and I imagined all kinds of dangerous otherworldly beings surrounding me.

Getting out of the alley became a priority. Telling myself all of my fears were only in my head didn't help much. Once my adrenaline started flowing, logic ceased to direct my actions, and I was ready to flee. The spirits of the alley blended with my sense of danger. Moving was the wisest course of action.

Logically, the rats were far more dangerous than any imagined spirits, but the image of wicked otherworldly beings sneaking around aroused my senses to every movement in the pitch-blackness.

Slowly, shakily, I moved my foot forward a few inches toward the dim haze of the street closest to me. I moved one foot a few inches, then the other. It probably took me a half hour to shuffle the quarter block to the street. The mist was turning to rain.

As I got closer to the street, the ambient streetlight made the raindrops shimmer like millions of gems. Even though the night was warm, the drizzle made me shiver when a breeze blew down the alley. Slowly I slid around the corner and stood in the dim glow from the corner streetlight.

I looked up and down the street, trying to decide where to go. I had been reduced to total helplessness, and I had to look for someplace I could at least get away from the rain. Squinting, I turned to the right and walked up the street whispering to myself, "One more step, one more step, one more . . . !"

Finally, I saw what I was hoping to find—an old office building with a large overhanging arch shielding the entrance. The front entry would be a reasonably dry place to spend the rest of the night. I was ready to collapse, but as I approached the door it became obvious I wasn't the first to discover it. Looking down the street, I saw another doorway with a similar entrance but a smaller overhang. It would have to do. I didn't want to upset anyone—especially someone who might be a cranky crook, like the guy who had stolen my wallet.

I began to pass the first entrance when a woman's voice called out, "Hey, you can get out of the rain over here if you want!"

I hesitated for a moment out of fear, but I was so exhausted and alone I gave in to the invitation, walked up the three steps and back about ten feet to the entry, and slowly, very slowly, sat down across from a couple who looked like they were in their late twenties or early thirties. While I was wary, having other humans around would make the night more pleasant and would keep me from feeling more depressed.

The doorway was easily big enough for the three of us. From my short experience, the couple looked too scared to have been on the streets for long. We reassured each other about our common plight. She called herself Josie. He said he was Max. Josie was short, athletically built, and pretty. Max was tall and lanky, almost unwieldy in appearance. I nodded, not telling them my name.

In a few minutes, we felt comfortable enough with each other to relax, at least a little. I leaned back against the wall and closed my eyes. Eventually, I slid onto my side and was soon asleep.

———

Morning light was just beginning to glow through the fog hanging over the horizon of the city when I felt a nudge. I heard a woman say, "Time to get moving before they chase us out of the doorway, or worse, call the cops."

I rolled over, sat up, and looked at the first rays of sun peaking over the top of the buildings. The streetlights were still casting misty shadows.

As I shook myself awake, I realized the voice had come from Josie—and she was right. I would need to be more vigilant about getting up early in the future, or I would have to find more private places to sleep.

We all stood and stretched. As they walked ahead of me down the steps, Josie looked back. Suddenly, she seemed confused and just a little concerned. She turned and whispered something to Max. Then he, too, looked at me. His face winced, and he let out the breath he was holding as he studied me. Sounding like he was asking himself the question more than asking me, he blurted out, "Aren't you the freaking murderer the police are after?"

I looked at them in horror. My expression must have confirmed their assessment.

Josie jabbed him with her elbow and said, "Let's get out of here!" They charged down the street as fast as they could. Max glanced back only once as he ran awkwardly away, trying to keep up with Josie.

I had a horrible moment of indecision. *Should I chase after them?* What would I do if I caught up to them? I couldn't even imagine killing them to protect myself. *Could I lie to them, telling them I'm not the criminal they assume I am?* If I tried to explain the truth about what had actually happened, would they believe me, and if they did, would it make any difference? The reward for turning me in was too big.

I quickly discovered I was in too much pain, and too weak, to try stopping them even if I wanted to. And if they told the police where I was, what chance did I have? All I could do was try to get as far away as possible.

About an hour later, as I hobbled down the street trying to figure out what to do and looking for a way to get some food, I heard multiple sirens blaring several blocks behind me. As fast as I could, I slipped into another alley. I had just ducked behind a large dumpster when a police car whizzed past and on down the street.

I looked around, and to my amazement, realized that it was the same alley Jane and I had come to just days before to meet Blake in the warehouse. I thought I had walked parallel to the neighborhood, but my sense of direction must have become confused. I was back where I had started. As more police vehicles circled the neighborhood, I hobbled deeper into the alley. I was sure that if my nighttime friends had reported me, it wouldn't be long before the police began driving down the alleys, too.

A door suddenly opened in front of me, and a hand reached out and pulled me into the warehouse, then bolted the door behind us.

Blake turned, grinned, and said, "Welcome. You're just in time."

Just moments later, I heard a car driving slowly through the alley. A flash of light flickered under the door I was behind, probably from a police spotlight scanning the depths of the alley for any sign of me.

My weakness and the stress of the situation overcame me. When I woke up, I was lying on a blanket on the floor with a wet washcloth on my forehead. Blake was standing over me holding a can of soda pop and a bag of potato chips. He handed them to me, and I pulled myself up against the wall. I slowly ate the chips and drank the cola.

Blake didn't say a word until I was done. Then he apologized, saying, "I would've given you something better to eat, but this was all I could find in the machines in the break room." After staring at me for several seconds and then looking across the dim room for several more, Blake said, "We'd better get out of here fast."

32

A medium-sized pickup truck sat near a garage door. Blake went over to it and got in. He drove past me so I was by the tailgate when he stopped. He helped me crawl onto the bed of the truck, then jumped up himself and opened what appeared to be three tool compartments sitting side by side behind the cab. Their interior was, however, one compartment about two-and-a-half-feet wide and high, and about six feet long. Blake said, "Because each individual toolbox looks too small for someone to hide in, I'm hoping the police won't check them if we're stopped."

Blake could go through any roadblock and look like no one was with him.

"Let me help you in," Blake said.

I slid over the side of the container and found a thick mat had been placed on the bottom with a small pillow on one side. That end of the box also had a hidden wire-mesh opening on the cab side to allow air to enter.

"I'm sorry I have to put you through this," Blake said, "but I've got no choice. We have to get you out of this neighborhood as fast as possible." As he lowered the lids he said, "I hope you're not claustrophobic." Then he snapped all three locks shut.

While the locked boxes might provide an illusion to keep the truck from being searched, Blake was right. The tight space made me nervous and I fought my urge to panic. The more I struggled against my confined space, the more likely I was to be caught. I could see some light through the vent by my head, and Blake had made the hideaway—if not comfortable—at least tolerable. I didn't have the strength to fight anyway, so all I could do was to lie still and hope it wouldn't become my coffin.

As Blake tossed some other gear into the back of the truck to draw attention away from the toolbox, I reflected on my dreams of being trapped in the bottle in the midst of Lake Superior's violent waves, with the storm raging all around me. Even that didn't seem so confining.

I finally relaxed, at least a little, when I remembered the more recent dream. I clutched my hand like I was holding the key to the Door to Refreshing Life. It had, after all, opened the door to life for me after the infection nearly killed me. I challenged myself, insisting that I could survive this time, too, if I just trusted in the key.

I heard Blake open the warehouse door and the reflected light against the cab brightened my box as he pulled out of the garage.

We were stopped almost immediately. I held my breath as a police officer asked Blake if he had seen the person in the photo. Then she explained to Blake that the photo had been retouched based on the description of a couple of vagabonds who had recognized me.

Blake, oozing the same charm we'd experienced, simply said, "Nope. Haven't seen anyone looking like that."

I sighed with relief when the pickup began to move again.

We drove for hours. I grew unbearably stiff and nauseated before Blake finally stopped. He unlocked and opened the end of the box that had been covering my face. I cried, "Let me out of here, please!" He responded to my extreme frustration by unlocking and opening the second box so I could sit up.

"Where are we?" I whispered.

"You don't need to know. It's safer for both of us if you don't."

Finally, he unlocked the bottom box to make it easier to get me out, but I couldn't seem to force myself into an upright position without his assistance. He helped me get down from the truck and supported me as I hobbled toward a small house in the middle of the woods.

As we approached, I could tell the house couldn't have had more than two bedrooms, and it was designed with lots of windows and expensive-looking oak siding. The front door was fitted with a stained glass window depicting vines and fruits. This place felt homey and inviting, not like a site of torment. I was glad it looked friendly, because memories of the place in Illinois where I had been tortured flooded back to me, threatening to drown my hope.

Blake helped me up the steps to the porch that extended the width of the cabin. He opened the front door and guided me to a large black leather recliner near a picture window. I fell into the armchair. Blake adjusted its back so I was lying at about a forty-five-degree angle. I was relieved to look out the window after being boxed in for so long. I hurt all over, but in spite of my discomfort, I fell asleep in minutes.

Blake didn't disturb me, and when I woke it was night. The only light came from a small lamp shining in the next room.

I lay as still as I could. I ached all over and a frigid darkness overcame me. Everything from the past few weeks seemed like a series of chilling nightmares, and I was waking up to find reality was even more chilling.

I focused on the light in the other room. My stomach told me I needed food, but I didn't dare move. I felt my nose tightening up for a sneeze, but I was afraid that once I made any noise, there would be no retreat back to the quietness of the night. I also feared I had so little energy that a sneeze would not only strain my injured face, but hurt to the bottom of my gut.

When I couldn't contain myself any longer, the sound I made was an overwhelming combination of blowing my nose, crying in pain, and an irritating wheeze.

A rustling noise came from the next room a split second before light exploded from a bright ceiling lamp, making my eyes blink and water. I realized I must be an awful sight to behold.

The stark outline of the figure framed in the doorway was Blake's. He gave me his toothy smile. "It's great to see you awake. I'll be right back." He walked back into the other room and a few minutes later returned carrying a steaming cup. Kneeling beside me, he handed it to me and said, "Drink this. It'll make you feel better, but take your time—you need to get used to food in your stomach again."

He handed me a few crackers to eat with the broth.

Normally broth tastes like medicine to me, but while it fell short of a gourmet meal, it wasn't bad. He could tell I was still hungry after sipping the last drops, but Blake said he didn't want me to get stomach cramps from eating too much too quickly.

I expected him to start questioning me right away, but instead he told me to rest a little longer, and he promised he would feed me again soon.

A short time later, I roused from a half-sleep to find that he had a bowl of chicken noodle soup ready. The smells filled the room, and I found I was even looking forward to eating another bland meal.

After I finished the soup, Blake eyed me with concern before he asked me his first question. It was simple enough, "What happened last night?"

I told him the whole awful story of what had happened since we'd last seen him. He smiled and said, "I heard the police report announcing someone recognized you. I was afraid they'd find you. Your reputation is growing. The FBI and the police are searching everywhere for you. A new photo, based on the description the homeless couple gave to a police artist, is now being broadcast. It was extraordinarily fortunate you showed up in my alley when you did."

"Thanks for being there!" was all I could say.

I was worried about Jane. I had no idea how she could have escaped the police search—or even where she was. I stared at the floor for a long time while I thought about her. I longed to ask Blake how she was doing, and though I was afraid of what his answer might be, I finally worked up the courage to ask.

"Jane; is she safe?"

"She's doing fine," Blake said. He explained to me that she had spent the first night at the homeless shelter with no incident, thanks to Cookie.

"In Cookie's disguise, no one even suspected she might be the fugitive they were searching for," Blake said. "Cookie also apparently ran interference, keeping her as isolated as possible to minimize the risk of someone seeing through her disguise."

Blake explained how Cookie had sensed the situation was becoming dangerous and called him. "She was careful to never mention Jane by name while making the arrangements for her. She said just enough about the police presence and the photos they were showing around of 'some dangerous people' for me to understand the urgency of getting her away as quickly as possible.

"Cookie slipped out with Jane early in the morning through a maintenance exit. They barely made it out. Only minutes after they left, the police surrounded the building, and presented a search warrant. From what we've heard, the police thoroughly searched the place. If Jane had been in the shelter when they were there, who knows what would have happened?"

"So where *is* Jane?" I said.

"Cookie and Jane walked several blocks in the opposite direction from my warehouse before angling around and heading back. They made it to the warehouse yesterday."

"So you know where she is." It was the first bright spot in a very dark day. "When can I see her?"

"Sorry, she's been relocated. Like you, I needed to get Jane out of the neighborhood as quick as possible," Blake said. "I'd already worked out a core identity for Jane so it was easy to move her. She's staying in seclusion for several weeks until her new identity is finished. Then she'll need to memorize the details before we move her to a final destination."

"So . . . when can I see her?"

That's when Blake declared, "For the safety of you both, I've decided you must be separated. You'll have separate identities in your new lives, and you'll be located in different places." Blake's words sucked all the light out of the room.

He refused to tell me where she was, where she would be finally located, or anything about her new identity. "Staying together has become far too dangerous for the two of you. For your own good, you need to have two separate IDs."

"Blake," I yelled, "you're not being reasonable. Tell me where Jane is!"

"I'm sorry, but you need to understand. I'm doing this for her protection—as well as yours. The fewer people who know her new identity and where she's relocated, the better. I've made it a practice to never tell anyone where another client is located, even if they were close associates in their past lives. I was almost ready to make an exception for the two of you, but after the last couple of days, I decided you must follow my rule."

"Please!" I cried. "Tell me where Jane is. You know I'd die before I would ever let anyone hurt her."

I wanted to wring the information out of him, but no amount of reasoning or emotion would get him to change his mind. He had his strict rule and he had decided to enforce it. Blake was adamant that he was keeping us apart to protect us. I told him we would rather risk our lives together than be separated, but my arguments made no difference.

In the end, all I could do was to sit down and cry inside, *Jane—alive—but dead to me.* She was someone else now, no longer Jane. She would still be the same person, but she was now disconnected from her past, and that included me, George Mercy.

I had always believed Jane and I would have new identities *together.* Blake had never, until that moment, indicated otherwise. I had assumed I would face separation from the past with the support of Jane—and she with me. We would lean on each other as we stepped into a new future.

In mere moments, I had lost my greatest hope for living. I would be forced to face a future knowing that somewhere there was someone who remembered me—and whom I remembered and loved dearly. But we had loved each other in a previous life, a life we could no longer have.

At least Jane was alive. I was certain she loved me today, but what about in the future? Would she eventually remarry under the guise of it being her first marriage, or would she always remain dedicated to our love? What were my chances of ever finding her when the best intelligence agencies in the United States couldn't figure out where she was?

It was almost like we were being reincarnated into new lives in different times and places. Jane would never be able to find me, and I would never find her. We might be thousands of miles apart, or we could be in the same city. If I saw her in a store or on the street in ten years, would I recognize her? And if I did, what would I do?

Likely, by then, we would both be dressing differently, talking differently, and have different interests. We might even pass on the street like perfect strangers, never realizing we were once lovers.

I stared out the window in frustrated anger. The stars looked so far away, but even the great expanse of the universe couldn't contain my longing.

I finally turned to face Blake. The look on his face told me he wasn't immune to what I was feeling. I didn't think my emotions would faze him. I had to take a chance. I screwed up my courage and asked him one more time, "Can't you please tell me where Jane is? We love each other, and I would rather die with her than live apart from her."

"Sorry," Blake said, pausing as if he were thinking, then continuing, "I must follow my rule for your best interests. I feel for your loss, but Jane needs to be safe—and so do you. You could blow her cover by finding her. She could also blow yours by trying to find you, but that's her problem. They'll expect to find you together. Separately, you have a better chance of escaping. In the end, you'll thank me.

"If they find either of you, of course, I'm also potentially in deep shit. I'm on my third identity now. Probably it's time for me to move on, too."

Fine! I won't be able to find my wife—or the person who in a previous life was my wife—and I won't be able to find the only other person who knows who she is. I was stuck.

Blake's lecture about new identities shifted into a kind of pep talk. "How many people can ever experience being more than one person? You can take on a whole new image, hang out with different people, and go to different places. You can become *totally new*."

"So, who will I become?" I asked, without my heart in the question. I didn't want to become a new person in a new life without Jane.

"I can't answer your question quite yet. I'm still working on a good fit for your profile. Who would you dream of becoming if you could be anyone you want in a new life?"

The question caught me off guard. *Who do I want to be, if I can become anyone?* I wasn't sure. The childhood question haunted me: "What do you want to be when you grow up?" I knew a lot of children wanted to become firefighters, police officers, or movie stars, but I had never thought much about it.

Finally, I said, "I could be a lot of things, but mostly, I want to be whatever it is with Jane."

"You're not playing the game right," Blake said, slowly shaking his head. "You're bringing someone from your past into your future. You could ruin your chances for a clean break. You know the police are looking for *a couple* matching your description. I repeat: it's too dangerous."

"I'd take my chance," I said. Then with some sarcasm I challenged him, "A smart man like you should be able to figure something out."

Blake mumbled that new identities weren't that easy to create as he left the room and slammed the door behind him.

When I last looked at the clock before I fell asleep, it was nearly midnight. I woke up to bright light shining in my eyes as it streamed through the window.

What will happen today?

I turned my head and saw Blake sitting at a small desk in the next room, typing on a laptop computer. That reminded me of the long hours I had spent typing and editing articles on my own laptop—the same laptop on which Jane and I had done our research of our beautiful, but evil, little book. Of course, at the time, we had no idea the book had such great value to the Guild for the Knowledge of Good and Evil. According to them, both good and evil were necessary to make men into gods. Now they were out to kill us. I guess they would consider that a necessary evil.

Blake must have heard me as I pulled myself into a sitting position because he turned and greeted me. He pointed at the table and said, "There's plenty of food to eat, but it's cold. You can microwave it if you want."

I was starved for solid food. After two minutes of agonizing patience waiting for the microwave to beep, I downed the spaghetti with no problem. It tasted fantastic.

After eating, I walked back to my chair. I wasn't sure how to handle my life without Jane. At least she was alive. But was she happy? I was quite sure she wasn't.

Can I ever be happy again? I was certain I could never again laugh freely, really enjoy a sunset, or find enjoyment in watching a play or movie without Jane. At the same time, I had come to believe that Blake would do his best to give Jane a good future—a safe future. Even if I never held her in my arms again, I could at least know she was somewhere, living a new life.

Blake walked over to the couch across from me and sat down. He took a deep breath, and ignoring my internal pain, began to describe what he had decided would be my new life. I was emotionally too numb to react to what he was saying.

"I've already told you how hard it is to create a new history, a set of credentials, and a credit line for you. We also must alter your appearance again so you don't fit the image of any of your photos or profiles.

"Jane was fortunate. I happened to already have a line on a lot of pieces that came together for her new ID. It wasn't quite as complete as I would've liked, but given the circumstances, it had to work. I'm still finalizing the last details, but I'll get them to her in plenty of time so she can learn everything before she's finally placed in her new situation.

"Your situation is more of a problem because of your publishing background, but I think a profile is beginning to form into a credible identity. It will take a couple more weeks, so be patient. I'll tell you what I've worked out for you when I'm ready."

I found myself unable to hold back my frustration at his calm. "What do you mean, 'What I've worked out for you?' Don't you care about me? I want to be with Jane. She's my wife. I demand you work something out so we can be together!"

"Be reasonable!" Blake snapped.

"Isn't it reasonable I would want to be with my wife?"

Blake looked away and then walked out of the room mumbling, "Okay, I'll see what I can do, but no, and I mean it, *no* promises!"

I finally felt a hint of optimism. Even the possibility that he would try to find a way for me to be with Jane was a huge leap for Blake, if indeed he was being honest with me. Still, I had always believed Blake was pretty straightforward. I was sure he would try. I had to hope that I might be allowed to move into my unknown future with Jane.

Once more I recalled my Lake Superior dreams. Only this time I was afraid Jane and I were floating on the expansive waters of the great lake in two separate bottles. Neither of us would know where we would come ashore. I could only hope we'd have been launched from the same rocky shore at the same time—and that we might drift in the same general direction. But what if Blake released our bottles in two locations or released us on different days when the waves were moving in opposite directions?

"No," I whispered to myself. "Blake will work out a way for us to find each other." I clasped my fingers together like I was holding the key to the Door to Refreshing Life. I hoped when I unlocked the door, I would step through to a new future with Jane.